Mud to Ashes

Also by Gayle Wigglesworth

GAYLE'S LEGACY,
RECIPES, HINTS AND STORIES CULLED FROM A
LIFELONG RELATIONSHIP WITH FOOD

TEA IS FOR TERROR

WASHINGTON WEIRDOS

INTRIGUE IN ITALICS

CRUISIN' FOR A BRUISIN'

MALICE IN MEXICO

MUD TO ASHES

by
Gayle Wigglesworth

Library of Congress Control Number: 2009938651

ISBN: 978-0-9800098-4-2

Koenisha Publications, 3196 – 53rd Street, Hamilton, MI 49419
telephone or fax: 269-751-4100
email: koenisha@macatawa.org
web site: www.koenisha.com

Acknowledgements

This story takes place in Belle Vista, California, a mid-sized town on the coast of California between the towns of Half Moon Bay and Santa Cruz. It is unfortunate, no town such as Belle Vista is located there, but I hope my readers will think, as I do, there should be.

The people, the dogs, and the story in this book are also products of my imagination built out of little snippets of stories in the news which started me to think, "what if...?"

I have spent many years in pottery studios and am still not an expert. And, while I may have modeled some of my characters on people I've worked with, I assure you my characters are fictional. I thank Roy Hanscom, potter extraordinaire, for allowing me to fire some beef bones in his kiln to see how they would come out, and Sharon Warrington for answering some of my technical questions. And, besides my normal reviewers, I want to thank Penny Shepherd and Nadira Lorin, who have both worked with me in different pottery studios and lent their expertise to make sure this story spoke of an environment similar to a real studio.

As usual, my husband David, my daughter Janet Hancock, and my friend Dr. Martin Lorin, put a lot of time and effort into editing this story and paying attention to the details. They keep me focused. As always, I appreciate their interest and their help, but if I missed any errors, I take sole responsibility for that oversight.

Dedication

I dedicate this book to all the men and women I have worked with in pottery studios in California and Texas. They are a remarkable and talented group of people who generously share their secrets and techniques on how to turn out fabulous works of art.

PROLOGUE

"Hello, my name is Alison Burkhouse and I'm looking for Augustus Aurelieus. Is he here?"

The woman holding the door partially open couldn't control her jerk of surprise. Then after a moment's hesitation she asked abruptly, "What do you want with Gus?"

"I'm a friend. He contacted me a while back to tell me he was here. He said he'd call me back and let me know how he was doing. But I haven't heard from him since then, so I became concerned. Since I didn't have a phone number for him I thought I'd just drive down here and see how he's doing."

"Come in," the woman said grudgingly, opening the door a little wider. Then after gesturing to a chair, explained, "I found him on the streets. I didn't know he had any family or friends."

Alison perched on the edge of a chair in the living room and said, "I don't think he has any family, but he certainly does have friends. I'm one of them." She looked around. "Is he here?"

"What kind of friend allows a man to live in the appalling conditions I found him in?" the woman asked, her disapproval clear.

"I'm not his mother, or his wife. I'm his friend," she said quietly, her manner calm and serene. "Gus has been living on the streets, off and on, for over ten years. Sometimes he comes into the mission where I work and joins one of the programs to sober up, but after a while he's out on the streets again. He knows I don't approve, but he lives his own life. It's his life and his choice." She shrugged, apparently accepting his strange life.

"However, he always stays in touch with me. His Social Security check is mailed to the mission, so he comes by to pick it up once a month. But it didn't come last month, or this month, so maybe he changed the instructions. Anyway, when I didn't hear I got concerned. I just want to make sure he's okay."

"I see," the woman said. "Well, he's not here. He checked into a clinic to help him sober up. He told me he was ready to make a change. He said he was tired of life on the streets. But he only stayed there a short time before he took off." She couldn't hide her irritation. "I don't know if he had his check mailing address changed. Maybe he did while he was at the clinic. It's such a shame he didn't stay. He's an intelligent man. He's wasting his life."

Alison nodded her agreement. "But some people are like that. He's had a lot of pain in his life and somehow living on the street is part of his way of coping with it. It works for him. And I'm not surprised to hear that even though he agreed to sober up, he went back to his life on the streets. I've seen it happen to him over and over."

"Well, he'll probably show up at some of his old haunts soon, so you'll see him again," the woman said, obviously expecting her guest to be on her way.

Alison didn't move. "Could I have the address of the clinic he was in? I think I'll stop by on my way home and talk to them. They may have some details that will help me locate him."

"Why would you do that? Why hunt him down, can't you let him alone?" She was angry and didn't mind showing it.

Alison didn't flinch as she explained gently, "We've been friends a long time. He would expect me to check up on him. He knows I will always be concerned about his welfare. It won't hurt to talk to the people. One of them might remember something to help me locate him. And surely they can tell me if he changed the delivery instructions on his Social Security check so I won't have to check with the Social Security Administration itself."

The woman's eyes widened slightly as if surprised at the lengths Ms. Burkhouse intended to take to locate Gus. She thought a minute and then said, "All right, I think I have the address if you'll wait just a minute." She got up and started out of the room, pausing at the doorway. "You are a good friend; Gus is a lucky man. You could have just called the authorities to check on him, but you took the time to drive down to see him. Gus should appreciate that."

Alison nodded. "Well, I didn't know what he was up to. I didn't want to get anyone else involved, you know, in case he could possibly get in trouble. It was just easier to come down myself to see what was what. This way no one knows anything but me."

The woman nodded, understanding, "Perhaps you'd like to come back here with me while I look for the address?"

Alison readily followed her into the small room set up as an office. She thumbed through the stack of papers handed to her, looking for the address, totally oblivious to the fact that behind her, the woman picked up a heavy metal bookend and swung it mightily. She clubbed Alison so hard across the back of her head, she fell to the floor, dead.

Later that night the woman struggled to drag Alison's body to her truck, position it in the truck bed and cover it with a plastic tarp before driving out to a lonely section of Belle Vista State Park, which jutted out high over the ocean. She carefully backed the truck to the edge of the cliff and then wrestled with the body in order to drop it where the high tide lapped at the rocks below. She watched a moment as the waves claimed the body, hoping it would float all the way to China before it washed up on a beach.

She was exhausted from her efforts, but she didn't dare rest; she still had work to do. She drove back to her house, where she carefully cleaned the bookend and the floor in the room where the murder had occurred. She then went out and cleaned the truck bed, wiping down all the surfaces to make sure no traces of blood were left.

Finally, she shed her clothes and got into the shower. The hot water revived her somewhat. She dressed in nondescript clothes and put her clothes, including her tennis shoes in the washer. While the washer did its work removing any trace of the crime, she donned a pair of gloves before she drove Alison's car to the San Francisco Airport long-term parking *garage. She parked it and left the keys on the floor mat. It took her hours to get home, first taking BART from the airport to San Francisco where she caught the Greyhound bus to Belle Vista. She then took a local bus to the bus stop nearest her house, where she walked the rest of the way home. When she finally got home she was happy to drop into a deep sleep and forget all about Alison Burkhouse and Augustus Aurelieus.*

CHAPTER 1

Karo looked up from her keyboard to find Captain and Rudy staring at her. Captain's excited dancing eyes, half hidden behind his tan hair, seemed to be willing her to move. Rudy's mournful gaze pleaded with her silently, but just as effectively as his buddy's. She felt guilt tugging at her and sighed. She couldn't ignore them, even though she preferred to stay glued to her computer until she was finished. She realized she had taken on other obligations.

She found the leashes, recent purchases from Petco, and secured them to the dogs' collars. While the dogs both dashed toward the front door, she grabbed a couple of baggies and a handful of doggie treats before shrugging into her jacket as she followed them.

Outside, the cool wind swirled the late morning fog around her. She drew in a deep breath of the damp air as she headed down her little street, realizing she needed this break.

She had been here almost a month and yet had only been down to the beach twice. Once when she was contemplating purchasing the house, and once when she was so tired from unpacking she had to have a break. But now, she told herself, she'd be doing this daily. It would be good for her, and it certainly seemed it was what you did if you owned dogs.

Sunset Lane wasn't a long street. It stretched only a block to where the sidewalk ended at the path which led over the sand dune to the beach. There were only ten houses along the way. Her house and two others were still in their original Craftman style, so popular when those houses had been built. The other seven had been bastardized over the years with so many remodels it was now hard to ascertain what style they had been originally. All the houses on her side of the street backed up against the Belle Vista State Beach, so there were no neighbors behind them. That privacy was a definite plus in her decision to buy. The houses across the street backed up against the houses from a newer housing tract which had its own entrances leading to the beach. So this street should have been very quiet.

That's what Karo expected when she bought the house. Unfortunately, there was a constant stream of cars going to and from the house closest to the path. That house apparently had active teenagers living there and attracted a lot of visitors. So far she hadn't been disturbed by anything more than the squealing tires of immature drivers, but she already knew to keep the dogs on leash on this street, lest they stray into the path of a speeding vehicle.

She looked carefully at the house as she passed. It looked innocuous, spread widely over its large unkempt lot.

She turned her attention back to her walk. Captain and Rudy were pulling on their leashes, trying to propel her forward at a faster pace, probably already smelling the ocean. She let them help pull her up the path and then over the dune to the beach. At the top of the dune when she saw no one else on the sand, she stooped and unfastened the leashes. The dogs took off in joyful leaps. It looked like so much fun she attempted to run through the sand behind them, but after a few steps she slowed to a walk. Later she would run, she promised herself.

When she reached the packed sand at the water's edge she ran, jogged and walked alternatively behind the dogs. Captain delighted in chasing the birds, while Rudy was more into splashing in the retreating waves and nosing drifting seaweed and other tantalizing items in the roiling surf.

Karo felt her own sudden burst of freedom. She twirled around, arms out-stretched, laughing out loud. There was no one around to remind her that at fifty-two she should act more circumspect.

She found two intact seashells in the sand. The delicate colors intrigued her, so she shook off the sand and put them carefully in her pocket. She imagined in a few months she'd probably have quite a collection lining the window sills in the sunroom off the kitchen.

Eventually she noticed it was getting late, so she called the dogs. Captain raced to her, circled her twice and then danced on his hind legs with excitement, just waiting to see what game she wanted to play. She laughed at him, he was just the kind of dog she wanted to have for a pet. She knew he was the one when she first saw him at the animal shelter only two days ago.

Unfortunately the attendant shook his head when she said she wanted that one, pointing at Captain. He explained the two dogs in that pen came in as a pair, and became so agitated and then morose when they were separated, the people at the animal shelter, driven to distraction by their constant whining, decided to let them bunk together.

"After all," the serious young man had told her, "It's not like they're going to be here very long."

"Umm," she had nodded absently, already looking in some of the other pens for a suitable pet, "Why not?"

"Well, no one has been willing to take them both, so they're scheduled for euthanasia in three days."

That got her attention. She looked at him with horror, hoping he just had a macabre sense of humor. When he just nodded, confirming the truth of what he said, she went back to Captain's pen and studied his friend, Rudy. He was a big dog of indeterminate lineage. Somewhere he had some hound dog relatives, which showed in his droopy ears and soulful eyes. His dark brown coat was rough, almost like a wire-haired terrier, but he was way too big to be a terrier. He was a homely dog. But apparently he was Captain's friend, and if she wanted Captain she was going to have to take Rudy. And if she didn't take them, their future wasn't hopeful.

She didn't want two dogs. She wanted one dog, a small one. She wasn't even sure she could become a dog person, never having owned one before. Years ago, when she had wanted to get a puppy for Lisa, Greg had been vehemently against it, finally insisting he was allergic to dog dander. Now, settled in her new house, she suddenly realized how alone she was. She had thought an older dog would be company. It had seemed a great idea. But now, peering at the two dogs, she wondered if she could ignore their hopeful expressions and just walk away as if she didn't know what would happen to them.

Of course she capitulated. She took them directly to the vet's, then to Petco, the big pet supermarket. It cost more than she ever imagined it could to outfit two dogs. The clerk kept showing her more things every dog owner needed. Finally, her SUV filled, the dogs each claiming one seat in the back, appointments made for grooming the next day, she headed for home. There, she was pleased to find that not only were they both housebroken, but they had exceedingly good manners. The dogs seemed determined to prove their value as they settled in as if they had been there for a long time. She didn't know why their previous owner had let them go to the animal shelter where their very lives were in danger, but she was beginning to feel exceedingly lucky they were there for her.

And after yesterday's visit to the grooming salon, she found Rudy wasn't nearly as pathetic looking as she thought. In fact, she was starting to think he was almost handsome. And she now suspected the small raggedy Captain might be a purebred Cairn terrier.

Now after giving Captain a pat and praise as a reward for coming when she called, she looked around for Rudy. Finally she saw him further down the beach, nosing in a pile of rocks that extended from the beach out into the surf. As she watched, he put his head up in the air and howled, sending a shiver up her spine.

"Rudy, come!" she called to him just as the dog book explained she should.

He couldn't, or wouldn't, hear her.

She walked toward him, calling again in a firm voice. "Rudy, come!" It was no use; something was just too intriguing to the dog. She clamored over the rocks, coming up behind Rudy. When she reached over to grab his collar, she saw what he was so excited about. She gagged, rearing back so abruptly she lost her balance, sitting down on the rocks with a spine-crunching jolt. She quickly scrabbled backwards, continuing to put some distance between her and the horror of that body floating in the little depression between the rocks. She took deep gulps of air, willing the contents of her stomach to stay down. She looked around wildly, but didn't see anyone or anything except the two dogs. She had to do something, but she was so frightened she didn't know what. Slowly she breathed in and out. Then she remembered her cell phone was attached to her belt.

When she found the phone had a signal, even here at the beach, she was suddenly grateful for those unsightly cell phone towers planted along the coast highway. It took a little effort to control her shaking enough to punch in nine-one-one. Her voice was squeaky with fright as she tried to describe exactly where on the beach she was. But when she hung up she felt calmer. Someone else was now in charge. She pulled a doggy treat from her pocket and called Rudy. While he was reluctant to leave his find for only a treat, eventually his insatiable appetite won. He came over for the treat and she snapped the leash on his collar while he was munching the biscuit. She secured Captain's leash too and then pulled them down the beach a bit where it was no longer possible to see where the body lay.

Her knees were still so shaky she wasn't certain how long she could remain standing. She went up to the ridge of dry sand where the early morning tide had stopped and sat down. Both dogs immediately sat down beside her. She gave each one another treat and patted Rudy. "Good dog. You're a good dog, Rudy." But they were just words; she didn't really appreciate his find. She would have much preferred Rudy had not found the body. Then she was ashamed; that body had been a person. In fact, she was pretty sure it was a young woman. Someone must be looking for her. Someone must be missing her. She shuddered. No, she couldn't even think how she'd feel if it were Lisa. That was too horrible to even contemplate.

She looked up and down the beach, but it was totally deserted. She didn't know which direction would bring help, but she was confident it would come. She stared at the waves relentlessly rolling on to shore in front of her, trying not to think about the body in the surf, trying to make her mind a blank. She wondered if death was always so horrible. She had rarely been confronted with it and certainly never in such a brutal, in-your-face way. When she attended funerals she never even went up to view the deceased. She had, of course, looked at both her parents when they had been laid out, but that was because as their daughter she felt it was her duty to make sure the undertaker had done a proper job. She felt the shudder move up her spine. She didn't want to think about her parents as it always distressed her. She thought instead about her friend Eileen's family.

She had always wished she had been a real member of Eileen's family. They treated her as if she belonged, but she knew she did not. She was just a visitor.

Eileen's parents were interested in what the children did, even what they thought, as Karo's never were. Eileen's father would go out and throw the ball with her two brothers. Sometimes he even insisted the girls come and join them. She remembered one weekend when she found everyone in the backyard, sawing, measuring and hammering. Eileen's mother handed her a hammer and some nails and told her where to pound in the nails in the corner of the tree house they were building. Just like that, the whole family worked together and the tree house was ready for occupancy by nightfall.

Karo's own parents were nothing like Eileen's. Oh, they didn't mistreat her, but they weren't really interested in her. She had realized at a very young age it was best when she was quiet and didn't interrupt them. When she was called down to say hello to their guests, she behaved demurely and politely and then escaped to her room to play with her paper dolls. There, the families she drew on cardboard and then cut out, acted the way she wanted them to act. They always played with their kids. They went to Disneyland. They had big, loud, birthday parties. They asked their children what they wanted to do on Saturdays.

When she was growing up she didn't understand her parents. For quite a while after starting school and observing the parents of her classmates, she thought her parents didn't like her. But now she understood it was mostly an age issue. Her father worked long hours and when Saturdays came he golfed. He somehow thought that providing the money to support her was enough participation.

By the time Karo came along her parents had built their own lives and were reluctant to change them to accommodate a child. Karo's mother was passionate about the bridge games she played at the club most afternoons. And since her mother was the only one amongst her friends with a child still at home, rarely was Karo included in any of her activities.

It was no wonder when she and Greg prepared for their first child, Karo insisted she had to be a stay-at-home parent. She was determined to do a better job raising her child than her parents did with her.

She smiled to herself as she remembered how much fun she had with Lisa. The school field trips, the Brownie Scout activities, the sleepovers, were all part of her memories, making up for much of what she missed as a child.

Her reminiscing came to an abrupt halt when she saw the ATV coming down the beach on the other side of the pile of rocks. She got to her feet and waved. When she got the driver's attention she pointed to the outcropping. She pulled the dogs' leashes in close and walked toward the ATV. She was reluctant to go close to the corpse in the rocks, although Rudy was eager to return, pulling hard against his leash. When she realized she needed to direct the ranger to the right spot, she allowed Rudy to pull her closer.

Now she could see another ATV and a larger vehicle approaching.

"Morning, madam. Are you the lady who called?" the ranger asked politely as he swung his leg over the ATV.

"Yes, my dog found her. She's up there. There's a little space between the rocks, and she's in the water, caught."

The ranger quickly headed over the rocks and then gestured to his colleagues as they arrived and left their vehicles. Karo stood a moment watching them, then turned and retreated to her safe spot in the dry sand. She would wait until they needed her.

A Belle Vista squad car, an unmarked car and an ambulance arrived next. This time they came from the opposite direction and Karo assumed there was a way to drive onto the beach from somewhere in the housing tract north of where she lived. She, Captain and Rudy watched with interest. It was like a TV drama unfolding before them. Two men in casual clothes approached her. Rudy sat up alert while Captain let a warning growl rumble in his chest.

"It's okay, fellers. They're the good guys."

The man in khaki trousers and a navy nylon Windbreaker appeared to be in charge. "Morning, madam." He eyed the dogs warily, but then relaxed when he saw the leashes held firmly in Karo's hand. "I understand you called nine-one-one with information on a body."

She nodded. "My dog wouldn't come when I called. Naturally, I went to get him. That's when I saw her."

The other man, younger, longish hair and thick dark mustache pulled a notebook out of his pocket, flipped it open to a page and started to write.

"You are?" the first man, who had approached her, asked.

Karo introduced herself and gave her address.

"I'm Lieutenant Myers, Belle Vista Police Department. This is Officer Keith Riesgo. We'll be investigating this case for the State Park Service."

Karo nodded, that made sense; she didn't suppose the Park Service had the manpower or the expertise for this kind of situation.

Lieutenant Myers apparently did, judging by the numerous questions he fired at her. Karo thought they would never finish. She found herself explaining far more about her life and situation than she thought was pertinent, but eventually he seemed satisfied. She headed back toward the path over the dune quickly, anxious to get home, realizing too much of the day had already gone by.

She let the dogs in the front door, following them across the hardwood floors to the closet where she hung her jacket. She only shrugged at the sand they all tracked in. She wasn't the super housewife anymore; she no longer wanted to worry about having a spotless house. She deliberately chose to refinish the hardwood floors and only use area rugs so she could just vacuum up the sand when needed. After all, she was living at the beach.

The dogs headed for the water dish and had a long drink. She handed them each a doggie treat and they settled near her computer as she sat down to finish the section of work she wanted to send in today. She wanted it off her desk because tomorrow she was starting her pottery class.

Pottery, she felt a little thrill of excitement. She couldn't wait to get her hands covered in mud. She found it so satisfying to repeatedly slam clay down to wedge out the air bubbles and then to manipulate it into different shapes. Actually, she thought, a pottery class was exciting enough for her; she didn't need the drama or the anxiety of finding a body on the beach. Just for a moment she wondered how accurate those neighborhood crime statistics were the real estate agent had shared with her. She shuddered. Suddenly she was grateful for the alarm system she installed and for the dogs' company. She didn't know what had happened to that girl on the beach, but she knew it wasn't good.

CHAPTER 2

His head was throbbing and his mouth felt sour and full of grit. He lay there for a moment, blinking, trying to adjust his eyes to the light. He put out his hand and tentatively felt around. He felt a surge of pleasure when his fingers felt the rough brown sack he had wrapped around the bottle. He picked it up and shook it cautiously. He was right! He had passed out before he finished it last night. He pulled the bottle out of the sack and held it up to his eyes. He could see there was at least a third left. He checked now to make sure the top was on the bottle securely, he didn't want to risk spilling it.

He rolled over and managed to get up on his knees. After a moment the world stopped spinning, and he lurched to his feet. He waited again, and then gathering his wits and his coat around him, he slipped the bottle into the coat pocket, ready to face the day. He stumbled away from the little pocket he had dug in the sand, toward the public restrooms situated at the base of the trail to the Recreation Center. He did what he could with the cold water, electric dryers and toilets, but he didn't try too hard, knowing he couldn't hide the fact he was living on the streets. He cupped a handful of water into his mouth and used one of his fingers to rub it round his teeth, trying to counteract the sour taste.

He straightened up and began his morning routine. He checked the change in his pocket and found only four quarters, three dimes, and a few pennies left over after he had purchased the bottle of cheap whiskey yesterday. He needed coffee. He decided to try McDonald's first. Sometimes one of their customers would buy a coffee and breakfast sandwich to thrust at him quickly when leaving the restaurant. He fantasized about the trash cans inside, knowing they could have yielded him enough discarded food for several meals, but he knew better than to go in. The manager there was definitely not sympathetic. He wouldn't allow him to come in or use the restroom, even if he planned to buy something, and in fact, any time he saw him hanging around outside he came out to shoo him away. Today, no one took the hint and bought him breakfast, although one young woman handed him a fistful of change. When he saw the manger heading his way he turned and shuffled off toward his second choice.

He leaned against the building a few feet from the entrance of Polly's Coffee Café, waiting. He had been lucky today because shortly after he got there he saw Lieutenant Delvin arrive. The Lieutenant nodded at Billy, lifting his hand in greeting before disappearing inside. Lieutenant Delvin Myers was a friend of sorts. A few years back Billy provided him with key information about a case under investigation. It was something Billy had observed while he was working a street. And when he heard about the crime from one of the other street people, Billy realized what he had witnessed could be important. So he took the time to contact Lieutenant Meyer. Since then the Lieutenant was always cordial. He treated Billy as a person which, when he was sober, Billy appreciated. Most people ignored street people, some didn't even see them and others were horrified if they were approached and their space was invaded.

Billy waited expectantly outside, knowing the Lieutenant would be coming out with a large coffee to start his day and one for Billy. If he saw him in the morning he always bought him a coffee, and sometimes the Lieutenant included a Danish pastry. Billy could be patient now as he could almost smell the rich coffee fragrance.

Sure enough, Lieutenant Delvin emerged with two large Styrofoam cups and a bag. He handed the coffee and the bag to Billy, wished him a good day, and was off to his shift at the Buena Vista Police Station.

Clutching his breakfast, Billy angled across the street to the small park in the center of downtown. He settled himself on a bench and had his first sip of coffee before even looking in the bag. This was going to be a good day, he thought. He had his breakfast, he had collected a few coins already, and he had the remains of yesterday's bottle still in his pocket. He felt good and his demons were quiet at present. He thought he would wander over to the big strip mall today; sometimes he picked up a fair amount of change from the shoppers there. His goal was simple and the same each day, he only wanted to collect enough money for dinner and for a bottle of whiskey to get him through the night.

* * *

It was a very short paragraph on one of the inside pages. If Karo hadn't been looking for it, she probably wouldn't have even noticed it. And it said nothing she didn't already know.

She sighed, drank some of her cooling coffee and stared out the window. While the gruesome event of yesterday kept her tossing and turning most of the night, it seemed it was not deemed to have much interest to the newspaper readers of Belle Vista. She hoped someone, somewhere, thought it a major news event. The poor woman deserved more of a goodbye from the world than a tiny mention in the local newspaper. She shuddered. Surely the woman deserved some notice of her passing. Anything else seemed too sad to contemplate.

She put the paper down, refusing to let the situation haunt her again today. She told herself briskly she needed to get moving. Today she was starting her pottery class. This was a major component of her plan to change her life. The divorce freed her from any obligations to her former husband. Her daughter's graduation from college and subsequent decision to accept a position with a company in Boston meant there was no longer a need to be a mother twenty-four seven. So she decided now was the time to find the person she had intended to grow into all those years ago. It was ironic that now after years of managing her family and anticipating their needs, she no longer knew who she was other than Greg's wife and Lisa's mother.

Greg had been delighted at her decision to sell the house. He was glad to be relieved of the obligation to continue the payments while she lived there. Selling meant the soaring California real estate prices would allow them to net enough to buy her a modest house in Belle Vista and him a substantial down payment on a condo for his use.

Freed from her former life, she now intended to move to the beach and find that artsy person she always thought she was. In those years while her daughter attended college, Karo had started taking a pottery class at the local college. She found she loved working in clay and suspected she had a natural aptitude for it. Now she was going to concentrate on developing her skills by working at the local studio in the Belle Vista Recreation Center. She planned to be working there three days a week, more than she had ever attempted before, which she hoped would result in a big improvement in her work. She dreamed of producing pieces good enough to sell and thus supplement her income derived from writing procedural manuals for a local bank.

She hadn't been in a pottery studio for months. When she and Greg decided to separate, her life had immediately become so chaotic she didn't have time for pottery. She chuckled to herself, thinking if she didn't start throwing clay, she'd soon be throwing other things, or she'd need some psychiatric therapy.

She was suddenly feeling in a rush as she put the dishes in the dishwasher and straightened up the kitchen. She filled the water bowl for the dogs and called them in from the backyard.

"You guys be good and I'll take you for a walk when I get home." She shook her finger at Captain. "And no sleeping on the sofa, mister. You hear me?"

Captain wagged his tail, but Karo wasn't convinced he would stay off the sofa. It was a bad habit he indulged whenever he thought he could.

Unfortunately for him, he left little strands of hair on the cushions which showed clearly where he had been sleeping.

The Recreation Center was a sprawling complex set in a grove of gigantic Eucalyptus trees near the middle of the Belle Vista State Beach, which stretched for miles from behind Karo's house, in the north end of the city, all the way to the south end of town. It housed a variety of classes for the community, meetings for civic groups, special events, and a daycare center. Outside was a picnic area, a playground, eight tennis courts and four basketball courts, in addition to three large parking lots with access to the State Beach. It was a busy facility and well used by the community.

When she pulled up in the parking lot near the wing of the Recreation Center where the pottery studio was located, she found several cars were already parked there. She grabbed her box of tools and a shopping bag containing her apron, rubber gloves and the other miscellaneous items she used and headed for the entrance.

She entered the studio and set her tool box down on one of the tables, and looked around with enthusiasm.

"You are?" The grey haired woman was short, solid and stern.

"Karo Meisner. I'm new," she explained smiling with pleasure.

"I'm Joy. I'm the workshop leader. This workshop is for experienced potters only. You can't work here until you've taken the class on Wednesdays. They should have told you that when you signed up." Her tone was sharp, not a hint of welcome showing.

Karo nodded, thinking Joy seemed the antithesis of her name. "They did explain the requirements at the desk when I registered. I just moved to Belle Vista, but I recently took Ceramics I and II at San Mateo City College. The woman at the desk said that qualified me to take this workshop."

Joy nodded grudgingly, admitting, "Well, I suppose so, but we have our own ways of doing things. Workshop here is like a co-operative. Everyone does some of the studio work in exchange for using the facility. Since I'm the workshop leader, I assign the tasks and oversee the work, but we don't have an instructor on site except on class days. So workshop participants need to be able to work on their own. You're supposed to know how things work."

"I understand. I'm sure I can transfer what I learned at San Mateo to your studio. I'll be sure to ask questions and observe what others are doing. Just tell me what to do and I'll do my best." Karo nodded seriously, hoping to convince Joy of her worthiness to belong in the workshop.

"Well, put your name on one of the shelves on the far wall and then, because workshop students also get one of the big cubbies on the end, mark one of those, too. Get settled and I'll send someone over to show you around." She turned away leaving Karo standing there.

Karo started stowing her things on an available shelf when the loud voice made her jump. "Hey, what do you think you're doing? You can't have that shelf. That one is mine."

A big blonde woman didn't even try to be friendly.

Karo smiled her apology and quickly moved her things off the shelf she had claimed. She was embarrassed, but she didn't see anything that would have alerted her to the fact someone else had claimed that particular shelf. Finally, she located one about knee high that was still empty. She pasted a piece of masking tape on it and wrote her name in bold strokes with a marker. Then she found a cubby at the end and did the same. She was arranging her things when another voice interrupted her.

"Hi, I'm Evy. Welcome to our pottery studio. Joy asked me to show you around; she said you've taken classes at San Mateo?" Evy looked to be of Latino origin. She was a short, middle-aged, slightly rounded woman who stood beside her.

Karo was grateful to see the pleasant face lit with a genuine smile.

Evy continued with enthusiasm, "I used to live in San Mateo and I worked at the studio in Central Park, off El Camino. Do you know it?"

Karo nodded. "Yes, one of the ladies at the college went down there to work. She really liked it, but she said they only have electric kilns."

Evy nodded. "That's right. No reduction or raku kilns there. That was disappointing. But don't worry, here we have it all. Let's go out to the patio area so I can show you the kilns."

She led Karo through the door to a covered patio area extending out from the studio. Here the cinder block walls didn't quite reach the ceiling leaving about a foot gap which had iron bars holding up the metal roof. Outside the covered patio was another patio. This fenced-in patio was a cement slab with several wooden benches, two picnic tables and a bench built around a large tree growing out of the middle of the space.

"We usually have lunch out there." Evy pointed as she headed for a couple of people busily painting the kiln shelves with a wash coating to protect them from the glaze drips during firing. Each shelf they finished was then carried to the patio to dry. Evy introduced the man and woman and then she led Karo to the far end of the covered enclosure. "These are the kilns." She nodded at the twin kilns sitting there. "This one we use for soda firings, which we do periodically. We accumulate the pieces waiting for soda firing on this set of rolling shelves and the pieces for the reduction kiln go on that set of shelves. We fire the reduction kiln once or sometimes twice a week, depending on the amount of work waiting.

The high fire kiln and the soda fire kiln were impressive. The high fire kiln's massive door was in the open position. Karo could see it was different than the kilns they used at the college studio. This one opened by pulling the door back from the kiln on tracks like train rails. The shelves were assembled on their stilts and were attached to the door so when the door was pulled open all the shelves were exposed between the door and outer shell of the kiln. Karo could see places where the stilts were missing shelves, probably the ones being painted and drying. This cavernous kiln was big enough to hold pieces that would need a forklift to load them into the kiln.

"Wow, this kiln can hold a lot. Do we all take turns firing?"

"Oh no, that's Joy's job." Evy looked shocked at the thought of everyone helping. "Joy is very precise about the firings. She has perfected the process and knows just how to coax it to the right temperatures to get the most out of the glazes we use. She usually comes in Saturday afternoons to load and fire the kiln. And she unloads it Mondays and sets the pieces out here," she pointed at two tables sitting near them, "so we can retrieve our work when we come in. But sometimes, if Joy needs a second firing, she'll ask some of us to load and unload. The important thing is that she always supervises the unloading. She says this kiln is a little peculiar and she needs to see how each glaze fires in various parts of the kiln. I have to say we have remarkable success with our firings and we can thank Joy for that. She can coax this kiln to achieve just the right reduction.

"But we also have this little kiln here." She pointed to a small kiln on the opposite wall. This one anyone can use and fire. In fact, if you chose to use it you have to load it, fire it and unload it. It's good practice. Sometimes when someone wants to do a Sagar firing or experiment with reaching a certain reduction temperature, then this is the way to go."

Karo nodded, thinking she'd have to find out what a Sagar firing was. Then she looked at the barrels on pulleys that Evy was now pointing to.

"These are our raku kilns. You can use them whenever you want, but you have to clean up after yourself. See, we keep the newspapers and sawdust over there." She pointed to some shelves near the door to the studio. "Have you done raku before?"

Karo nodded. "But only a few times. I'm not sure I'm competent enough to do a firing on my own."

"Well, don't worry. Just buddy up with someone the first couple times. It's easy; you'll be an expert before you know it."

Evy led Karo back into the studio. There on the far side, a room held the bisque kiln. This kiln was used for the first firing of the pottery pieces, done before each piece was glazed and then fired in one of the other kilns for finishing. She then took Karo into the glaze room and very carefully went over the procedures for mixing and using the glazes. There was a long list of do's and don'ts which were listed on posters hanging on the wall, but it seemed to be a very efficient set up. The room had lots of lights and a strong exhaust fan which, Evy warned Karo, was to be switched on before mixing any glazes.

By the time they returned to the main studio Karo was reeling from all the rules Evy had recited to her. It was obvious that this studio was controlled with an iron hand. She hoped she wouldn't embarrass herself by forgetting some.

Now there were many potters busy working at the electric wheels and the tables. Evy, perhaps sensing Karo's eagerness to get her hands in the clay, suggested they get some clay for Karo so she could start work.

"The first bag of clay is included in the cost of the class, but any subsequent clay needs to be purchased at the front desk. They will give you a receipt which you turn in when you get the clay from the supply stored in the shed." Then as Karo carried her bag of clay in to the wedging table she said, "Joy will be having a meeting in a little while, after some of the stragglers arrive. She has one each time class begins and you can meet the others then. Do you want a wheel or do you do hand building?"

"Oh, a wheel, definitely."

"Well, you can pick any wheel not being used, but after two hours if they're all busy you have to offer it to another person. That way everyone gets a chance on one. That wheel on the end is Joy's. We usually just leave it free for her. If you do use it, be prepared to clean it well afterwards. She's pretty picky. In fact, we like you to clean it with a damp rag, not a sponge. The sponge leaves a clay residue behind."

Karo nodded.

"Okay, if you have any questions just ask. We're all glad to have you here, Karo. We need to augment this group with fresh blood to keep us fresh. Have fun." And she headed back to a wheel she had obviously left to show Karo around.

Karo gathered up some tools and a bucket of water and set them down at one of the vacant wheels before returning to the wedging table to prepare some lumps of clay by wedging the air bubbles out. Finally ready, she sat down at the wheel, laid the old towel she brought over her knees and started centering a lump of clay on the wheel, hoping she'd remember what to do.

She had been working for over an hour before she became conscious the man sitting next to her had spoken.

"Hi, I'm Rich Jay. You must be the new kid."

Karo took her hands off the clay cone she was forming between her hands. She looked at the man sitting at the wheel next to her. He was lean and his face was hawkish looking. He had a head of short blond wiry curls and his gray eyes were friendly.

She smiled in response. "Yeah, I'm new. I'm Karo. Karo Meisner."

"Welcome, sorry to interrupt. I see you've just about got it. Are those your's?" He nodded towards the two pieces sitting on the ledge in front of them. Seeing her nod he said, "Well, I guess you're experienced. They look good. Where did you work before?"

"San Mateo City College, but I'm afraid it's been a while. I'm feeling the strain. Some of my muscles don't seem to want to cooperate."

Rich laughed. "I hear you. Frankly, that happens to me after a few days away, say nothing about weeks. Some days I even wonder what I'm doing here, but I love getting my hands dirty." He started his wheel and quickly forced the lump of clay into a semblance of a balanced cone.

Karo watched him deftly insert his fingers in the center, widening the hole as the clay spun until he had the beginning of a bowl. After all this time she was still fascinated watching how quickly and smoothly a bowl could be shaped by experienced hands. She looked at the clay before her and wondered if others felt the same when she worked. Then she started the wheel once more, forgetting Rich, concentrating on forming this piece in precisely the shape she envisioned.

"Okay everyone, meeting time." The loud words broke through Karo's concentration. She rinsed her hands in the bucket of water and quickly dried them on the towel in her lap before joining the other people gathering around one of the tables. There were quite a few people here now. They must have dribbled in while she was on the wheel. She counted fifteen waiting for the meeting to start.

The tall, stern-faced, gray-haired lady, who had made the meeting announcement, turned to Joy with a flourish. "Everyone's here, Joy."

Joy smiled at the assembled potters. Karo was glad to see she could.

"Welcome back to another session. I just want to mention a few things; reminders, if you will. We have a new potter, Karo Meisner, joining us today." She gestured toward Karo and all eyes swiveled in her direction. Karo squirmed a bit under the scrutiny, then everyone turned their attention back to Joy as she continued talking.

"Evy has given her the tour of the studio, but I'm sure she'll appreciate your help from time to time. Introduce yourselves and make her feel welcome.

"Now, Mary Louise tells me we're very low on newspaper since we used so much at the last sale. Please start bringing it in."

The tall gray-haired lady, who was apparently named Mary Louise, said somewhat crossly, "And don't forget to remove all the slick colored ads and magazine sections. We can't use those and they take up too much space."

Immediately two other voices chimed in about how messy the newspaper pile became when the unwanted papers where included. The large blonde woman complained rather snidely about "some people" who didn't even bother to bring newspapers even though everyone used the supply they kept there.

"Well, if that's a subtle complaint about me, Liv, I'll say it once more." All eyes swiveled to a woman on the other side of the table. "My husband reads four papers daily, so I have lots of papers I'd be willing to donate. But I'm not wasting my time by sorting through them to discard the pieces you don't want. I am too busy with things I want to do. You either get them all, or none."

"It doesn't take much time to sort through them, Marge."

"I don't choose to spend my time doing it. If you want the papers I'd be glad to bring them, if you don't want them the way I bring them, fine with me. But don't bother to complain about me not doing my share because I'm not following your silly rules." The woman folded her arms across her chest and glared down the table at the woman who had launched the original complaint.

Joy said emphatically, "We only want the standard newsprint, no colored sections or slick magazine pages or ads. As you know we use a lot of paper on a daily basis, so we need everyone's contribution. But we want the newspapers the way we've stated, understood?

"Now, Betty is working up the list of glazes that need to be replenished for this session. I'll assign those on Friday. I will expect all the glazes to be completed and strained within a week of assignment, so plan your time accordingly.

"And one last thing. I've noticed some of you are getting a little sloppy with the wedging table. Remember to clean the surface after you use it with a wet sponge or rag to remove excess clay before it dries. When it gets hard it's apt to make pits in the plaster when it's removed. We just had that table redone last session. Let's make sure it lasts us for a while."

"Joy, can you remind Sandi to make sure someone watches the beginners when they start to glaze. I know someone contaminated the Celadon last session. I ruined several pieces," A woman complained, her voice a trifle whiney.

"And they need to clean up after themselves. Every Friday it's the same thing. We have to clean all the tables and wheels before we can even start work. Who's coming on Wednesdays?" Mary Louise looked around as Karo and several others raised their hands.

"Rich, can you check and make sure the room is clean?"

"I told you before, Mary Louise, it's clean. Those people are very conscientious about cleaning up after themselves. Perhaps it's the night class who is leaving the mess. Joy should talk to the instructor."

Joy nodded. "I'll leave him a note and remind him."

She looked around. "One last thing, the refrigerator needs to be cleaned weekly. We had some forgotten lunches in there that would have made great science projects, but they smelled gross. I've decided that every Friday afternoon someone is going to have to clean out and throw away any lunches still in there. So mark your items and date them. Cream and condiments we'll keep for a reasonable length of time, but bagged lunches are going in the trash weekly.

"Now, Hal and PJ have cleaned all the kiln shelves, and this morning Jeff and Lydia started painting them with new wash. From now on, any pot which drips glaze on a shelf will mean the potter responsible will clean the shelf or buy a new one. Pay attention to your glazing. Clean off the bottoms and if you use a glaze on top of a glaze leave enough room for it to flex. Let's not mess up the shelves." She looked around and seeing the nods she waved a hand, dismissing them.

Karo was glad to get back to the wheel and her clay. She wondered only briefly if she would like being a part of this group. It seemed to contain some very picky people and there were lots of rules. But then she concentrated on taming the clay in front of her.

"Lunch time. It's lunch time everyone," was the next call which interrupted Karo's work. There was a general stir as people stopped working on their projects and gathered their lunches.

"Did you bring a lunch, Karo?" Rich asked. When she nodded he continued, "We usually sit on the patio unless it's too cold or wet. Get your lunch, and I'll save you a seat."

Karo slipped out of the studio and fed coins into the soda dispenser in the hallway, then grabbed her brown bag and joined the others on the patio. Sometime in the last hour the sun had finally broken through the fog and it had turned into a very pleasant day.

Karo sat down next to Rich, smiling at the women sitting across the table. Rich introduced her to the potters sitting close to them and then she busied herself eating her sandwich while she listened to the conversation.

"Did you read about that woman? The one who won the lottery?"

Several nodded or said they had.

"I think it is a crime. They should take the money from her. She's on welfare. She's living on our money and using it to buy lottery tickets. That should be against the law. She's probably not even a citizen. She had a Mexican sounding name." The big blonde woman with the unpleasant expression on her face obviously had very definite opinions.

"Well, Liv, at least now she will be able to get off the welfare rolls. That should make you happy," Rich commented drolly.

"Well, it doesn't," Liv snapped back. "I think it's a crime. She has no business buying a lottery ticket when she can't even support her family. Those are my tax dollars she's spending!"

"I agree," Joy added. "We have too many people expecting the rest of us to support them. I think we should just cut them all off. They can work or starve."

"But what about the children? The welfare benefits are to insure the children have food. Surely you don't want to deprive them?" Evy's expression reflected her horror at Joy's suggestion.

"Well, that is tough," Liv conceded before offering a solution. "Maybe the children could just be gathered up and placed in a home somewhere. If we did that, I bet we wouldn't see all those women having baby after baby just to collect the welfare checks. I'm tired of people living a life of ease off of my hard earned money."

Rich snorted with disgust. "Life of ease? Joy, Liv, do you have any idea how much they get per child? No one could live a life of ease on that amount of money. Get real! Those checks barely keep them from starving to death and some of them can't even afford to pay for a roof over their heads. I say good luck to the one who won the lottery. Who better to appreciate it? So they spend a dollar to buy a bit of hope for a brighter future? It worked for her."

Liv and Joy glared at Rich and then, with looks of disgust, turned away from him to talk to the woman on the other side of Joy.

"Well, Karo, how do you like Belle Vista?" Evy asked from across the table.

"I like it a lot. I'm still finding my way around, but I like the way it feels like a separate little town and that the country seems so close."

"Where are you living?" Rich asked.

"Out in Vista Cove. Do you know where that is?"

"Oh, it's nice out there, good beach access. Betty lives near there. Betty, don't you live in Vista Cove?" He called down the table.

A woman with brown hair, streaked liberally with grey, nodded. "Yes, I've lived there for about thirty years. I love the beach. What street do you live on?"

It turned out that Betty lived only two streets away from Karo and she cordially invited her to stop by for coffee some morning. Then everyone was finished and eager to head back to their projects. The patio was quickly empty of everything except the wet pottery lined up on the benches to dry to the leather-hard stage suitable for trimming, the next stage toward completion.

CHAPTER 3

The dogs were waiting right at the door, dancing with excitement when Karo came in. Or perhaps they weren't excited to see her; rather they just needed to go out after being locked up in the house for several hours.

"Come on." She led the way to the back door and watched as they bounded into the backyard. She left the door ajar and went to hang up her jacket and check the mail that had been dropped through the slot into the basket that sat in the front hall. She walked through the house, checking the stack of mail for anything interesting as she headed for the kitchen and took a diet Coke from the refrigerator. Then, before she had pulled the tab, the phone rang.

"Eileen? How are you?" She and Eileen had remained close over the years in spite of Eileen's move to St. Louis many years ago. They visited occasionally, wrote and called as often as they could. They constantly updated each other as to the activities of each family, and so they still felt close. Karo noticed that since her breakup with Greg, and during the resulting period of upheaval, Eileen had been calling much more frequently. It was Eileen's way of providing support, despite their miles of separation.

Now the friends spent a few minutes going through their usual discussion of their children, Eileen's husband, and their extended families before getting down to a serious discussion.

"How are you doing, Karo?" Eileen's voice projected her concern.

"I'm doing better. I started my pottery classes today." Then she gave her friend an abbreviated description of the day she had. "I'm excited about working there, these people are really good potters. But I've noticed there are some strange-acting people in the group. It will be interesting getting to know them. Maybe they'll turn out to be more normal than they seemed today."

Just then Rudy pushed the kitchen door open with his head and he and Captain hurried to Karo, eagerly looking for a treat. She took the phone with her to the cupboard and managed to get the dog treats while still talking.

"Actually, Eileen, one of the reasons I'm doing so much better is that I took your advice. I went to the animal shelter last week and got myself a four-legged companion." She smiled at Eileen's enthusiastic response. "Well, actually, I got two. Captain and his friend Rudy now call it home here. Captain is a Cairn terrier mix, but I swear he looks like a purebred. He came with a friend, Rudy, who is a little harder to describe. He's big, and clumsy, with brown short bristly hair, and he's very lovable. Anyway, they came as a pair. And they were scheduled for..., you know. They were going to be put down if I didn't take them."

Karo couldn't hide the distress in her voice. "Eileen, I just don't know who could have trained these guys, and then allowed them to be taken to the pound where they were at risk of losing their lives. It doesn't make sense. These two are very sweet, well behaved, and a lot of fun."

"Two? Karo, I can't believe you've gone from a no dog person to two. Do you have enough yard space for two dogs?"

"Oh, there's plenty of yard. And I can walk them on the beach every day. They love that." She paused, stricken by the memory of yesterday's walk, surprised she could forget so quickly what had happened.

"Oh, Eileen, something awful happened yesterday." Then hearing the sound of Eileen's sharp intake of breath, she realized she had alarmed her friend. She quickly explained. "Not to me. I'm sorry. I didn't mean to scare you. Yesterday I took the dogs to run on the beach. We had a wonderful time, but when it was time to go home I couldn't get Rudy away from something he had found in the rocks. When I went over to get him I saw he had found a body." She shuddered now just thinking of it. "It was just awful."

"A body? Dead? Who was it? Was it a drowning and the body washed up on shore?"

"I don't know. The only thing it said in the paper today was an unidentified woman's body was found in the surf on the Belle Vista Beach. So I don't know what happened. And of course, I was so horrified at the time I didn't look closely." She didn't intend to tell her friend she had looked closely enough to see the crabs and other creatures of the sea had been feasting on the woman already. It was too horrible to share.

But she did proceed to tell Eileen every other detail and, by the time she hung up, she was wondering if she really wanted to take the boys, what she had started calling the dogs, down to the beach for a walk again this afternoon. She could see they were eager to go, so she decided a compromise was in order. Today they would go the other way on the beach and explore the north end. That should be safe enough.

The next day Karo went to the pottery class taught by Sandi Weir, a local who was also the Director of Ceramics at San Francisco State University. Unlike her experience in meeting Joy yesterday, Karo found she liked the easygoing Sandi immediately. In fact, the studio on Wednesday seemed like an entirely different place than the workshop on Tuesday. The Wednesday class contained ten brand new students, who would be doing hand building; and seven intermediate students, who would be learning to throw on the wheel this session. In addition, there appeared to be at least another twelve advanced students. These included people from the workshop like her, Rich and Betty as well as several, who for some reason hadn't attended the workshop the day before. Even though the studio was big, it was obvious that with a class this size they would have to take turns using the equipment and carefully share the space.

Sandi started the class with an explanation of what they could expect during the session. She explained that each of the three groups, beginning, intermediate and advanced potters, would be working on different projects during class. She would give the new students a tour, and then they would begin work on pinch pots, little balls of clay the students would pinch with their fingers to form into small bowls or cups. While she was working with the new students, the intermediate students would be working with Betty to begin their training on the wheel. Betty, the older woman Karo met yesterday, was going to demonstrate how to center and open a piece of clay on the wheel. While all this was going on, the advanced potters would start the day on their own projects, but later Sandi promised a demonstration on how to make an altered pot. They would be expected to produce several variations of an altered pot as their first class assignment.

Karo was happy to claim a wheel and start trimming the three pieces she had thrown yesterday and hadn't been able to finish before leaving. Karo paused for a little while to watch as Betty deftly demonstrated how to center and open a piece of clay explaining each of her movements to the fascinated audience.

"It looks so easy, doesn't it?" she whispered to Rich, standing beside her. "Betty's very good. Has she been here long?"

"She's one of the originals. She, Joy and Mary Louise have been coming since they built the studio. They were instrumental in setting it up and designing it, so no wonder they sometimes think they own it." He grinned. "But several of the others have also been coming for years. Liv, P.J., Jane and Iris are all old timers."

"What about you? How long have you been coming?"

"Me? Oh, about four years now. But I've been potting since college. I found this place not long after I moved to Belle Vista. I used to have a studio in my house, but I find this works much better for me. I keep the mess here."

"So is Betty a teacher's assistant or something?"

"Yeah, something like that. It's too big a class for one teacher, so Betty gets her tuition and all the workshops free for helping Sandi on Thursdays. The guy who is teaching the night class does it on his own, but he has only about half the number of students and, since it's only a three hour class, it's more manageable."

Karo looked around. "Where are all the people who were at workshop yesterday. Don't they come to class?"

Rich shook his head. "Most of them don't. And it's odd because they have to pay for the class whether or not they attend. It's a requirement for the studio workshop to be enrolled in the pottery class." He shrugged. "Too bad for them, because Sandi is a great potter and a good teacher. But this is a class and she does require the projects she assigns be completed. Some people only want to do what they want to do, so they just pay the fee and don't come to class.

"And, I'm sure Joy doesn't come because Sandi is in charge. Joy is in charge of the workshops, but she still reports to Sandi. Sandi is the boss, so if Joy is never around Sandi, she can pretend she doesn't exist unless she wants Sandi to do something for her. And Sandi doesn't mind. I know Sandi likes having Joy take care of all the work assignments and firing all the kilns. It would be a much bigger job for Sandi if she had to do all of that in addition to teaching the class.

For sure, without Joy's help, Sandi wouldn't be able to manage here and her obligations at S.F. State. So Sandi gives Joy a lot of latitude in the studio. She just leaves notes for Joy or sends messages through Betty. It all seems to work out."

Karo stared at Rich with amazement thinking their system was a little strange, but he acted like it was no big deal and as it obviously worked, she just returned to her work. She finished the pieces she was working on and then, after Sandi did her demonstration, she threw two more pots to alter as she had been shown. She found a place at one of the tables and used a small turn table to alter the thrown pot by stretching the wet clay into a different shape. She then added clay extensions on the piece and stretched them even more, letting her imagination move her. It was different and it was fun. She thoroughly enjoyed her first day of class and went home tired, but satisfied.

When she got home she made the phone call to confirm her appointment for tomorrow at the bank that had hired her to write their procedural manual. Then she organized her notes for that appointment, before she was ready to take the boys out. It was much later than she planned when they left the house. As she walked past the end house she saw a young man standing in the shadows by the garage, smoking. She waved and smiled cordially, but he just stared at her a moment and turned away without acknowledging her. Well, she thought, how rude! She wondered for a minute what his parents must be like if the kid was so devoid of social graces. But she realized some teenagers were very moody and forgot him as soon as they reached the beach. She headed north again, not willing yet to go south, although that was the way the optimistic Rudy wanted to go. The sun was sinking toward the horizon and, while she had promised Eileen she wouldn't go on the beach at night, she told herself this was just late afternoon. However, by the time she returned to the path over the dune it was definitely getting dark, making it difficult to find the way. She saw the fog bank heaped up on the horizon, and shivered in the cold wind blowing off it. She realized that soon the fog wouldn't be burning off every morning. It would be sitting here all day, sometimes hiding the rain clouds above it. When they reached Sunset Lane she was happy for the streetlights. She vowed to herself that in the future she would make the time to leave for the beach earlier. She realized it would have been smarter to organize her notes after the walk on the beach.

So Karo's new life on the beach took on a satisfying rhythm. She was pleasantly busy and, between her writing for the bank, working in clay, the demands of the dogs and the chores required to settle into her house, she was kept challenged and interested. She certainly didn't miss the demands of a husband or the irritations of the last few years of their marriage, but she still missed Lisa, who had been the focal point of her life for so many years. She satisfied that longing by calling Lisa every Sunday on her cell phone, using up her monthly allowance of minutes on a conversation she really cared about.

Even her work was going well. The bank was so pleased with the completed sections of the manual they were thinking about extending her contract to include maintenance of this manual as well as to have her write a product manual for the marketing department and a procedural manual for the business banking division. Knowing she would be having a steady income for a while calmed her and allowed her to concentrate on other aspects of her life.

* * *

The cold autumn day was a definite harbinger of the winter coming. Suddenly Captain raced for the front door growling and barking with Rudy right behind him. Rudy's bark was more menacing and the ridge of hair that stood up on his back meant he was serious. With that warning Karo wasn't surprised by the doorbell and peered through the little window in the door to see Rich on the porch.

She pulled the door open, smiling. "Hey Rich, what's up?"

"I thought today might be a good time to take care of that tree for you."

Karo, busy calming the dogs, stepped back to allow him to step into the house and only then saw he was followed by another man.

"This is my friend, Winwey," was his casual introduction.

Winwey dipped his head. "He really means that today he has help. He's drafted me and my chainsaw, ma'm." His grin lit up his face before he stooped over to address the dogs. "Hey guys, how ya doing?"

The dogs couldn't believe their luck and didn't know whether to lay down for a belly rub or sit still for an ear fondle. They obviously forgot all about their roles as guardians of the abode.

"So, is this a good time?" Rich peered around the house reminding Karo of her manners.

"Are you kidding? Anytime is a good time. Come this way." She led the way down the hall into the kitchen and then pointed out the mud room window. "That's the villain there. You can see how it's only still upright because it's leaning against the back of the garage. It can't be good for that structure, now can it?"

Both men crowded forward, peering through the window.

"Piece of cake. We'll take the top limbs off first and then do the trunk in pieces. Where can we stack the wood? You'll want to use it for firewood, won't you?" Winwey seemed to be in charge.

"Don't you or Rich want the wood? That seems fair considering the work you'll be doing."

"I don't need it. I have a forest on my property. Rich?"

Rich shook his head. "Don't have a fireplace. Wish I did. No, Karo, you may as well make use of it. Is your ladder in the garage and can we get into the backyard through that gate?"

Karo showed them where the ladder was and opened the back gate. Then she dragged the protesting dogs back inside, knowing as soon as the chainsaw was fired up they'd be cowering under her desk for protection. She watched the men for a minute from the kitchen, but it was obvious they knew what they were doing. So she checked the fire under the kettle of soup simmering on the stove and returned to her office and the work she was doing.

She was surprised by Rich's arrival, but she shouldn't have been. He said he could take care of the tree for her when she told him about the sagging tree and her worry about what it was doing to the little apartment at the back of the garage. Rich Jay was a surprising man. It turned out that he was a nurse in the emergency room at the Carruthers Medical Center, the big hospital on the east side of town. He worked nights, Friday through Tuesday, if he was lucky, and didn't have to work extra shifts. He admitted working in the pottery studio helped keep him sane. He was a gifted potter and, while he was shorter and thinner and younger than Karo, his wiry strength allowed him to throw amazingly large pieces. Karo thought if he was only half as good a nurse as he was a potter, he must be a valued member of Carruthers staff.

Karo thought Rich was about thirty-five, and she assumed he was gay. After all, he was a nurse. But they had clicked from that very first day in the workshop and soon found themselves good friends. Karo was grateful. Starting a new life in a new area meant she needed all the friends she could find.

Now, thinking about Rich's friend, Winwey, Karo thought he was pretty nice to help Rich do this project for a complete stranger. He looked older than Rich, judging by his weathered face, which needed a shave, and the bits of gray peppering the hair above his ears. He was taller than Rich and heavier, but good looking in a rugged outdoors way. Karo wondered if they were romantically linked. But she told herself sternly, that wasn't any of her business. He was Rich's friend and he was helping her. That was enough for her.

It was getting dark by the time the chainsaw was finally quiet. Rich and Winwey crowded back into the warm fragrant kitchen. Karo realized taking care of that tree had not been the "piece of cake" they had claimed it would be. The men had spent several hours of hard labor and she felt as if she had imposed on them.

Finally, coats and gloves shed, hands scrubbed, they sat at the kitchen table with their cups of tea, which they selected over a choice of wine or beer. That choice made Karo feel even more guilt, because it had obviously been darned cold out there. She put a bowl of tortilla chips on the table and took another bowl of con queso (hot cheese dip) out of the microwave.

"Now, how is it you just happened to be in this end of town, Rich?"

"Pure luck, hey Winwey?"

Winwey nodded, pausing a moment with a chip halfway to his mouth. "We got a call from our fishing captain friend. He said he had too much fish and if we wanted to help him by taking some of it off his hands we'd better hightail it down to the dock right after we got off work."

"Hell, we're smart enough to act on that kind of message," Rich explained. "He owns a charter fishing boat and sometimes they catch more than the customers want to take with them. This time he had a group of business people who had flown in for the trip and they hit it big. There was no way they could take all that fish with them and they didn't want to have it processed and shipped. So, Captain Jack had to get rid of it."

Rich looked at Karo. "Say, do you want some? We must have a hundred pounds of filleted rock cod in the ice chest in the back of Winwey's truck. You can just freeze it. It's great fish, even frozen it will be fresher than what you get in the market."

"Do you like fish?" Winwey asked.

"I love it, but I can't have you work all afternoon and then take your fish too. That's too much!"

"Don't be silly, Karo. Did you hear me say we have a hundred pounds? Do you know how long it would take us to eat that? We'll be giving lots of it away. You may as well have some too."

"Well, if you're sure." She smiled. "I'd love some. But speaking of food, could I interest either of you in some tortilla soup? I have a pot simmering that is ready to be eaten."

"So that's what we're smelling?" Winwey asked and seeing her nod said, "Hell yes, I'd love some. I'm famished even after inhaling these tortilla chips. I didn't know what you were cooking, but it smells great. There's nothing better than a warm kitchen full of good smells after a little outdoor work."

Rich went out to the truck for some fish while Karo set the table. She got out shredded cheese, sour cream and fresh cilantro which she placed on the table along with a refill of tortilla chips and the silverware. She put the soup kettle on a trivet right on the table and after Rich put the fish in the refrigerator she sat down and began dishing up the soup.

"Now, I sprinkle crumbled tortilla chips on top, then cheese, then cilantro, if you like it, and finally a dab of sour cream." She demonstrated. "See? It's a little spicy, so be prepared."

The men finished their first bowl and handed the empties back for a refill, exclaiming, "That's great."

"Wow, I didn't know you could cook, too?" Rich deftly added the condiments to his filled bowl.

The two men paused from time to time to make conversation and when they passed their bowls again they indicated Karo should just give them half a bowl.

The screech of brakes startled them all, but the unmistakable crunch had them up from the table and heading for the front door even as they heard the squeal of wheels spinning and someone yelling.

Rich got to the door first, pausing only a moment to push Captain back, as he went out. Winwey was on his heels, so Karo had to drag Rudy out of the way, not even bothering to shush Captain's frantic barking before she, too, was outside. Rich was talking to the driver in the car stopped in front and then the driver turned off his motor and got out. It was the neighbor who lived across the street and down two houses from her. He and his wife worked, didn't seem to have kids. She rarely saw them, but recognized the car.

"Crazy kids! Probably a friend of those kids at the end of the street." The man was looking at the front of his car, shaking his head with disgust. "Scared the stuffin' out of me, I'll tell you. I turned into the street like I always do and here's this car headed right at me. I slammed on my brakes. He swerved and just nicked me, and then instead of stopping to make sure I'm okay, he steps on the gas so hard he fishtails around the corner. Look, you can see the marks where he burned rubber."

The men gathered around the front of his car, checking the bumper and the smashed headlight.

Karo stood on the curb and talked to her neighbors, who came out to see what was going on. The people on the right of her were very vocal about the people at the end of the block. "All the time the cars are going up and down. Cars going too fast; never paying attention. It's a crime. And do you see any of them coming out to see what's wrong? No, they don't even notice."

Another neighbor agreed and told a story of when her grandchildren were visiting and someone drove over her curb. She thought the children were going to be hit. She said she was so mad she went down the street to complain, but the people wouldn't even come to the door. "But I know they were in there. I saw the curtain move. So I just stood there and yelled at them."

"Did it do any good?"

"Well, it seemed quieter for a while and it let me blow off steam at least. I just wish they'd move. This used to be a quiet peaceful street, but since they've been here it's gotten worse and worse."

Rich and Winwey turned back toward the house so Karo said her good-byes and followed them in.

"Whoa, it's cold out there tonight." Winwey rubbed his arms.

"This kind of thing happen often here, Karo?" Rich asked as they sat back down at the table.

"No, generally it's fairly quiet except for the house at the end. I guess they have teenagers or young adults, not very friendly. I spoke to one of the boys once, but he didn't even nod in return. You know how some kids are." She shrugged, then, picking up the abandoned bowls asked, "Anyone up for some ice cream and cookies?"

Both men nodded, obviously happy to find the meal wasn't over yet. Karo plated the cookies she had taken out of the freezer a while ago and scooped out the ice cream.

"This is a great meal, Karo. Thank you so much." Winwey dug into his bowl of ice cream with gusto.

"Hey, I like these cookies," Rich said. "They remind me of some my aunt used to make for me and my sister."

Karo smiled happily. She loved cooking and enjoyed the praise and the men's obvious appreciation. "Well, it's small payment for your work today, and while I can't always guarantee an *ad hoc* meal like this, I do try to keep things in the freezer, just in case."

Finally, Winwey said he had to get home and get some sleep and Karo remembered the men had come over after working all night and hadn't been to bed yet. Rich gave Karo some instructions about how to best freeze the fish he had put in the refrigerator.

With a final pat for the dogs, they were off with a final caution. "Best stay far away from those kids at the end. It doesn't sound like a good situation. You have an alarm system, don't you?" At Karo's nod Winwey continued, "Be sure you use it. I think you should even set it when you take the dogs to the beach. After all you pass that house on your way, so they can see you're gone. And that would be just the time for mischief if they were so inclined."

Rich nodded, agreeing with Winwey, and then they were both gone and suddenly the house seemed very empty.

CHAPTER 4

"Coffee? Hot coffee?"

The mound of cardboard and dirty blankets moved. The woman waited and was rewarded for her patience by a dirt encrusted hand at the edge of the flattened cardboard box, then an eye appeared, swollen with sleep and red from the wine consumed the night before.

"Would you like some hot coffee?" the woman kindly inquired.

The man emerged fully, nodding his head, and holding out a shaking hand for the Styrofoam cup filled with the hot brew, liberally laced with milk and sugar.

"I'm sorry, but I only have it with cream and sugar. Would you like more?"

He nodded, holding out the now empty cup eagerly.

She took the cup and held it under the spout in the vacuum jug, pumped the top and watched the light brown stream fill the cup again. She handed it back. "I have sandwiches, would you like some?"

When he nodded, she put a baggie holding three meat and cheese sandwiches in his hand. She then picked up her thermos and canvas bag of sandwiches and moved down the lot to the next pile of trash, which most likely contained another homeless person.

He was munching the last of the sandwiches, still watching the woman distribute her largess when another derelict squatted near him and nodded toward the woman.

"Who's that? What church does she represent?"

He shook his head. "Don't know. She's called the Coffee Lady. She comes by once in a while with coffee and sandwiches. One time she gave me a fiver." He grinned, the memory of the wine it purchased still sharp in his mind. "Don't think she belongs to a church, just a do-gooder."

"Just gives out coffee and sandwiches and money for nothing?" The other guy was skeptical as were most of them who refused to go to one of the missions on these cold nights. They refused a warm bed and a hot meal, because it came with the obligation to sit through a church service and sermon.

The man finished his sandwich and looked around, gathering up his cardboard and blankets. "Yep, once in a while she takes someone with her. She cleans them up and helps them get a life again."

"No!" He didn't believe it.

"Yep, she took Gus a while back, and he left me his stuff." He pointed to a rickety grocery cart, leaning against the on-ramp support pillar behind him. "Said he wouldn't be needing it anymore."

"And what happened to him?"

He shrugged. "Don't know, but he never came back here so I'm guessing he did get his life together again. He was a good guy, very smart, just had a lot of bad luck in his later years."

He squinted down the lot, but the woman was out of sight now. "Whenever she offers coffee and sandwiches I'm always happy to accept. She's got a heart of gold, that one. For sure she does."

* * *

"Rudy, sit!" Karo called out sharply when she saw Rudy bounding toward the figure stooping over on the beach. She need not have worried because Rudy behaved like a gentleman, stopping short of the old woman and waiting for an invitation to approach. Captain, on the other hand, was wriggling with excitement, cavorting around Rudy and the woman, who was now patting Rudy's head.

Karo hurried up, full of apologies. "I'm so sorry. I hope they didn't startle you... Oh, Betty, it's you. Good morning. What are you doing out on the beach so early?"

Betty seemed to hesitate a moment and then she apparently recognized Karo. "Oh, Karo, I didn't know you had dogs. Aren't they fun? And this one is such a gentleman." She patted Rudy's head and stooped, managing to pet Captain at the same time.

"These are my boys. This is Rudy," Karo indicated the large dog," and this one is Captain. We're out here everyday, but I've never seen you on the beach before, although I do remember now that you live out this way, too."

"Yes, I live on Seal Rock Circle, over there." She vaguely waved in a northerly direction. "After a storm like the one last evening I try to get on the beach as soon as possible. You just never know what you'll find."

Karo noticed the burlap bag sitting on the sand near Betty's feet.

"Do you collect shells?"

"Shells, driftwood, and sea glass, if I can find it."

"Sea glass, what's that?"

She stooped over and rooted in the bag coming up with something in her hand. "This is a part of a bottle which has been worn down by the wave action and the storm tossed it on the beach."

Karo picked up the piece of brown glass, turning it over in her hand. The edges had been worn smooth; the finish was matte and the color deep gold. It was attractive.

"I use it for decoration, or I just sell it."

"Is it valuable?" Karo was a little skeptical.

"Only to people who collect it. Some use it in crafts. Some people make jewelry out of it, and some people just like to collect it for the different shapes and colors. It's not like finding gold, but it has a special look to it. I have a booth at the flea market once a month where I sell my pottery and things I find on the beach. I sell enough to keep me scavenging whenever possible."

"I've heard about that flea market. It's at the fairgrounds, isn't it?"

"Yes, the second Friday of each month, Friday, Saturday and Sunday. You can buy anything there. The farmers bring in their crops to sell. Some people rent a booth instead of having a garage sale. People sell all kinds of homemade goods there. You should come. I'm sure you'd enjoy it. It's kind of a Belle Vista thing, you know."

"I will. I have heard about it, even before I moved here. I just haven't had time to check it out."

Betty slung her bag over her shoulder. "I'm heading home now. Would you like to walk with me and see my studio?"

"You have a pottery studio?" Karo asked eagerly.

Betty nodded. "Yes, I'm only at the recreation center studio three days a week and Thursdays I'm helping Sandi, so I work at home the rest of the time. I just love that reduction kiln we have at the Rec Center and there is no way I have the space or money to put one in at my house. So I save up certain pieces to fire there, otherwise, I make most of my things in my own studio."

"I'd love to see it. Do you mind the dogs?"

"Of course not! I love dogs. I sometimes think I should get a dog. Or a cat. A cat sits on your lap and is such a comfort, but a dog could go to the beach with me and is more of a companion. What do you think?"

So they walked along the beach while Karo told Betty about her own mission to find a pet only to return with two instead of one. By the time they reached Betty's small ranch style house, Betty was seriously considering a visit to the animal shelter.

Betty's roomy two-car garage had been finished, plumbed and heated so it now was a very efficient studio. The electric kiln was in a small alcove attached on the yard side of the garage. And the place was immaculate.

Karo tied the dogs up outside with stern orders to "stay." Then she followed Betty into her studio. Once inside she was glad she refused to let them in as Betty had invited her to do. She could just imagine one of them knocking down a row of teapots sitting there drying, or bumping something and causing some other tragedy. She stood looking at a half dozen finished teapot sets with Japanese style cups. One in particular caught her fancy, done in a black and green glaze.

"Oh, Betty, are these for sale?"

She nodded and seeing the one Karo was looking at she said, "That's Reitz's Black to Green glaze. It turned out rather well, didn't it? This glaze works as well in the electric kiln as it does in the reduction kiln, but the look is different when it's fired in the electric kiln."

"Could I buy it? I love this set. It's such a lovely shape and the cups feel so good in my hand." She was fondling one of the cups.

"Well of course, but I didn't bring you here to sell you my pottery."

"I know that, but I just love this set. If I don't get it, I know someone else will snap it up."

Betty laughed at Karo's earnest expression. She took the rest of the set down from the shelf and started wrapping it up in paper.

"I don't have to have it right now. In fact I don't even have any money with me, but I can come back to get it."

"Don't be silly. You can take it and bring me a check for thirty dollars on Tuesday. You'll be there, won't you?" She saw Karo nod and continued wrapping the set. "This way you can have tea in it tonight if you want."

Betty finished packing the set into a bag with handles and then said, "There, all finished. Now do you have time for a cup of tea?" At Karo's nod she led the way to the house, pausing long enough to instruct

Karo to bring the dogs. "They're probably ready for a drink of water, don't you think?"

They all spent a pleasant hour in Betty's kitchen, sipping tea and lapping water while Betty told Karo how her husband, Ralph, had built the studio for her to work in. "He was such a precise man; it had to be perfect he said. And I think it is. I can't think of one thing that needs to be changed. I do miss the man." She sighed.

"I'm sorry, Betty. Has he been gone long?"

Betty's eyes widened and she gave a start, saying quickly, "Oh, I didn't mean you to think he died. No, he's still alive, but he's suffering from dementia. I'm afraid I couldn't cope anymore and for his own safety I had to place him in a full care facility. They take wonderful care of him, and I get up there to see him as often as I can, not that he even knows who I am anymore."

"It must have been very difficult for you. Do you have children?" As soon as she said it she knew she shouldn't have, because a look of sadness washed over Betty's face that almost broke Karo's heart.

"We had a son. But we lost him when he was still a teenager. It was a stupid, tragic accident and then he was gone." She shook her head. "But enough of that, Karo. Let's talk about you. What brought you to Belle Vista?"

Karo told her briefly about her divorce and her decision to move to Belle Vista. "I'm so glad I did. I'm loving this area and this town. It makes me feel young and excited about my life again." Then noticing the time, she jumped to her feet. "Oh, Betty, I've stayed too long. I have work waiting for me."

Betty stood up. "Well, I'm so glad I ran into you and the dogs today. We live so close, you'll have to stop by again soon."

Karo hooked the leashes to the dogs, gathered her bag containing the teapot set and listened carefully while Betty explained the route she needed to take through the housing track's twisted streets to bring her out at the end of her street. As she ambled toward home with Captain and Rudy checking out every tree and shrub along the way, Karo thought about the stream of events which led her to Belle Vista.

She realized that she had become lost sometime between when Lisa was born and when she went away to college. Looking back, she guessed she started to change when she decided to stay home and become a fulltime mom. Somehow, being a mother and housewife didn't seem to be justification enough to escape the unrelenting demands of the work world. At first, motherhood and housekeeping were like a game. She only had to play all day with the baby and keep the household going. Each evening she presented Lisa, herself, the house and a dinner like a beautifully wrapped gift to Greg, when he came home beaten down from frustrations at work and stretched to the breaking point by the inevitable traffic. When things didn't go exactly as she anticipated, if Lisa had a bad day, she just absorbed it, not wanting to burden Greg with her minor frustrations. When Lisa started school and she had more time for herself, Greg began moving up the ladder and needed more support from her, so that free time just disappeared. He was traveling a lot then, and they were entertaining. Somehow her days filled up with running errands, taking care of the house, volunteering at Lisa's school and being Lisa and Greg's cheering section. That's when she really started to forget her dreams.

She spent an inordinate amount of time on Lisa. Having been raised by disinterested parents she had vowed that would never happen to her child. Her child and her husband would enjoy a life she directed, just as she had dreamed up lives for her paper doll families when she was young. Karo was so busy smoothing the path for Lisa and Greg she didn't even realize she no longer had any interests or hobbies of her own. When Lisa went off to college it hit her.

Greg was gone on business much of the time and when he was home he was very particular about how the house was run and how they spent their time. Karo realized now that she had put so much effort into sparing Greg from the difficulties of running their house and raising their child that he now regarded her efforts minimal and her contribution as valueless.

So with too much time on her hands, Karo let a friend talk her into signing up for a couple of art classes at the local junior college. The classes gave her days purpose and still allowed her the time she needed to attend her chores to keep her household running efficiently. And surprisingly, she didn't stick out in a sea of young faces as she expected to. There were several members of the older generation attending classes and she didn't feel at all odd. When she signed up for the pottery class she found she loved working with the clay and she had to have more.

Then Lisa finished college and accepted a job in Boston. Karo and Greg realized she wasn't coming back soon. They also realized whatever they had between them originally was now long gone. Greg became more and more critical of Karo, how she dressed, how she acted and even how she thought. And Karo was finding Greg had somehow become a pompous overbearing bore. She thought his friends were more of the same, and while she had originally attempted to be part of the group for his sake, she now found it hard to be interested in the subjects that seemed to amuse them.

She wasn't surprised when Greg finally admitted he wanted a divorce. He denied there was anyone else, but the signs were all there. The new sports car he drove, the younger more fashionable wardrobe he bought, the regimen he started at the gym were all signs of a change coming. She wondered how long it would have been before she suggested a separation, if he hadn't?

She turned the corner and her house appeared in front of them. Home! She smiled to herself with satisfaction. The dogs lurched forward against their leashes, apparently as anxious as she was to get home.

* * *

"Now look what you've done?" Liv's shrill voice cut through the quiet murmur in the studio.

"That wasn't my fault. You got in my way," Marge defended herself.

Karo looked up from her work in time to see Liv give Marge a mighty shove. Marge grabbed onto the table to keep from falling and subsequently dropped the bisqued bowl she was carrying. That unique sound of pottery shattering got everyone's attention.

Marge charged at Liv furiously, arms flailing as she screamed, "You bitch; you did that on purpose."

Liv struggled under Marge's onslaught, her face red, contorted with anger as she started kicking and slapping back.

"Hey, you two. Liv, Marge! Stop it right now!" Joy's voice rang sharply through the shocked silence of the room.

Liv and Marge froze in place.

Marge slowly let her raised arms drop. "She pushed me and I broke my bowl." Marge's voice quivered with rage as she attempted to justify her actions.

"She knocked into my piece and broke the handle," Liv defended loudly, out of breath.

"I don't care! If you're going to act like kids take it outside. I don't want any more pieces broken as a result of your childish tempers. And none of us want to witness your petty squabbles."

Both women looked around, startled to find everyone in the studio was staring at them with opened mouths. Liv and Marge's expressions immediately turned from anger to embarrassment. They sheepishly turned away to other tasks. Liv went to the glaze room and Marge knelt down and started picking up the pieces of her broken bowl. Quickly, everyone else went back to work, as if nothing had happened. Later, when Karo was alone in the glaze room with Evy she asked, "What was that all about?"

"They just hate each other. They have been feuding so long I don't even think they know what started it," Evy explained with a shrug.

"But they were actually physically fighting. I've never seen adults act like that. Has it happened before?"

Evy reluctantly admitted, "Well, they're always bickering and making snide remarks about each other. But I've only seen them actually fight once before. I heard once it was so bad that they were on the floor screaming, pulling hair and gouging each other. Apparently that time they knocked into an older woman, Flo, and bruised her pretty badly. But then Joy had a serious meeting with them both and it's been better."

Karo stopped what she was doing and stared at Evy. "I can't believe that! Why doesn't one of them quit coming? Or come on a different day. That seems like an easy solution."

"That's all part of it. Neither of them wants to give it up because of the other. Frankly, I think they enjoy the feud. I'm sure you've noticed they both are very opinionated and try to boss everyone around. Most people just ignore them, but each of them refuses to do that to the other so they get into arguments and that leads to very unpleasant confrontations. I think they enjoy the excitement. It gets their blood in an uproar." Evy laughed. "But you saw how quickly Joy stepped in. She's not about to let them damage anything or anyone in the studio. And they pay attention because she can bar them from the studio and they know it. Joy never has them work together on the assignments. If you notice they never take a wheel near each other. In fact, even at lunch you'll find them at opposite ends of the lunch benches."

Evy was finished with her piece and left Karo to her glazing with plenty of time to think about the strange dynamics of the pottery group.

She felt she was learning lots at this studio, partly because she was devoting more time to her work, partly because of Sandi, who was a wonderful teacher. However, most of her improvements she attributed to the other people working in the studio. In particular Betty, Rich, and Mary Louise were excellent potters and turned out pieces which really appealed to Karo. Just seeing the quality of their work, the detail they achieved, inspired her to do better with her own. And the others, while maybe not as good as her three favorite potters, still came up with innovative ideas and occasional pieces that spurred her to attempt new techniques with her own work. But she noticed there seemed to be an inordinate number of wacky individuals in the group.

Joy, their leader was plainly just a grouch. She wanted everything her way and didn't mind letting everyone know if they didn't measure up. Karo wondered idly if she had always been that way. One of the women whispered once that Joy's husband left her suddenly several years ago. He apparently employed the old technique of going to the store for cigarettes and just kept going. Karo wondered if Joy's personality drove him away, or if she was grouchy as a result of that abandonment. But whatever the reason, Joy's negative attitude seemed pervasive in the workshops she supervised.

On Wednesday, the day she took class with Sandi, the studio had a whole different atmosphere. It was much freer and the students more light-hearted. Laughter frequently sounded through the studio. They only worked five hours on class day, but they did as much as the longer workshop day. And everyone seemed to have fun doing it.

Well, she told herself, it wasn't likely Joy would change her attitude or her style. She just tried to stay out of Joy's way as much as possible. She had already noticed that while Joy was abrupt and sharp with other people she seemed overly sensitive to criticism herself. And she didn't like direct confrontation; she frequently employed a technique where she got her lieutenants such as Liv and Mary Louise agitated about some infraction of the "rules" and then sent them to straighten out the guilty party. That way they got into the shouting matches, not her. Then she would play the good guy, calming the waters. Working with Joy could be unbearable if you let her bother you. Joy usually left about one in the afternoons, leaving either Betty or Mary Louise to lock up the studio at five, so it was easy to avoid Joy in the afternoons. Her defenders said she did this because she worked many extra hours when she was firing the kilns, coming in to load and unload and to mind the big kilns when they were being fired. This was always said with admiration for Joy's dedication to the studio, but Karo could see by the pieces Joy produced that she used those times in the studio to her advantage. It was as if she had her own private studio to use on those days.

Several of the women watched over the studio as if it were their own house. They spent hours organizing the glazing room, and alphabetizing the formulas for the glazes. They checked the wheels and tables to make sure they were pristine; and of course, they reported any infractions to the housekeeping rules. Naturally, this caused some resentment and sometimes a few sharp disagreements among them. However, the altercation between Liv and Marge was still the first time Karo had seen one of these disagreements lead to physical blows. It was very upsetting and hard to ignore. She vowed that she would just try to avoid working near either of these two women.

That decision made her laugh. Now she realized her plan was to avoid being near Joy, Liv and Marge, just a few more people to avoid would almost put her to work outside the studio. She shrugged. She'd just take one day at a time and hope she wouldn't have to give up attending the workshops altogether.

CHAPTER 5

The cold rainy Saturday morning in November made it seem more like winter. Karo didn't mind. She decided it was a perfect day to hole up in the house and finish the section of the manual she was writing. When the doorbell interrupted the quiet and the dogs ran barking and growling to the front door, Karo reluctantly followed. She peeked out the small window in the middle of the heavy dark oak door, but didn't recognize the misshapen dark form on the porch. Cautiously she held Rudy's collar tight and ordered Captain to sit before opening the door.

It was Winwey, Rich's friend, dressed in bulky warm clothes and balancing a basket heaped with apples on his shoulder. "Hi, sorry to barge in unannounced, but I was hoping you'd be glad to have some apples." His smile was boyish and friendly.

Karo pulled the door open, still holding onto Rudy. "How nice of you. I'd love some apples. Take them through to the kitchen if you don't mind."

Once Winwey was heading for the kitchen she let go of Rudy and signaled to Captain he could go and they all followed. The dogs went scampering and leaping, but Karo managed to keep to a sedate pace behind him even though she was thrilled to have both the apples and the company.

"I think I mentioned I live on a piece of property up in the hills a ways and I have an old apple orchard. Anyway, this time of year I have apples, apples and more apples. I try to gather as many as I can and distribute them to people who will make use of them. I remembered those cookies you baked when we were here and thought you might be a person who could put some apples to good use."

Karo had a large smile on her face as she picked up one of the apples and inhaled the tart, yummy scent. "Umm, I can taste applesauce already. You bet I can find a use for them. This is so nice of you."

Then remembering her manners, "Sit down, take off your jacket. Would you like some coffee, or tea?"

Winwey nodded, removing his jacket he sat down at one of the chairs around the sturdy oak kitchen table. "Tea would be nice, if it's not too much trouble."

Karo filled the tea kettle with water and put it on the burner while she moved around the kitchen assembling the teapot, tea and sugar. "Cream?" she asked, and when he shook his head she put the pitcher back in the cupboard. She ducked out to the freezer in the mudroom and reappeared with a package which she popped into the microwave to defrost.

"I love your kitchen, Karo. I noticed the last time I was here how comfortable it is. It's so big and roomy and..." He looked around trying to find a word to describe his feeling.

"Old fashioned?" Karo offered.

"Well, yes. It looks like the kind of kitchen my aunt had at the farm. You know, everyone lived in the kitchen."

Karo laughed. "I know, I loved it when I saw this house. The realtor was apologetic, describing how I could update it, but I love it just the way it is. That stove may be fifty years old, but when it was new it was at the top of the product line and it still works beautifully." They both glanced at the light yellow and chrome stove with its four gas burners and griddle on top, the oven and broiler on one side fueled by gas and the narrow rotisserie on the left side powered by electricity.

"I had a Wolf range at my former house, but this one works just as well, is more compact and it's easier to keep clean. And somehow it fits in the kitchen. I admit I did replace the refrigerator and added the dishwasher, but everything else is just as it was. How many kitchens do you see with this charm?"

They both looked around at the room with the light yellow tile counters, the painted white cabinets and the fresh looking white and yellow café curtains at the window. It looked sunny and cheerful even on this gloomy day.

He nodded. "It's just right, it all fits together. Except that." He pointed to the elaborate brushed chrome coffee machine."

Karo laughed. "That's my Jura–Capresso coffee maker. You push a button to select coffee or espresso and it grinds the beans and makes a cup of coffee, presto." She snapped her fingers. "My ex-husband had to have it. He liked gadgets. He liked showing off to his friends so, of course, he had to have one no matter the cost. But surprisingly, after using it, I fell in love with it too, so here it is. Part of the divorce settlement." She laughed and then realized how callous she sounded, explaining further, "I wasn't just being mean. It's a great machine. I knew I'd never spend the money to replace it, but he will. In fact he probably already has."

Winwey nodded.

Karo said, "Well, it's been a while since you guys took down my tree, for which I'm still very grateful. So what's up in your life?"

"The usual and lately, picking apples."

"That sounds a lot like work."

"It is, but I had help. I arranged with a local scout troop to spend a day picking. We donated half to the Food Bank, and the other half we split. They all took a bunch home to their families, and their scout master chalked it up to community service. I think they'll get a badge for their efforts. It worked so well we're going to do it again next year." He looked pleased with himself.

"What a good idea." Karo got up in response to the whistle of the tea kettle to make the tea. While the tea seeped she took the package out of the microwave and cut the loaf of blueberry pound cake into slices and set the plate of cake on the table.

"Whoa, this looks good." Winwey didn't wait. He had a slice of cake in his hand and was taking a sizeable bite before Karo could pour the tea.

After a couple of cups of tea and several pieces of cake, Winwey commented on the tea set. "This is a great tea set, yours?"

"I wish. No, I bought it from one of the women in the class. She does beautiful work. I aspire to be this good."

He nodded. "I've seen some of the work from that studio and it's all good. Rich does amazing things. I asked him why he bothered being a nurse when he could produce such wonderful pottery."

"And...? What did he say?"

"He said nursing was his vocation, pottery was his fun. That made sense to me. Why do you do it?"

"It lets me be creative. It's fun trying to learn all the little tricks, and someday I hope to supplement my income by selling some of it. At least I'm hoping to sell enough to support the cost of the—"

The kitchen shook, followed immediately by a huge boom which rattled the cupboard doors and the windows. Both dogs immediately dove under the table.

Karo and Winwey stared at each other stunned. "That wasn't thunder, was it?"

Winwey shook his head, getting up from the table, and reaching for his jacket at the same time. Karo followed at his heels, grabbing her jacket from the coat rack as she passed it. They headed out the front porch and then headed for the house with the flames and smoke billowing out, at the end, the one nearest to the path over the dunes.

"Call nine-one-one. I've got to see if anyone's in there," Winwey ordered over his shoulder, already running ahead of Karo.

When Karo returned to the street it was now clogged with residents from the other houses, and more people were coming around the corner from nearby houses to see what had happened.

Winwey was shouting at some of the bystanders; warning them to back away from the blazing house. He was kneeling beside a figure on the ground near the sidewalk.

Karo ran up to him. "What can I do?"

He looked at her and shook his head. "Not much. Too late! Maybe someone has a blanket we could use to cover him."

Karo stricken, nodded as she backed away, the smell emanating from the blackened figure gagged her. She was glad to ask one of the neighbors standing nearby for a blanket or sheet. The woman returned shortly and thrust a bundle at Karo. When she handed it to Winwey, she held her breath and didn't look beyond his face. Now she could hear the sirens, there were a lot of them.

Karo shifted back with the crowd to make room for the fire trucks and the firemen to get to the house. Then the police were there directing the increasing number of people crowding in, trying to see what had happened. She found herself talking with some of the neighbors about this house.

"Sounded like an explosion to me," the old man who lived across the street from the house said. He nodded his head sagely. "At first I thought it was another earthquake. It rattled everything in the house, but that boom got my attention. When I got outside it was already blazing and that young man over there was running up the block to help. He pulled that guy out through the back, but I guess it was too late."

"Oh, dear, how did this happen? And I never did even meet the couple who lived there. Every time I went over to introduce myself they weren't home. I just gave up after a while." One of the neighbors was shaking her head sadly. "I hope they weren't home today."

"Ahhh." A collective exclamation of horror went up from the crowd when the second story looming over the back part of the house collapsed. The crowd on the sidewalk moved back of their own volition to avoid the subsequent shower of sparks released into the air.

The lady who had brought the blanket moved quickly away from the group to intercept the firemen, who were headed toward her house.

"They'll need to get into the back to make sure the flames don't spread to the area of park land behind the house," one of the men observed knowingly. "We certainly don't need the complication of a brush fire."

It was amazing how quickly the firemen seemed to be winding down their battle with the flames. The smoke was still pouring out of what was left of the structure; a tow truck had pulled away a car parked in the drive and was now loading it on the back of a flatbed truck for transport. An ambulance had quietly moved up the street, but when the shrouded figure on the front lawn was loaded in the back, the ambulance still didn't move away. Karo thought it was like a hovering bird of prey, waiting for more bodies.

She saw Winwey heading back toward her house and headed that way to intercept him. "Hey, are you okay?"

He grimaced. "Yeah. I saw another body when I pulled that guy out. The fireman said it will be hours before it cools down enough to check for more remains."

Karo nodded. "Everyone said they had never actually talked to the people who live there. Some have seen some younger people they assumed were the kids. I saw someone there once, a young man was standing outside smoking when I passed on my way to the beach."

Winwey shook his head. "People are very strange. I see it all the time in the emergency room. They live on this street for months and yet have made no contact with any of their neighbors. Then tragedy strikes and no one knows anything about them, or how many are in the house or even if they are in the house."

"The neighbors said they just kind of showed up one day. No one remembered seeing moving vans, but one day they noticed the empty house was occupied. And, of course, everyone's noticed all the cars going up and down the street. I've only been here six months myself, and they were already here when I moved in."

They had arrived at her porch by this time and paused at the top, looking over the crowded street.

"We may as well finish our tea. I don't think you'll be able to get your truck out of the drive for a while, do you?"

Winwey nodded, following her in the house, where the dogs were still huddled under the table, waiting for reassurance that it was safe to emerge.

* * *

It was late that afternoon before Karo finally got back to her writing project. When the doorbell pealed once more, the dogs again ran barking and growling to protect her. She had finally been making progress on the section of manual she had to have finished by Monday, so she didn't really want to stop at this point. But when the bell pealed again she hurried to the door.

"Ah, Ms. Meisner, we meet again." The man on the porch smiled, before reminding her, "I'm Lieutenant

Delvin Myers with the Belle Vista Police Department. We met on the beach a while back."

She nodded, recognizing him. She cordially opened the door gesturing him to come in, holding Rudy's collar and directing Captain sternly to sit.

"Hello again to you guys, too." He stooped and let the animals smell his hand and then patted each one before saying, "I'm sorry to bother you, but I have a few questions for you."

She led him into the living room taking a chair across from where he perched on the sofa to wait for his questions.

"So, what can you tell me about the house down the block?"

Her head jerked with surprise, and then she said, "Are you investigating the fire? Was there something criminal about it?"

"Why would you think that?" He raised his eyebrows.

"Well, maybe a police lieutenant coming to my door to ask questions about it? And...," she paused thinking, "The boom. It was definitely an explosion. It rattled everything. The people right next door said two of their windows on that side broke."

"It did seem a little fierce for a normal house fire, didn't it?" He offered a ghost of a smile this time and Karo was surprised to notice he was attractive. And today he was dressed in slacks with a sports jacket over a dress shirt that was opened at the neck. Yes, today he looked like a different person than the man who interviewed her on the beach. Or maybe she just noticed him today, on the beach she was so numb from shock she hardly knew who she was talking to.

"So what happened? Do you know yet?" she asked eagerly although she didn't really expect him to say anything. But he surprised her.

"We pretty much know. It was just a normal neighborhood meth lab blowing itself up. It's a very dangerous business, you know. We're all lucky the house next to it didn't go up with it."

Stunned, it was a moment before she realized her mouth was hanging open rather unattractively. "But, but what about the people who lived there? What about the kids?"

He shook his head. "What people? No one ever saw them. The people, who everyone apparently thought were the kids, were probably the people who were processing the drugs. All the traffic up and down the street should have clued some of you in on what was going on."

"A meth lab? On my street?" She shuddered. She read the newspapers, she had seen the programs on television, and she knew how dangerous they were. Abruptly she stood up. "I need a Coke, would you like something?" She headed for the kitchen and then glanced back, surprised to find Lieutenant Myers right behind her. She chose a diet Coke and opened a Dr. Pepper for him, found glasses and ice cubes and then sat at the kitchen table. After finishing the drink she was ready to talk again.

"So do you think that house could have had anything to do with the body I found on the beach?"

He shrugged. "Makes you think about it differently, doesn't it?"

"You never identified her?"

"No, she's still labeled as a Jane Doe. She could have been a visitor to the area. We didn't find any identifying tags on her clothing and no purse or identification. She was apparently bludgeoned to death and either fell or was dumped into the ocean."

"Murder?" Karo shuddered. "How awful. Somewhere, someone is looking for her, wondering where she is. God help them."

"So tell me what happened this morning and about your friend, Dr. Doug Winwey."

That surprised her. Doctor Doug Winwey? She had realized he worked at Carruthers with Rich, but somehow she just assumed he was a nurse as Rich was, or a technician. "Well, first of all, I don't know him very well. He's a friend of a friend. I didn't even know he was a doctor. He stopped by this morning to deliver those." She pointed to the basket of apples still sitting on the kitchen counter. "While we were having tea, we heard the boom. Well we felt it too, the whole house shook. We ran outside and saw the flames and smoke. He yelled at me to call nine-one-one as he headed down the street to see if he could help. By the time I got down there he had already pulled the guy out to the front lawn, but he said it was too late to do anything for him. I got one of the neighbors to get us a blanket to cover him. It was awful." She paused and shuddered. "And the smell was horrible. I thought I was going to be sick. But right about then the fire trucks started to arrive. Winwey said he saw another body inside near the back door, but couldn't get to it."

She looked at Lieutenant Myers. "That's it. I don't know much. Anything else I learned was from the neighbors on the sidewalk."

"And, what was that?" he said hopefully.

"No one knew anything about the people living there, but I guarantee no one thought it might be a meth lab. Although now, I'm thinking we're all very stupid. It was obvious, wasn't it?"

"Nobody thinks it's happening in their neighborhood. That's how these people get away with it. Of course, they don't usually blow themselves up. That only happens occasionally," he said cynically.

"Did you ever see the woman you found on the beach there?" he asked crisply.

"No, I've never seen anyone there, except once on my way to the beach there was a young man, a kid, I thought, standing outside smoking. I waved, but he just ignored me. Now I understand why, but then I just thought he was rude."

Then she added, "I'm only down that way once a day when I walk the boys here to and from the beach. I've really never seen the cars going past my house stop there. I just assumed that was where they were going."

She thought a moment. "And frankly, I don't really know what the woman on the beach looked like. I mean...well, you saw her. She would be pretty hard to identify.... She was so bloated, and the crabs..." She stopped appalled. A violent shiver ran up her spine. She suddenly realized that while she had never before been involved in any violence, now, since moving to the beach, she had been drawn into two occurrences.

He nodded. "Yes, I understand. Well, it was where all the cars were going. The people across the street and the ones in the house next door saw the drivers of the cars going in and out. There was plenty of traffic and lots of visitors. They should have been suspicious." He drained his glass of soda and then closed his notebook. "We showed them this artist's sketch of the dead woman, but so far no one recognized her." He handed her a copy of the sketch, looking hopeful. When Karo shook her head he folded it up and stuck it back in his pocket. "Well, we're still working on it."

He stood up. "Thank you for your help. I hope the next time I see you it will just be at the grocery store, or somewhere in town. You seem to be involved in more than your share of Belle Vista's nasty situations." He headed for the front door, stopped to pat the dogs once more, and then handed her his card. "If you think of anything else, or have another problem, call me." And he was gone.

* * *

Karo was elbow deep in apples when the phone rang.

"Hi, Mom, whatcha doing?" Lisa's cheerful voice came over the line.

"Making applesauce. I already have three pies made and in the freezer, so when you're here at Christmas I'll bake one for you. You're still coming for Christmas, aren't you?" She had been so upset when she heard Lisa wouldn't be able to get away from her job long enough for a Thanksgiving visit she had immediately sent her plane tickets for Christmas to make sure she'd be home.

"Yummy. I love your apple pie. Yes, I got the days off, my plans are set. I'll be there. But Mom, I'm only going to be there five days and I need to spend some time with Dad." Her voice was hesitant, wary of how her mother would react to that news. She hurried on.

"And I want to see a couple of my friends while I'm there too, so don't make too many plans."

"I understand, don't worry. Of course you need to spend time with your dad and your friends. But I can't wait to see you. I want to show you my house, and my new town, and my boys." The last was said with pride and love.

"Boys? Oh, you mean your dogs. Mom, I can't believe you have dogs. Two dogs, in fact. And after all that time I spent begging for a puppy when I was a kid, as soon as I'm gone you get a dog."

"Well, it's because you're gone I have a dog. I need someone to boss around." They both laughed.

"I'm really sorry now we didn't get you a dog, Lisa. I'm really having fun with them. But your dad was allergic. What could we do?"

Then she changed the subject. "So why are you spending your money on a phone call? If you waited a while I would have called you as usual."

"I'm going out to meet some friends for an early dinner, so I thought I'd call you and then you won't have to panic when you call and I'm not home." She didn't really mind that her mother insisted they talk once a week. It helped her stay connected and avoid bouts of homesickness when she realized how far away she was from her family. "What's with the apples? Do you have a tree?"

So Karo told her about the basket of apples Winwey brought by, and then she told her about the fire down the block.

"Meth lab? Right down the block? What kind of neighborhood did you move to, Mom? Did you check it out before you bought?"

"Of course I did. It's a very nice old neighborhood. These things happen everywhere, Lisa, you know that. It's just that it was so surprising to find one under our noses, and no one in the neighborhood apparently even guessed at what was going on there. So, what's happening with you this week? Did you resolve that problem you had with Wanda?"

And Lisa, distracted by thoughts of her life was off on a description of the most recent chapter of her exciting life in the city.

* * *

Early Monday morning Karo pounded on the locked studio door, waiting impatiently for Joy to answer. She knew Joy was in there because her truck was in the lot. She knocked again, rapping her keys against the door to make more noise. The door knob turned and there was Joy, scowling at the interruption.

"What? What do you want? The studio isn't open today, Karo. You can't just come barging in whenever you want." Joy was obviously crotchety this morning.

"I'm sorry to interrupt you, Joy, but I suddenly remembered yesterday that I hadn't wrapped up the piece I was working on Friday. I'm hoping I can catch it before it's ruined. I know you're sometimes here on Monday mornings attending the kiln, and I hoped I could save it by wrapping some wet paper towels around it and then putting it under plastic sheeting." She smiled tentatively hoping she looked properly contrite so Joy would feel sorry for her and accommodate her. She was really mad at herself for her stupidity. She had been working on this modified piece for several hours and was very pleased with how it was turning out. She didn't want to lose it by letting it dry out before it was finished just because she had been distracted and forgot to properly wrap it and put it away before she left.

"Oh, all right. Just this once, but don't think you can make a habit of this. I need to use these mornings to get things done before Tuesday workshop. Usually I don't even come to the door. In fact, I didn't hear you at the door until I came into the studio to get one of my tools." She turned around and trudged back into the covered patio.

Karo wasted no time in finding her piece sitting just where she left it. When she finished she went out to the kiln room to thank Joy and tell her she was leaving, but the noise was tremendous. "What are you doing?" she shouted, pointing at the machine which was emitting a clattering, banging, whooshing din.

"Ball Mill," Joy shouted. "I'm grinding up some bones. I put some beef bones into the kiln and now I'm grinding them up to use later."

In answer to the surprise on Karo's face she pointed to several pieces of her pottery sitting on the table, still warm from the kiln. "See those? That flash of color on the unglazed clay came from the beef bones. Nice, huh?"

Karo nodded picking up one of the pieces and turning it over in her hands. "Very nice. What is it?"

"It's a bird bath. See?" Joy took the shallow bowl from Karo's hands and set it on top of the gracefully sloped column. It was suddenly a charming birdbath about a foot and a half high. The color ranged from a light golden brown to dark rust and she could see how attractive it would look in a yard.

"Will it hold water without glaze?"

Joy nodded, shouting, "Sure, it's been fired at about 2200°F, no moisture is going to leak out of that. And the texture is nice, I think."

Karo nodded. "Very nice. Do you sell them? I think I'd like one for my yard."

"I do sell them. Unfortunately these are already promised. I could make you one, or you could even make one yourself. You can see how simple they are to make. You just need to use the right kind of clay. Use something with a lot of grog to hold up to the outdoor temperatures."

Karo nodded. "Maybe I'll try to make one. It looks like fun. Well, I've got to go, as I have an appointment. I'm sorry to have disturbed you, but I think I saved my piece. Thanks again."

Joy nodded and turned back to her work, not even looking up as Karo left.

Karo paused before climbing into her car to check her gray wool slacks for clay dust. She didn't want to arrive at her appointment looking messy. Satisfied, she headed toward the highway and Redwood City. Already she was composing a list of items she wanted to clarify at today's meeting. And she decided she would stop by at the local branch afterwards and talk to the operations manager about the process.

It was later than she expected when she drove into the bank lot in Belle Vista. She glanced at her watch and debated if she shouldn't just go home. But then she told herself sternly it was better to get this matter settled now so she could spend Tuesday and Wednesday on her pottery and write on Thursday. If she went home, she'd just have to come back here

Thursday. You're here, just do it, she told herself sternly.

So she entered the bank in a better frame of mind. The particular task she was writing up seemed to be a bit complicated, mostly because no one could agree on the way it was to be done. So she was going to observe the process as the operations manager here did it. She had met Sally Schmitz shortly after she first moved here. Sally was considered an expert by her colleagues in the bank and had been helpful to Karo in the past.

"Hi, Karo. I thought maybe you weren't coming today."

Karo smiled apologetically. "I'm sorry to be late, Sally. Is it too late?"

"No, I waited. I have a long list today so it's a good time to show you how the process works. Come on back."

Karo walked through to the back area, smiling as some of the tellers nodded or waved, then followed Sally to her desk, which sat positioned so she had a clear view of everything behind the row of teller windows.

"So how did your meeting go this morning?" Sally asked.

"You know, everyone has a different way to do it. It's amazing how passionate people can be about those differences."

"Well, I'll show you what I do and point out all the control issues and then we can discuss the differences. You can tell me if I do it differently than the others."

Sally tapped into her keyboard and while messages were flashing on her screen, Karo pulled over another wheeled chair and took out her notepad and pen. They worked together for a while, their concentration on the report they were checking was only interrupted occasionally when one of the tellers had a question, but then Sally was called to the teller window to talk to a customer about a problem leaving Karo sitting alone at her desk. Karo checked her notes and looked at the screen. She was surprised to notice a name she recognized on the screen. The names Joy Ledbetter and Hiram Wilson were followed by the account number, two dates and the amount for the automatic transfer. She supposed this was the Joy Ledbetter she knew. After all how many could there be in Belle Vista? She was surprised to see a joint account with a man after hearing that Joy's husband ran out on her. And, she mused, she was almost certain she heard that Joy lived alone. She reminded herself it was really none of her business. After all, this Hiram Wilson could be Joy's brother, nothing odd or scandalous about that. Or perhaps he was a business associate. It wasn't until Sally came back and they were almost finished with the report they were checking that she saw a second entry for Joy. This one was in the name of Joy Ledbetter and Robert Lang. How odd was that?

Sally noticed her start of surprise. "Someone you know?"

Karo nodded.

"Well, Belle Vista is a small town. You'd be surprised at how many of the citizens bank with us. Many of them find the big banks are too big and they feel lost in them. We have a large share of the Belle Vista market." This was said with pride.

"So, is this amount transferring to another account in the bank or is it going outside?" Karo pointed at Joy's account.

"Remember what I said. This field gives the code. So what does that tell you?"

"It's an outside transfer." Karo looked at the list she had. "Bank of America, right?"

Sally nodded, pleased with her student. "Right. Every month on the fifteenth of the month this amount transfers from this account to this account number at Bank of America automatically, unless something prevents the transfer from taking place, such as if there wasn't enough money in the account to meet the request. Otherwise, no one ever has to touch the transfer, it just happens. Automatic transfers are very convenient for the customers. The customers pay bills, they put money in their savings, and they send money to their kids away at school. There are a million ways to use the service."

Karo smiled at Sally. "I think I understand now. Thank you so much for your patience. There is nothing like doing the process to clarify all the little sticky points. I appreciate you taking the time to work through the process with me."

"No problem. After all, your manual is going to rule my life. I'm just protecting my turf." Sally laughed and escorted her to the door. "Come back anytime or call if you have more questions."

As Karo was pulling out of the lot she thought about the two entries for Joy Ledbetter. That's very strange, she thought. Then she remembered the non-disclosure agreement she signed with the bank before she started to work for them and realized she had promised to never reveal anything she learned in the bank to anyone. She shook her head. No matter how strange it seemed, she would just have to forget about it.

CHAPTER 6

Karo tasted a piece of the crusty bread, smiling her approval while the vendor explained how they ground the wheat fresh to make it. Finally, she shook her head regretfully at his plea for a purchase and moved away.

"I'm surprised you even tried it. I would have thought you baked your own bread."

She looked up surprised. "Winwey, uh, Dr. Winwey, I mean. What are you doing here?"

"Winwey is fine, or Doug, and I'm shopping just like half the city seems to be doing." He held up the plastic bags he was toting. "How are things on your street? Quiet I hope." He fell into step beside her and they moved down the path between the stalls set up in the produce section of the flea market.

"Everything is very quiet. Did you hear it was a meth lab?" She looked at him and seeing his nod, "And they found two more bodies." She shuddered. "It's so dangerous. They thought they were going to get rich and instead, they ended up dead."

"Yeah, Rich told me about it. He said the whole neighborhood was shocked. No one even suspected what was going on." He looked at her and noticed her grim expression and decided to change the subject. "So what are you shopping for?"

"Well, nothing, or anything. I thought it was about time to check this market out. So far I've managed to escape buying anything, but I've been tempted." She laughed. "I would have thought you'd be working or sleeping on a Saturday morning. That's how Rich tells me he spends his Saturday mornings."

"We work different hours. The doctors are scheduled more like firemen, working continuously for forty-eight hours on and then three days off. Our work days on are always changing."

She looked at him with surprise. "Well, when do you sleep? How can you work for forty-eight hours straight?"

He smiled. "It seldom works out that way. We have breaks. We just nap whenever we get a break. They keep a couple of beds available. When it's busy we're all there and then when it's slow we take turns napping. Carruthers is responsible for covering all the emergency work on this part of the coast and they have to have good ER coverage. The support staff works regular shifts, only the ER doctors do this. They seem to think it works best for the patients. They have three teams working, just as if they would if they did eight hours shifts. But since the shifts change over fewer times there is much less risk of a patient getting lost when the change occurs. And I have to say emergencies have no regard for shift turnover times.

"Anyway, I've gotten use to it and I like my time off. Of course, I don't have a family on an entirely different schedule so that helps me."

Karo nodded. "But you can't plan anything else can you? It means your whole life has to be revolving around your work."

He nodded. "Well, that's true, but frankly, my work is the most important thing I do. I don't mind having everything else revolve around it. I do some volunteer work, and some gardening and sometimes I fish, but very little else I'm afraid. And since I'm new to the area I don't have a lot of friends, which means I don't have a big social life. But it works for me."

She was a little embarrassed. "I'm sorry; I didn't mean to pry, or to criticize your lifestyle."

"No, don't worry. I wasn't offended. Many people have hobbies and families and try to arrange their work around them. For me it's the other way around. I arrange everything around my work."

She nodded, beginning to understand. "Well, then it's lucky you do what you love most. Did you always know you were going to be a doctor?"

He nodded. "Always, since I was a small boy."

"And did you always want to work in the emergency room?"

He laughed. "No, that was destiny. I was in the first Gulf War. That was like emergency room duty for forty-two days. But I found I was really good at it. So when my tour of duty was up I went to work in the emergency room at a big hospital in Chicago. And that's what I've been doing ever since."

"And you came to Belle Vista because?" As long as she was being nosy she thought she may as well get all her questions answered.

"I don't know...I needed a break. Big city ER is intense; it never stops. It never lets up. I dreamed of living in the woods and going fishing when I wanted to.

I was tired of the streets, the noise and the confusion of the big city. So when the recruiters offered me a good deal, I thought a change was in order. I decided to move west. And so far I'm still enjoying it. I'm still making a contribution, but it's not like working in the inner city. That position was becoming more and more like working in a war zone, with gunshot wounds, and knife fights. All that violence and waste of life just burns you out."

He looked at her. "So why are you here?"

"Nothing very dramatic I assure you. Mine is the usual story of mid-life changes. You've heard it all before, middle-aged woman emerging from divorce, whose only child has gone off to seek her fortune, moves to another area to start again."

He nodded. "By starting again I assume you don't mean at the beginning and doing it all over again."

"God, I hope not. I hope I've learned something. No, I felt that I got lost somewhere. And I wanted to simplify my life. I was spending a lot of time doing things I didn't particularly like. I think life should be fun. Or at least it should be interesting."

"That seems reasonable. So is it working for you?"

"I think so. I love working at the studio. I love my house and being so close to the ocean. I'm enjoying my dogs; I've never had a dog before. And I even like my work. So far, so good! Like you, being new in the area I don't have a large network of friends, but I think that will come after a while. It takes time, you know?"

"Hang on a minute, I need a drink. Would you like one?" They paused in front of a drink stand.

Karo nodded. "I wouldn't mind a glass of lemonade."

Winwey returned shortly with a drink for each of them, then after taking a sip he said thoughtfully. "You know since we're both short of friends in the area, we should just become friends. That would be good for both of us, don't you think? What do you say?"

She looked at him with a questioning look on her face. "Well, how exactly do you define friends?"

"Well, you know, getting together for a meal sometimes, or maybe going to a movie together, just hanging out, or even talking on the phone. You know, just friendly kind of things?" He looked at her closely. "The kind of friend you can call if you need a favor, or are lonely and just want to talk. Doesn't that sound good?"

She laughed. "I don't think I've ever decided to have a friend. It's always just happened."

He nodded. "You're right, that's how it usually happens. But why wait? I've been here for a year and haven't made much headway in making friends. I liked you when I first met you. I think I'd like to be friends. Isn't that what they do now on all those websites that are so popular? You send an email and say let's be friends?"

She looked at him a moment, thinking about what he said. "Well, I think you'd be a good friend. Okay!" She stuck out her hand and he shifted his bags and drink around so he could clasp it and they formally shook hands.

"Wow, I feel good. This is better than being a friend on Facebook, because my reception in the hills is pretty spotty. If I could do this every week or so, I'd soon have a hell of a social life."

She laughed. "Well, I feel good too."

"So, as friends, we should get together one day next week and chat, okay?"

She nodded.

"I'm on duty Sunday and Monday, so I'll call later in the week. Maybe we can take your dogs for a walk on the beach and then have a casual meal some place. What do you think?"

"Sounds good. Call me."

"Okay, so now I'm going home and finish raking the leaves in my yard. When we get to be really good friends you'll probably want to come and help me do my yard work, won't you?"

She laughed again. "I don't know if we'll ever be that good of friends, but maybe." She waved to him and then headed toward the area of the market where the arts and crafts booths were set up.

Karo still had a smile from her encounter with Doug Winwey when she arrived at Betty's booth. Betty nodded in acknowledgement of her arrival, but continued her conversation with a customer. The conversation was apparently successful because Karo watched her wrap up a set of six small pottery bowls, which the customer happily carried off.

"Hi, I see you decided to check us out."

"Wow, this is a great flea market. I'm sorry I waited so long. I shudder at all the opportunities I've missed. And I'm amazed at the variety of stuff for sale. And, the crafts are wonderful. I love this. I'm coming again for sure."

Betty looked at her empty hands. "Doesn't look like you've bought much?" she said dryly. "The vendors need buyers, not lookers."

"But I saw several things I want. I'm going to buy when I head back to my car. I decided to wait, so I wouldn't have to carry everything with me."

"Oh, that's smart. Or at least it is if the things are still available when you go back."

Karo frowned, then brightened. "If it's meant to be, they'll still be there waiting for me." She reached out exclaiming, "Betty, is this the sea glass you were talking about?" She fingered the pieces of glass, smooth rounded edges in a variety of colors.

Betty nodded. "Look at this piece." She held up a piece of light turquoise glass that was beautiful.

"What do you suppose it was originally?" Karo took it and turned it over. "A bottle?"

"Maybe a canning jar. Do you remember some of those old Ball jars were a light turquoise?"

"Well, it's certainly beautiful. I can see why people want to collect it. If I ever see any on the beach I'll pick it up for you." Karo put it down and moved over to the display of Betty's pottery. While she was examining a candlestick, a woman came up and started going through the sea glass. She was obviously a repeat customer judging by her conversation with Betty. She bought several pieces, including the turquoise piece they had been admiring.

When the woman left, Betty asked apologetically, "Karo, are you in a hurry?"

Karo shook her head, so Betty asked, "Could you watch my booth while I visit the restroom? I'll only be a few minutes. And if you get a customer all the prices are marked on the pieces, and add the sales tax. I take cash or checks." Betty pointed to the tin box she used for her money.

"Sure." Karo waved her off and continued examining the pottery available.

When Betty hurried back Karo had sold the candlesticks and was wrapping them for the delighted woman. "Oh, here is the potter. Betty, this lady just bought your beautiful candlesticks."

"Oh, I love them. They'll look absolutely perfect on my mantle. Your work is lovely. I'll be back again, for sure."

"Thank you for watching the booth. I can get a minder, but it takes a little time so I appreciate your letting me take a quick break."

"No problem, glad to help. Actually it was fun. They all thought I was the potter." Karo smiled with pleasure. "Someday."

"Karo, you do lovely things. You could sell your things now. Why don't you rent a booth here?"

"Not yet. I'm not ready yet, but someday."

"Well, we're having our pottery sale at the studio in a few weeks. For sure you'll want to put some of your things up for sale then. We have a good turn out and people love our pieces. Joy sells the most, but once in awhile Mary Louise beats her, and most everyone makes enough to pay for their pottery classes so everyone is happy."

"I've heard about it. Actually, I was at one of the sales you had in the spring one year. I was very impressed. I'm going to participate if only to see if anyone will want any of my pottery.

"I'm going to head out now, Betty. Have a good day." She left to finish exploring the whole market. She wanted to know what goods were sold there and in what locations. She had a feeling that the Flea Market was going to be one of her favorite haunts. For sure she would be buying fruits and vegetables from the farmer's stalls every month.

* * *

The Monday before Thanksgiving was sunny but cold and, while it was only four o'clock, it seemed like it was evening already. Karo and the boys came down the path over the dune from the beach and carefully skirted the barricades and machinery gathered around the perimeter of the end house, well really, all that was left of the end house. Bulldozers and dump trucks had been working there for the last few days clearing the charred remains and carting off the debris. The whole neighborhood was looking forward to the time when the house and what happened would only be a dim memory. As they approached their own house, Karo was surprised to see Lieutenant Myers get out of a car parked in front and wait for her to come up to him.

"Good afternoon, Ms. Meisner. I see you've been on the beach again. I trust you didn't find anything alarming." He nodded soberly.

"Just some seaweed, Lieutenant. Were you waiting for me?" She headed up the walk, gesturing him to accompany her. She fumbled a little with the key before she got the door open and the leashes unsnapped so the dogs could scamper eagerly for their water bowls. "Come in. Let me get the dogs taken care of and I can make us some coffee. Or, would you rather have tea or a soft drink?"

"I would appreciate a cup of coffee, thanks." While Karo put fresh water out for the dogs, Lieutenant Myers took off his jacket and sat down at the kitchen table.

She set the large mug brimming with fragrant coffee in front of him, watching him take a sip.

"Man, that's good coffee. It tastes like something you'd get at Peet's." He took a big sip while she brought her own cup to the table and sat down.

"Well, what's going on? Why are you here?" She studied his face for clues.

"We identified your woman on the beach. I thought you'd want to know."

"Thank God. It seemed so sad that she died and yet no one seemed to know she was gone. I've worried about her, about her family."

"Her name was Alison Burkhouse. She worked at one of those missions in San Francisco. You know the kind. They're the people who provide shelter and food for the homeless. She had been with them for over ten years and then she went missing. They found her car in the long-term parking lot at the airport, but no trace of her. Anyway, the dental records match, so we're certain it's her." He took a few papers out of his shirt pocket and handed a snapshot to Karo. "Look familiar? Have you seen her in the neighborhood?"

Karo looked at the woman in the picture. Alison Burkhouse looked like a nice middle-aged woman posing with a pleasant expression on her face. It was sad to realize the woman was dead.

Karo shook her head. She had never seen the woman in the photo and she didn't look anything like the body she saw floating in the pool amongst the rocks, or even the artist's sketch Lieutenant Myers had shown her previously.

CHAPTER 7

Thanksgiving came and went. Karo was glad when it was over. It had been a little grim for her this year. Lisa hadn't accumulated enough time at her job to take time off to come home. Karo had separated herself from her former life, so those friends hadn't thought to include her in their plans. And she hadn't yet built strong enough connections in Belle Vista to be included in her new friends' holidays. Rich went to his sister's house in Oregon for the week and Doug was working Thursday and Friday. Her friend, Eileen, tried to talk her into flying back to St. Louis for a visit over the holidays, but Karo didn't want to put the boys in a kennel while she was gone. She thought the kennel would be too much like their experience in the animal shelter. So she decided to tough it out, using that time to get ahead of her writing schedule. That way, she reasoned, she wouldn't worry about the time she was going to devote to pottery in the following week, to get ready for the studio sale.

The anticipated sale had everyone at the pottery studio in a dither. The potters sold their work twice each year, the first weekend in December when the

Recreation Center hosted a Holiday Craft sale, and in the spring during the Annual Arts and Crafts Fair. The studio had an extensive mailing list which included many people who looked forward to attending each sale. The customers loved the reasonably priced, unique pottery pieces they sold. The potters loved the sale because it was a monetary endorsement of their skills in pottery. And the Recreation Center liked the sale as it always generated new students and because ten percent of all sales went into a fund used to buy equipment for the studio.

Karo had volunteered to print the address labels for the flyers on her printer. One of the other potters designed the flyers, which the Recreation Center ran off on their big copy machine. The potters spent a lunch hour folding the flyers, labeling and stamping them for the mail. And, of course, throughout the days preceding the sale countless stories were told about the previous sales and the wacky customers they attracted.

Rich whispered for her ears only, "You think these stories about the customers are funny, wait until you see the set-up process in the studio. Heads sometimes roll." He winked to lighten his ominous words, but nevertheless Karo understood with this volatile group it was an event which would try everyone's patience.

And she was nervous about the pieces she was going to sell. What if no one wanted to buy any of her pieces? The whole pricing strategy was mindboggling. Some said price low and sell everything, some said price high to get the most possible. She had already witnessed one altercation between Mary Louise and that nice Jane Eng. Mary Louise accused Jane of under pricing her pieces at the last sale so she could steal sales from the other potters.

Jane explained she priced her pieces to sell. Since she lived in a small condo she had no storage available, so she wanted to sell everything. That sent Mary Louise off on a tirade about the importance of valuing her work, herself and her craft, and while Mary Louise didn't come right out and say it, she hinted that the only reason Jane's pieces sold was the low price.

Karo didn't believe it; she thought Jane's pottery was lovely. She especially admired the sushi plates Jane made and was planning to buy one for herself at the sale.

And she overheard Liv loudly complaining to Hal about the pottery one of the night students put in the last sale. "Worse than seconds. It was disgraceful. We should tell her to just throw away that trash."

Hal murmured some response trying to calm her.

"Well, I'll tell her," Liv continued loudly. "I'd rather embarrass her than be embarrassed by having that junk in our sale. It reflects badly on us all."

Karo was alarmed by what she heard. She imagined how hurt the potter would be if Liv called her work trash, but Evy assured her Liv wouldn't say anything. "Liv talks big, Karo, but she knows Joy always checks on the work displayed and if it doesn't meet her standards it comes out. So if it was in the sale, then Joy had accepted it. Joy's rule is no damaged pieces can be offered for sale, even as seconds, but lots of damaged pieces are accepted as 'modified'." Evy laughed. "Art is in the eyes of the beholder, you know."

Evy shook her head. "Liv is just sounding off. Joy won't put up with that kind of interference and Liv's not going to take a chance on being barred from the studio."

One day at lunch after listening to a couple of the women hassling Marge about bringing in newspapers again, Karo volunteered to sort through the papers if Marge would bring them and remove any of the unwanted glossy colored pages for her. Liv, at the other end of the table, just threw up her hands in disgust and even Joy looked irritated at Karo's peace offering. They wanted and needed the newspapers, but somehow they preferred Marge to acquiesce.

When set-up day arrived, Karo was ready. All her pieces had been selected and priced. She was certain she had complied with all the instructions about sticker size, color and placement. She had collected, flattened and stacked grocery bags and newspapers, and she had her dolly ready to wheel the three heavy plastic bins full of wrapped pottery into the studio. She parked her dolly and bins on the patio along with the others and joined her fellow potters in the studio as the work began. They covered the shelves and counters with plastic sheeting, arranged the tables and pottery wheels in locations specified by Joy, washed counters, swept the floors and stacked the chairs. Finally, Joy's critical eye was satisfied and they were given the nod to start the decorating. Out came the cloths, the risers, and the display platforms. It was obvious they had all done this before. Three of the potters, Helene, Iris and Hal acted as design coordinators. All had previous experience in design; Hal was considered the senior consultant as he had spent years as the window display artist for a large department store in San Francisco before retiring to Belle Vista.

Soon everyone was unpacking their pottery on the patio and carrying it in piece by piece to set in strategic spots for display. Karo now saw what Rich was talking about when he said heads would roll. Some of the potters went to amazing lengths to secure what they deemed the most advantageous places to display their pieces. Sometimes they brazenly moved someone else's pot so they could place theirs in a particular spot, murmuring sanctimonious comments about balance and color. She could barely contain her laugher as she watched Liv perform that maneuver and then when Liv left to bring in more of her pieces, Marge came along and replaced Liv's piece with her own, setting Liv's piece to the back of the table behind another piece. Karo waited, holding her breath, for the resulting fireworks, but when Liv came in she went directly to another area to place her pot and didn't even notice hers had been moved.

Karo vowed she wasn't going to play that game. She just unwrapped and set her pieces in various parts of the room until she only had bins filled with rumpled newspaper waiting to be loaded back in her SUV.

When Rich arrived, Karo finished with her own pieces, helped him with his. So she was on the patio when Joy came through the gate towing a big shiny aluminum box on heavy duty wheels. "Wow Joy, what kind of box is that?"

"It's a toolbox like some of the construction workers use. I just modified it to meet my needs," Joy said proudly. "I have a winch in the back of my truck so I just slide the ramps off the back and connect the box to the cable and winch it up and down. And this handle allows me to easily pull it around. Believe me, I really appreciate it every time we have one of these sales."

"Very clever, but it looks more like something you'd use to hide the bodies in," Karo said, looking at it closely.

Joy jerked with surprise and said hotly, "What do you mean?"

Karo laughed. "Relax, I'm not accusing you of anything sinister. It's just that it rather resembles a coffin, don't you think?"

Joy glared at her and then apparently deciding Karo didn't mean anything by her remarks, relaxed, admitting, "Well maybe it does a bit, but it holds all my pots, and it fits in the back of my pick-up, so I don't care what it looks like." She opened her box and walked into the studio with her arms full of pottery.

Jane and Mary Louise had been gathering branches of eucalyptus and holly from the grounds and now added the greenery to the displays. Karo was amazed by the transformation of the studio. In a matter of a few hours the space had changed from being a working studio to becoming an upscale boutique. All the pottery looked attractive and saleable. She thought the customers would be tempted to buy more than they anticipated.

By the time Karo left everything was done. Some of the night students would be coming in after they left work for the day to bring their pieces. And while some of the potters were still making minor adjustments to displays, the sales table and wrapping desk were ready, so they just needed the customers.

That readiness was a good thing because the next morning customers were clustered around the doors demanding an early entry. Joy nodded and the doors were unlocked. It was exciting, just like a super midnight sale at one of the electronics stores with a hot new product. People were snatching up pieces and building piles of their selections on the sales table while they dashed off to search for more bargains. The cashiers were frantically calculating tabs while the people at the wrapping desk, which is where Karo was assigned, were trying to keep up with the sales. They wrapped and bagged and smiled even as the waiting pots piled up.

It was after noon when Karo's relief took over. She was grateful for the chance for a quick visit to the restroom. She grabbed a cup of coffee and a piece of coffee cake, which someone had brought, and cruised through the studio noticing how much had already been sold. She helped rearrange pieces to fill the gaps in the display made because of the pieces sold. That first onslaught was over, however, customers and sales were still heavy. Karo snatched up the last one of Jane's sushi plates and a couple of other pieces she had been admiring before they were sold to someone else. She did a quick run through of the craft booths set up in the halls and big rooms of the Recreation Center. Fortunately she didn't find anything she needed to buy so she was free to head for home and her walk on the beach with the boys. She was glad to be finished with her shift at the sale and very happy that many of her own pottery pieces had already sold. All her concern about the acceptance of her work was unnecessary. It was obvious from the customers' response that they liked her work. She still had her shift to work tomorrow and the tear down process after the sale on Sunday evening, but she was much more comfortable about the whole process now.

She had only come in and greeted the dogs when the phone rang.

"Hey, whatcha doing?" Doug's voice inquired.

"Getting ready to walk the beach. What are you doing today?"

"I was thinking about getting a late lunch and then checking out that famous pottery sale. Want to come?"

"No, thanks. I just got home. I've spent enough time there today. I'm worn out."

"Sounds like it was busy. Did you sell a bunch?" Doug knew how anxious she was over the sale, so it was considerate of him to ask.

"We sold a ton of stuff and I sold most of my pieces already. It's really funny how customers wander around and manage to select pieces made by one or two potters exclusively. I asked one lady who was buying three of my pieces why she selected that particular potter and she didn't even notice they were all made by the same person. She said she just liked those pieces. And when I told her I made them she was excited and very flattering."

"That's interesting. Well, I'll see if I can find any of your pieces and Rich's left. How are they marked?"

"Mine all have Karo on the bottom and Rich uses R and J. See what you think. I think you'll be surprised at what you see. You may even end up buying another potter's work. And if you feel like it, stop by afterwards and we can have tea or coffee. I'll be home from the beach by then."

"Okay, I'll do that. See you later."

Karo gathered up the things she needed for the beach thinking about Doug. They truly were friends now and she enjoyed their relationship. They talked frequently on the phone, went out to dinner and to a movie on occasion. Sometimes he just dropped by. Once she met him and Rich and a couple of others from Carruthers at a breakfast spot they favored. And her friendship with Doug wasn't the only one that she was nurturing. Betty had been over a few times and Karo and the boys had visited her again. Karo loved to look at Betty's work in various stages of completion in her studio. There was something about looking at the bisque ware sitting there waiting to be glazed that was inspiring.

Betty's bisque ware was so beautiful Karo wished it could be used in that state. Betty was such a perfectionist, if the bisque ware was not what she considered perfect, she smashed it and threw away the pieces. And she was just as exacting when it came to the glazed pieces. She said sometimes a piece didn't come out as she expected, and then she just sold it because many times other people loved it even though she didn't. However, if there was a problem with the glaze, if it bubbled, or the piece cracked or was chipped, out it went.

Karo tried to emulate Betty, but found it difficult to destroy some of the pieces she had worked so hard to make. Still, she was trying to be more objective about her work.

Karo had also become friendly with Diane, a thirties something woman and her eight-year-old daughter, Tiffany, who lived next door. Tiffany came over occasionally to visit. She loved to go to the beach with Karo and the boys, especially if she was allowed to hold onto one of the leashes as they walked down the street. Karo liked both of them, and she understood how hard it must be for Diane as a single parent and having the entire responsibility for Tiffany.

Since the fire at the end of the block, the neighbors had gotten together and started their own version of a neighborhood watch program. They were all getting to know each other better and were committed to keeping their street secure. The owners had started cleaning up the property at the end of the block thanks to the groups' pressuring the insurance company and the city officials. With that success under their belts they felt they were ready for anything.

Christmas was coming and Karo, inspired by the decorations on the houses along the street, decided to decorate her own house. Consequently, she had draped icicle lights across the roof of the porch on the front of the house. The squatty square pillars reaching from the low wall around the porch to support the porch roof she festooned with large candy canes and red bows. As soon as her tree was up and lit in the front window, she expected her house to look as festive as any other house in the area.

She then turned her attention to the inside. She had saved the Christmas decorations from the big house in San Mateo and she filled the little house on Sunset Lane with it all. The front door opened into a generous entry hall with double pocket doors opening off each side leading to the living room and a study. She draped both doorways with fragrant swags of evergreen. Besides the big decorated tree sitting in front of the window, she draped the mantel with more greenery and lots of scented candles. She set out the caroler figurines, and all the Santa Clauses she had collected. The two bedrooms and a large bath in a row behind the living room got everything from greenery and candles, to a variety of angels, little Santa soaps and the red and green reindeer towels. The master bedroom and bath at the back of the house got its own small tree, covered with tiny ornaments specifically selected for it. On the other side, directly opposite the living room was a study, off the entry hall. There on the table she moved in for this purpose, she set up the crèche, so it could be seen from the other window on the porch as well as from inside the house. In the dining room between the study and the kitchen she'd unpacked and set out Christmas-themed serving pieces, and even a wonderful bright red linen table runner to set off the table centerpiece she had put together for the table. The kitchen got the dish towels, the collection of mugs with Christmas themes, and a few odds and ends that made it seem festive.

She admitted she may have gone a little overboard, but told herself it was her first year in this house and so she wanted it to be special. And besides, she had decided to have an event on Christmas Eve.

Lisa was only going to be arriving the afternoon before Christmas Eve. Karo would have her that day and Christmas Eve, but Greg was picking her up about noon on Christmas. So in order to celebrate properly, Karo invited several people, Doug, Rich, Betty, Diane and Tiffany, and a few of the other neighbors, over on Christmas Eve. She announced there would be a gift exchange, so everyone should bring a wrapped gift they made, or something from their house they no longer used, but thought someone else would enjoy. She explained the object was to share without spending money. Only Tiffany was excused because Karo had purchased the perfect gift for her, which was already wrapped and under the tree.

Karo was so excited when she picked up Lisa at the airport she could hardly stop hugging her long enough to drive to the beach. The ride was filled with stories and questions until finally they arrived and Karo could proudly introduce the boys and give her daughter a tour of the house. After Lisa had settled her things in her room, they went down to walk on the beach with the dogs, returning to bake the last of the cookies for the party the next night. And during all this time they talked as if they hadn't spoken at least weekly since Lisa left home.

Lisa was enchanted with her mother's house and especially the dogs. "They are so right here, I feel as if they've been part of the family for years. They're perfect for you," Lisa exclaimed, a hand on each dog's head.

Karo nodded. "I feel that way too. I can hardly remember not having them."

Then changing the subject, "Did you reach your friends?"

Lisa nodded. "I'm meeting Janiece, Annmarie and Leslie for lunch tomorrow at Max's in the Stanford Shopping Mall. It will be crowded, but the place is central for everyone and besides, I can pick up a couple of last minute things and still catch up on what's happening with our old crowd. That will be fun.

"Mom, are you sure you don't mind me taking your car? What if you need to go out to get some last minute thing for the party?" Lisa's eyes showed her concern.

"Don't worry. I have everything I need and I'll be busy all day making the stew and finishing up. And you have your cell phone, so if I need anything I'll call and you can pick it up on your way back.

"Go and enjoy yourself. Just be back by six when everyone will start arriving. And be careful driving over the mountain in the dark. That road can be treacherous."

"Yes, Mother," Lisa said in a droll tone.

Karo laughed. "Okay, okay, so you're grown up now. But once a mother, always a mother. We're required to say these things or we lose our membership in the union."

Lisa laughed with her mother. It was so good to be together in the warm, good smelling kitchen.

* * *

Christmas Eve the house was glowing with candles, the fire, and the lights on the tree. Christmas carols played softly in the background. Karo glanced at her reflection in the mirror. She liked the look of her bright red sweater trimmed in shiny beads over the long black skirt. She stood tall and proud studying her reflection critically. She realized after giving birth to Lisa she had never returned to her lithe willowy shape. In fact, she had morphed into a sturdier shape to fill her five foot seven inches. Greg hadn't been pleased, perhaps feeling the loss of that woman he married. Now, examining herself in the mirror she realized while she was admittedly not the person she was in college, she was still attractive, and she noted with surprise that she looked happy.

Well, she was happy. She loved her life. Her daughter was home and life seemed good. The bell rang and the dogs raced barking for the front door.

"I hope we're not too early? Tiffany has been driving me crazy asking if it was time yet. I thought we may as well come over."

Karo smiled in welcome. "Of course you're not too early. Come in. Here, let me take your coats. Ooh, Tiffany, don't you look beautiful. Is that a special Christmas dress?"

Tiffany nodded shyly, pirouetting so Karo could see her dress better.

"Is that for the gift exchange? Just set it over there near the tree," Karo told Diane while Tiffany ran to hug the dogs.

"Oh, Karo, your house looks so festive. I love how you've decorated it." Diane looked around with admiration. "It must have taken you days."

Karo had the pocket doors open so the front of the house was one big room. Additionally, the doors opening to the dining room revealed the table had been pushed back against the far wall and was now loaded with plates of cookies, cakes, candies and savories. A big glass punch bowl sat on a base filled with ice and held eggnog. A second bowl held red punch, a large chunk of red ice, embedded with glowing candles, floated on top.

"Can I get you something to drink, Diane? Eggnog or fruit punch, or if you'd rather, I have wine in the kitchen?"

"Eggnog? You made eggnog? I haven't had it in years."

Karo laughed. "I'll tell you the secret. I buy the commercial eggnog, lace it liberally with dark rum, squirt a can of whipped cream in it and gently mix it all together. It's delicious, you'll see. And it's really easy." She poured a scoop in one of the cups and handed it to Diane.

Diane's face lit up when she took the first sip, but before she could say anything the doorbell rang again.

Clyde and Molly, neighbors from down the street came in, followed closely by Rich.

Karo took coats, introduced people, offered drinks and went to the door to let Doug and then Betty in. Just as she finished those introductions, Lisa emerged from the bedroom and she started again. When the bell rang again she opened the door to Gil and Donna, the older couple down the street across from the burned out meth house.

"Merry Christmas, come in."

Karo ushered them in, and did the introductions one more time. It was a lot noisier in the house now. People were enjoying eggnog while they talked. It felt like a party.

Later, Karo looked around at her living room strewn with people holding empty bowls of fish stew, still drinking wine and nibbling on the oyster crackers, satiated and content. She smiled, pleased with how well the party was going. "All right, let's get this stuff cleared away. I think it's time for presents."

Tiffany bounced up off the floor where she was sitting with the dogs, eager to help, excited about the promise of presents. Lisa, sitting on the floor beside the coffee table talking to Doug, started gathering up bowls.

Donna carried a load to the kitchen. Putting the bowls in the sink, she said, "That fish stew was wonderful. I don't know when I've enjoyed a meal more than this. I guess I just get into a rut and cook the same things over and over. I'll have to try your recipe."

"Sure, it's simple and easy with fish so plentiful here at the beach. I'll write it down for you next week sometime, okay?"

Donna nodded and left with the wine bottles to pour refills for those who wanted them. Karo made coffee for Gil and Rich and then delivered them to the living room.

"Okay, if it's all right with everyone I think Tiffany should have her present first and then the rest of us will play a game to earn our presents."

They all watched Tiffany tear the paper and ribbon off the large box which held a stuffed toy dog. It looked a lot like Captain and when squeezed in a certain way, it barked. She was thrilled with it and couldn't stop squeezing it.

"I think you may live to regret that gift," Doug said to Diane, laughing at yet another bark from the toy.

"Maybe the barking mechanism will wear out?" Diane said hopefully.

"Not a possibility," Molly said, laughing. "Trust me, I've had experience."

Karo waited for their attention and then gave the instructions for the game. "Okay, now everyone will draw a number. We'll select gifts by the number starting with one, each subsequent person can take a gift already opened, or one from the pile of gifts. If the one you opened is taken away, then you can select another from ones which have been opened or from the unopened pile."

"Oh, we'd better have a limit on how many times a gift can be taken, hadn't we? Otherwise we'll be here all night."

Karo nodded at Donna's suggestion. "Good idea. How about twice? A gift can only be stolen twice and then it's off limits."

Fingers eagerly dipped into the bowl with the numbers, hoping for the highest number.

"Who has number one?"

Clyde smiled, lumbered to his feet and selected a beautifully wrapped package containing a gorgeous ceramic salad bowl made by Rich. Everyone was still oohing and ahhing when Betty held up her number two and selected a package which contained a birdhouse Gil made.

"Gil, it's charming. I didn't know you made birdhouses," Diane said as she eyed it.

Betty smiled slyly. "But I did. Every once in a while he takes a space at the flea market to sell his work. I saw him carrying this in and hoped it would be a birdhouse."

They all laughed, and then Doug held up his number three and said, "Thanks for your sleuthing Betty, but I have some feathered friends that need a place to live."

"Oh, darn." Betty handed it over, already looking at the pile of presents under the tree. The next one she selected and unwrapped was a luxurious shawl, hand knit out of a soft, multi-colored yarn. She wrapped it around her and sighed, then glared ferociously at the others. "Don't any of you think you can take this. It was meant for me."

"Who made that?" Lisa asked looking around.

Diane shyly nodded. "Me. I knit while I watch television."

"It's beautiful." Everyone nodded, envying Betty.

Rich was number four and he selected a package containing one of Betty's set of ceramic candlesticks, but gave them up to Lisa, who had number five. Rich then picked a very heavy package which revealed six pints of homemade jams and jellies made by Donna.

"Wow, I'll really enjoy these, Donna. I love jam on my toast every morning. And look, this one is strawberry-rhubarb. My grandmother used to make this. Thank you so much." Rich looked like he was already tasting the jam.

Gil selected one of Karo's gifts, a set of six dinner plates she had made which both he and Donna seemed to appreciate. Then it was Diane's turn. The package she unwrapped contained a gleaming, ornate silver teapot.

"Ooh. It's gorgeous," she whispered. "It's way too expensive. I can't take this. Who gave this?" Her voice was husky with emotion, betraying her reluctance to give it up even though she thought she shouldn't keep it.

"My dear, Karo said bring something you made or something you no longer use and thought someone else would enjoy. That was Clyde's great grandmother's teapot. Frankly, it's too precious to sell, and I'm tired of polishing it. I'd like someone else to have it. None of our kids wanted it; they'd only sell it in one of their garage sales. If you would like it, I would appreciate you taking it and cherishing it." Molly nodded firmly; she had no intentions of taking it home again.

"Oh, Molly, it's so beautiful!" Diane hugged it to her, tears springing to her eyes.

Molly's turn was next and she carefully eyed the presents already unwrapped. She shook her head at the silver teapot Diane hugged protectively, her eyes skimmed over the shawl Betty had wrapped around her and lighted on the birdhouse sitting in front of Doug. "Sorry Doug, but I have just the spot for that birdhouse. You'll have to find another present."

Everyone laughed at Doug's disappointed look. He picked up the second package Karo had contributed for Lisa which contained four coffee mugs. He seemed delighted.

Karo was next. She picked one of the last two packages to find it contained two framed, mounted black and white photographs. It wasn't until she saw the signature in the corner that she realized Doug was the photographer. "Doug, these are lovely. Are they taken on your property on the mountain?"

He nodded. "One is the apple orchard last spring, and one I took down by the creek this last summer. Do you like them?"

"They're lovely and if I manage to keep them I have just the spot for them."

"Ah, if you keep them? I have number ten, I believe that entitles me to choose from any of the gifts or open the last one, right?" Gil was relishing his position, waving his slip of paper with the ten written on it. He slowly, circled the room, looking carefully at each gift, ignoring the owner's attempt to shield each item from his gaze. "The birdhouse is out, it's been transferred twice and besides I made it. And fortunately for you, Rich, I have an endless supply of jams available, married to the cook you know." He looked carefully at the candlesticks, moved over to closely examine the photos. "Well, much as I would like to have some of these, it is Christmas so I'm feeling generous. I think I'll just take the package that is remaining."

Everyone smiled their relief, especially Diane and Betty, who both looked as if they wouldn't let their presents go without a fight.

Gil opened the box on his lap, pushed the paper aside and sat looking at the object in the box.

"What is it?"

"Who is it from?"

"Hold it up so we can see it."

Gil carefully picked up the object and held it up. It was a small, polished brass instrument, similar to a clock. But it wasn't a clock.

"What is it?"

"It's a barometer. Rather old I think. I found it in a garage sale and fixed it up. It works now. I think it looks good," Clyde said with pride.

"It's great," Gil said as he carefully looked it over. "It's a perfect present for me. Thanks, Clyde. I know I'll enjoy using it."

Karo looked around. "Is that it? Are we done?"

"I think so. That was a lot of fun, Karo. Thanks for thinking of it."

Rich and Lisa started gathering up the wrappings strewn around the floor.

"Who would like some coffee, or more wine?" Karo asked remembering her hostess duties.

"I'm afraid I need to take Tiffany home to bed." Diane looked at the sleeping child who was stretched out on the floor, her toy dog clutched in her arms.

"Here, let me carry her for you," Doug offered, as Diane gathered up her things.

"Karo, it was a wonderful Christmas Eve. Thank you so much for doing this and inviting us. We had a wonderful time and I know this evening will be one of our special memories," Diane said with appreciation as she left.

Clyde and Molly went next and then, when Doug returned, Betty left with Gil and Donna. Gil and Donna insisted on walking Betty home, overriding her protests of taking them out of their way with assurances that they would like to walk around and see the decorations in the neighborhood.

"Okay, let's get this place spruced up," Rich said, starting to clear the remains from the table.

"Wait, you don't have to do that. Have another drink and relax," Karo protested.

"Yes, we do have to do this. What are friends for? After everything is clean then we'll relax with another drink before heading for home." Doug was firm, and with them all pitching in they made short work of the clean up.

CHAPTER 8

Christmas morning was a lazy time for Lisa and Karo. They sat around in their bathrobes, unwrapping their presents to each other, enjoying their coffee while occasionally mentioning something from the party the night before. Later when Greg arrived at the door to pick up Lisa, Karo invited him in. He shrank back from the dogs with such alarm Karo put them out in the backyard. Then Greg relaxed enough to come in. Karo saw him assessing her home with a critical eye and thought, with annoyance, he was probably pricing the property and the furnishings.

His comment surprised her. "Nice place, Karo. You look very at home here."

"I am. I love being this close to the beach," she admitted, feeling ashamed of her earlier assumption. She stood at the door watching them drive off while thinking it hardly seemed possible that she had been intimate with Greg for all those years. Now he seemed as remote as an old acquaintance she hadn't seen in a very long time, totally disconnected from her current life. She remembered all the irritations and the anger during those final years of living together, each trying to turn the other into their ideal mate. But after all,

Greg was Lisa's father and Lisa had been looking forward to her time with him, so she hoped they would have a pleasant day. She shut the door on the sight of his pricey car heading down the street, content to spend the rest of Christmas day with the boys.

The next morning Karo had been working for a couple of hours before Lisa finally poked her head in to tell her mother good morning.

"Hey sleepyhead, you got home late." She got up from the computer to accompany Lisa to the kitchen. "Want breakfast?"

Lisa nodded, still looking groggy. "I'm starved. But just eggs and toast, I feel like I've eaten way too much the last few days."

"How about poached eggs on a toasted English muffin?" At Lisa's nod she got busy while Lisa pushed the button for coffee. "Well, you must have had a good time or you would have been home earlier."

Lisa nodded once more. Taking her coffee to the table she sat down and said, "Mom, did you know Dad has a girlfriend?"

Karo stopped what she was doing, turning around she looked at Lisa. Then she said slowly, "No. No, I didn't know. But you know, Lisa, I suspected he did. Before we even decided to divorce he suddenly started acquiring a new, more updated wardrobe. And that car seemed to be more than just a toy. It was kind of a statement, you know? So I just assumed someone had caught his eye.

"So did you meet her? Did you like her?" she asked her daughter gently, wondering if the meeting had been traumatic for Lisa.

"She's okay, but really young. She's closer to my age than Dad's. That's kind of weird. You know, having your father date someone your own age? I mean, what if he dated one of my friends? Ugh, gross."

"Is it serious? Do you think they're going to get married?" Karo was trying to analyze how she was feeling about this conversation, how she would feel if Greg married a beautiful young woman as soon as he was freed from his old middle-aged wife.

Suddenly, she realized she really didn't care. Yesterday seeing him here in her house only confirmed their relationship had disintegrated to a point where she wasn't much interested in what he did, except for how what he did impacted Lisa. She didn't want Lisa hurt.

She turned back to the stove to slip the eggs into the boiling water. "What's she like, what did you do until all hours of the night?" She might not care if Greg had a new interest, but she was still curious about his girlfriend.

"Her name is Kelli Madison. She works for a company that does business with Dad. That's how he met her. She's nice, dresses very well and seems completely taken with Dad. Actually, she's so gaga over him it's almost embarrassing. I mean of course I love him, but he's my dad, you know?

"We had dinner with some friends of theirs, then we went to a movie and afterwards we went out to a couple of clubs. I didn't know Dad could dance like that."

"Your dad used to love to dance. Don't you remember how we used to dance at the parties we had while we were living in San Mateo?"

Lisa shook her head. "I guess not. But he knows all these great clubs, so we had a good time. And fortunately, I didn't have to get up and go to work today like they do." She laughed. "They're probably wishing we didn't hit that last club in Redwood City before they brought me home."

Karo listened to Lisa's description of the club while she carefully scooped out the eggs, drained them and slipped them onto the toasted muffin. She placed the plate in front of Lisa and then went to get herself a cup of coffee and joined Lisa at the table while she ate.

"So what would you like to do today? Any thoughts?"

"A walk on the beach, and then could I see your pottery studio?"

"Oh, dear, I'm afraid not. The studio, actually, the whole recreation center, is closed up tight for the next week. There's no way to get in until January. But we can go for a walk on the beach and we could drive up to Half Moon Bay and visit the shops in town and have lunch at the beach. Do you want to do that?"

Lisa nodded. "Sounds good. I haven't been there in years. I told Janiece it was okay for her to come over tonight for a visit. Is it okay with you?"

She saw her mother nod. "And Dad is going to come by tomorrow to take me to the airport. He wanted to do it and I thought it would save you a trip."

Karo nodded again. "I would have been happy to take you, but it's nice of him to offer. Oh, Lisa, I wish you could stay longer."

"Next time, I promise. I just haven't worked there long enough to accumulate the vacation time. If they didn't give everyone the day before Christmas and the day after, I wouldn't have been able to get here at all."

Karo sighed. She remembered how it was when she first started working. It was the way life was.

* * *

He moved aside the paper which covered his head to find the day was cold, gloomy and weepy. He was stiff from crouching in the doorway and was not looking forward to another cold rainy day. He put his hand out and the warmth of the Styrofoam cup filled with hot coffee enticed him to shrug off more of the papers covering his ratty sleeping bag.

Last night, shaking from cold, huddling in the doorway to escape as much of the rain as possible, he had vowed to himself that today he would move to one of the shelters. After the cold of the last few days he was now willing to give up his freedom for a warm bed, a hot meal and a chance to shower. He was even willing to sit through the service and sign a pledge of sobriety if he had to do so. But this morning things were looking up. Here was the Coffee Lady. Here was hope from a different direction.

He finished the coffee and held out the cup for a refill. He took the sandwiches gratefully, nodding his thanks. And this time when she offered him the chance to go with her, he didn't scrabble away in panic as he had previously. No this time he looked at her and thought about it while he tore into the sandwiches.

She hunched down in front of him, cajoling him, promising him hot food, a clean bed, a big television and even a gradual withdrawal plan from the booze he just couldn't seem to live without.

"Why?" he barked rudely. "Why would you do all that for me." He was just playing her, making her work for it. He knew he was going with her; it was a much better solution than the missions offered.

"My brother died on the streets. I didn't even know where he was. I couldn't do anything for him, but I vowed to help others to make up for my failure to help him," she said piously. "You know me, Charger. You can trust me. Remember, what we talked about before? This would be a good thing. You could get your life back together. I could help you get your pension and Social Security funds so you could live a decent life. You would have enough with your retirement benefits coming in each month to have your own place, manage your own life."

He nodded. He could use her help. Once before she had told him when he turned sixty-five, as he had last year, he could collect the retirement benefits due to him from both the government and from the union. That would mean a monthly income, probably enough to pay rent, buy food and still have enough for booze when he really needed it. He knew it was sensible to do something about his life; he just hadn't been ready then. But after the last few days, he was realizing he couldn't continue living on the streets, existing each day by his wits. It was too cold, he was too old, and life was too mean.

"But what about my things?" He looked around at the treasures he had collected, tied up in bundles and propped in the doorway to lean against as he slept.

"You don't need them. Leave them for one of the others. I'll get you clothes and whatever you need. When the money starts coming in you can buy what you want. Just come with me now, you won't regret it." She made it all seem so easy.

He struggled to his feet, rooted through one of his bundles. Finally he found what he was looking for. He stuck some papers in his pocket, checked to make sure his ratty old wallet was in his pocket and then said, "First, I need to use the bathroom. Let's go by the train station and then I'm ready to go."

She nodded, standing up and picking up the bag of sandwiches and the thermos of coffee. "You go on and I'll follow behind. That way I can give out the rest of this food, before I leave. My truck is parked down that way a bit. I'll meet you in front of the depot. Wait for me there."

Charger finished up in the grubby restroom at the train station and even washed his hands and face in honor of the importance of the occasion. When he emerged he saw Howie hovering in the shadows, panhandling for money for breakfast. He waited until one of the commuters dropped a few coins in his hand before he went over to him.

"How's it going?"

"Not so good. I could eat a horse this morning, but will have to settle for coffee and a donut." He looked at the paltry number of coins in his hand.

"I'm out of here, Howie," he announced abruptly.

Howie looked at him, his jaw dropped. "What do you mean?"

"I'm going with the Coffee Lady. She's going to straighten out my money and help me find my own place. I'm gone! I'm not living on the streets any more."

Howie looked at him, wide-eyed and disbelieving. "You're leaving, just like that?"

"Yep, and I left my things in my doorway back there. If you want them, go get them before someone else realizes I'm gone."

"You're sure?"

Charger nodded. "I'm sure. Good luck to you, buddy. And take care." But Howie had already sidled off, quickly heading down the street toward the derelict building Charger had formerly claimed as his own.

* * *

It was a quiet Friday at pottery. Many of the regulars were absent. The holidays were over, there was nothing fun to look forward to until Valentine's Day and the heavy rain which had been falling since yesterday probably convinced many of the potters to stay home. Rich wasn't in, so Karo assumed he was working a double shift as he sometimes had to do. Evy was babysitting one of her grandchildren this week. Even Betty wasn't in. That was a surprise. She was always there. So because there were fewer people to talk to today, Karo seemed to be getting a lot done. She had spent a couple of hours this morning trimming the cups she had thrown Wednesday. She had always made mugs for coffee, but these were a more refined shape for tea. She had each cup sitting on a footed base, with a narrow bottom, gracefully sloping out to a wider top. And while they weren't going to be thin and translucent like fancy teacups, they were made of porcelain, so she thought they would take the glaze very well. Now she was finishing them by attaching the handles and adding little touches to the decoration. She was quite pleased with them, and was admiring them when she became aware of the voices behind her.

"You can't come in here. This studio is open to enrolled students only." Joy's voice was abrupt and mean.

"But, but Sandi said..." The other voice trembled.

Karo looked up to see Joy scowling at the woman facing her.

"Sandi works on Wednesday. If you want to talk to her, come then." Joy was dismissive, making a rude shooing gesture with her hands before turning away.

Karo recognized Connie from Sandi's Wednesday class. She saw the distress on Connie's face and couldn't help from leaping up to try to help her.

"Hi Connie, what are you doing here?" she asked gently, afraid the quiet, shy woman was going to burst into tears.

"I just came in to finish that casserole so it could get fired this weekend. It's a present and I need it next week. Sandi suggested I come in today to finish it. She said since I missed so many classes last session because of the flu, it would be all right. But she," she pointed to Joy, who had stopped and turned to glare at her, "says I can't work here, even though Sandi said I could."

Connie looked at Karo, a tear slipping out of one of her eyes. "I don't know what to do. It's a wedding shower present for my best friend's daughter and I need to get it out of the kiln by Monday." She shook her head. "I guess I'll have to buy her a present over the weekend..."

Karo turned and looked at Joy, thinking fast. "Joy, Connie is one of Sandi's advanced students. She's an experienced potter and been coming here for a couple of years. She never asks for favors or special treatment and Sandi wouldn't have suggested she come in today if she hadn't thought it was an exception."

"I don't care what Sandi said, I'm in charge of workshops. We have rules about who uses the workshop. We only allow people, who have signed up for the workshop, access on Tuesdays and Fridays. That's the rule! And we have that rule because we don't have a teacher on the premises to watch out for the blunders the inexperienced student might make. And I don't have time to watch everyone who would like to stop by to make up for a missed class."

Karo offered, "I'll be glad to work with her so she can finish her piece. Can't you make an exception? I'm sure she won't do this again. Will you Connie?"

Connie shook her head, looking hopeful.

Joy didn't look like she was going to change her mind, so Karo decided to apply a little more subtle pressure.

"I know it's not usual. I know you are very fair about keeping to the rules for everyone. But with me taking responsibility for her, you could bend the rule a bit to accommodate Sandi and avoid an incident which might develop into another battle." She saw Joy's eyes widen slightly before her face tightened in a frown, which meant she was thinking about it. Everyone knew about the fierce disagreement Joy and Sandi got into just before Christmas about how the studio was going to handle some aspect of the pottery sale. Joy had been enraged when she had to back down and accept Sandi's decision on the issue. She had been fuming about it since then. But Joy also knew that Sandi had threatened to make changes in how the workshops were run and thereby curtail Joy's control of them. Karo didn't think Joy would want to confront Sandi again just when things were beginning to quiet down.

And she was apparently right.

Joy shrugged. "All right. You can stay for the afternoon and Karo will supervise your work. But don't expect this to happen again. If you want to work in the studio you have to sign up for my workshop, pay the fee and take responsibility for some of the work. These workshops are not just for the convenience of the potters who find themselves in a bind.

"And don't tell anyone else I allowed you to work here because they'll expect the same treatment, and it's not going to happen." She stomped away leaving Connie almost quaking with fear.

The other students, who had been watching surreptitiously, turned their attention away from the fracas and back to their projects.

"What do you need to do with your casserole to finish it, Connie?"

"I just need to finish glazing so it can go in the kiln this weekend. What with all the rain we've been having, the glaze didn't dry. But since it's for a special gift, I didn't want to rush it and ruin it." She looked at Karo with a grateful expression. "I hope I won't mess up your plans for the afternoon, Karo. It's really nice of you to help me." Her eyes turned to the other side of the room where Joy was working on her wheel and she couldn't seem to control the shudder running through her. "I had no idea my request would cause such a problem."

"Don't worry about it. I've noticed Joy is a little grumpy today. It's probably the weather affecting her. She sounds worse than she means to be. As it turns out, I have some pieces I need to glaze too, so I'm happy to work in the glaze room with you and that way I can watch you do that beautiful design work you're known for. I've always wondered how you did it. Get your piece and I'll meet you in the glaze room as soon as I put these cups away."

CHAPTER 9

"Captain, sit down!" Karo said sternly to the dog trying to get out of his seat, while slowing the car to search for the driveway Doug had described to her. She maneuvered the car into the sharp turn and carefully rolled over the small bridge spanning the creek. The dirt and gravel road circled endlessly around the hill, before she was finally coasting into the cleared space near an old corral. The dogs were really excited now, fairly dancing in their seats, wanting to be free of the seat belt constraints attaching them to the backseat.

"Hey, you found me." Doug came out of the house to help.

"I wouldn't have without your directions. They were great. In fact, I'm wondering how you ever found it when you were house hunting." Karo paused looking around with amazement. The little house sat in a flat clearing at the top of a rounded hill. On one side was a barn, or maybe it was a large garage, a couple of worn out buildings and the old corral. Behind the corral was the apple orchard. Today, on the crisp cold winter day the trees were leafless, but she could imagine how beautiful it would look in the spring and summer. And behind the orchard more hills piled up against the mountain range that ran up and down the coast separating the coastal towns from those on the peninsula.

The dogs were on the ground now, dancing around Doug, trying to get his attention. Karo left him to pat Captain and Rudy and went around to the back of the car to unload the pies she had brought.

"Here, can I carry one?" Doug was practically drooling over the Ollieberry pie.

Karo carried the apple pie as Doug led them into his house.

"Doug, this is a beautiful house. Somehow I was expecting a rustic cabin in the woods. You know one of those falling down shanties with a decrepit porch across the front they show in pictures from the depression."

She looked around at the three large rooms that made up the living part of the house. The dining area, living room and kitchen were all one large space furnished with comfortable looking chairs, couch and tables with lots of bookshelves. The fireplace was on a wall where it could be seen from all three rooms.

"Well, it is, kind of."

"Not! It's roomy and comfortable. And it smells good. What are you cooking?"

He laughed. "Don't get your hopes up. That's just the corn pudding cooking in the crock pot. We're having rock cod baked in salsa, a corn pudding and a big salad. Very simple, but there will be plenty, and of course for desert we're having your pies. Okay?"

"Sounds better than just okay. Do you need me to do anything?"

"No, everything is under control. Seeing this is my first dinner party, I'm keeping it low key and very simple. The others I invited won't be here for a couple hours and everything is ready, so I thought maybe you and the boys would like to check out the property."

"Oh, could we? We'd love to see this property we've heard so much about. Is that little creek under the bridge down by the road where you fish?"

"No, that's a little too small for decent size fish. It's mostly good to carry off the rain, although in the summer the blackberry bushes growing along the sides are generous. Remember that if you'd like to make blackberry pies as well as Ollieberry. I have another creek that runs through the back of the property further up the hill. That one sometimes gives up a trout. I spend a lot of time there, trying. Come on, I'll show you."

Karo put down her purse and headed out the door behind Doug. The dogs were already racing in circles in front of him, just waiting to see which way he was going.

"At least you're dressed for the terrain," Doug commented eying her worn jeans, leather hiking boots and the windbreaker she wore over her sweater, with approval.

"You said casual and I knew you were in the hills, so I was happy to get out my comfortable clothes." She followed him into the orchard where they walked side by side. The dogs ran here and there, chasing scents and each other only to pause now and again to check if they were still coming, running back to greet them, and then running off again. On the other side of the orchard they came to an old dirt road and started following it up the hill. When they came around one of the curves they found the dogs, noses down, snuffling at something.

"Ugh, gross. What's that?" Karo made a face. "Captain, Rudy, leave it."

Of course the dogs paid no attention to her order, finding the lime green, eight inch slug much more interesting.

"Haven't you seen a banana slug before?"

"No, and I can't say I'm sorry. It looks awful."

"Well it is, kind of. It's really just a big, yellow-green, slimy slug. We have a lot of them up here in the redwoods. They apparently thrive in this climate."

Karo shivered. "Not my kind of wildlife, thank you very much." She gingerly passed at the edge of the trail, as far from the slug as possible. Soon the dogs, afraid of being left behind, abandoned their find to catch up again.

The road gently wound through the thickening forest until it petered out near the crest of the hill. This was a very remote area. It was so quiet, the air was so crisp, it made Karo's heart swell with the joy of being alive.

Karo and Doug sat on a boulder at the edge of the road and Doug fished into his backpack for a bottle of water and a small plastic dish. He poured out a drink for each of the panting dogs while Karo just enjoyed the air. After a while they headed back down and Karo remembered. "Hey, I thought you said there was another creek. Did we pass it?"

"No, we have to go off the trail to reach it. We'll go that way, you'll see."

A bit further on he veered off the road onto a small trail which led them through the brush down the hillside. Karo lost all sense of where they were in relationship to Doug's house and even the dogs stayed close as if afraid to wander too far.

They heard it before they saw the water, and suddenly there it was gurgling and splashing over rocks and felled trees as the stream wandered down the hillside.

"Oh, it's beautiful." Karo stared at the moving water enthralled. "I'd love to just sit here and watch the water move past. It wouldn't matter if I caught a fish."

Doug nodded, smiling. "That's what I think. I come out here for a couple of hours, especially after a really intense session in the ER, and afterwards I feel revitalized, as if I could tackle anything. And sometimes I even catch a trout." He led her to an area where some rocks provided perfect seating, and they sat there for a while. The dogs seemed happy to lay down for a rest.

They chatted idly about the twenty acres that was attached to the house and the State Forest land that stretched behind it, enjoying the solitude and the fresh air.

"We'd better be starting back, people will be coming soon," Doug said after a glance at his watch. He led the way and they emerged from the orchard just as a car drove up. A couple seemed to just explode from the vehicle that stopped in front of them.

"Dotty and Norm," Doug explained as Dotty threw herself at him for a hug and he reached out his free hand to shake with Norm.

"Are we too early? What a great place. Remote doesn't even explain how far away from everything you are." Dotty's enthusiasm seemed to just spill out.

"You're not too early, and it's not as remote as it seems. And this is my friend, Karo. Karo, meet Dotty and Norm. Dotty works at Carruthers with me, and Norm is a fireman with the Belle Vista Fire Department."

Karo smiled and shook hands and they all trooped into the house. Doug was dispensing drinks when Rich came in the door followed closely by two guys who were obviously a couple. Everyone else seemed to know each other, so Rich introduced Karo to Scott and Byron. Byron worked at Carruthers' in the administration area and Scott, his partner, was an accountant with a local firm. And then as Dotty helped Doug set out the hors d'oeuvres and Norm lit the fire, two more people arrived. They were two more doctors who worked the Emergency Room at Carruthers. Janice, a thin, red haired woman in her early thirties was on Doug's team and Eldon, a tall, solid man with coffee and cream colored skin, was on another shift. Both were available for the party as the third shift was on duty today.

The house became very noisy. "Oh, aren't you a cutie?" Janice leaned over to pet Captain. "Doug, I didn't know you had a dog," she amended, "two dogs," as Rudy wandered over looking for his share of the attention.

Doug shook his head. "I don't. They belong to Karo and just came for a visit. Captain is the little hairy guy, and Rudy is the big guy with the sorrowful eyes."

Byron was scratching Rudy behind the ears and Karo relaxed. The dogs were behaving and no one seemed to mind their presence. At home when someone came through the door they were right there ready to protect their house, but they seemed to understand they were guests so they were minding their manners tonight.

It was a congenial group and very soon Karo felt as if she belonged. While many of the funny stories came from incidents at Carruthers, the group made an effort to include the three guests, who were not connected to the big medical facility.

Karo watched Doug and Rich interact with their friends, remembering her discussion with Lisa about them. During the Christmas visit Lisa had asked her about her relationship with Doug. Karo explained they were friends and that he was gay, but Lisa stared at her with disbelief all over her face.

"What, you don't believe me?"

"He didn't act gay. In fact, he seemed pretty interested in you."

"Well, he's not. He's way too young for me. And he's a friend of Rich's. I'm sure Rich is gay. They may be a couple."

"What makes you so sure about Rich?" Lisa challenged.

"He's a nurse, for God's sake. And a potter. And he's single. Well, I'm sure they're both gay. But they're nice and they've been nice to me, so I don't care about their sexual orientation."

Lisa had just snorted, leaving Karo feeling as if she was missing something obvious.

So tonight she took the opportunity to watch how Doug and Rich interacted and how they both related to Scott and Byron. But frankly she couldn't see any difference in how they treated the gay couple versus Dotty and Norm. Or the two doctors who were apparently an item.

"Hey, Doug, I love this place in the woods, but how do you keep from getting creeped out? I mean isn't it kind of scary, so far from everything?"

"Yeah, every horror movie I've ever seen starts in some remote place." Byron shuddered. "I think I'd be awake all night listening for strange noises."

"Not if you worked the hours I do. Trust me, when I go to sleep, I sleep. And actually being so remote is great for that. I don't have all the road noises and neighborhood noises to keep me awake when my shift is over." He grinned a minute, obviously thinking, then he seemed to make up his mind. "Well, when I first came, I found it very different from living in the middle of a big city. I wouldn't say I was scared, but I admit maybe I was a little spooked. I woke up one night hearing noises out here and realized I had an intruder. My heart was pounding almost out of my chest. My knees were quaking, but most of all I was just plain mad at being disturbed."

Everyone was leaning toward Doug, breathless with anticipation.

"I had this old rifle, a 30-30, I had been using to shoot cans off the corral fence, so I grabbed it and tip-toed out here. I flipped on the light switch and aimed the rifle..." He demonstrated with arm gestures pretending he was holding the rifle. "And there was my intruder, frozen in my sights, a gigantic rat. Somehow, he gnawed his way in and found a big bowl of apples I had on the table. He had eaten so many he literally couldn't move. No way could he run away and he never would have fit back through the hole I found later. He just sat there and stared at me."

"Oh, no. What did you do?" Dotty said through her laughter.

"You didn't shoot, did you?" Janice asked with concern.

"Are you kidding? And fill my living room with more holes? No, I got a hammer and hit him over the head, took him outside and dumped him down the ravine behind the shed. The next day I found the hole and repaired it. I've slept pretty soundly since. But, I still keep that 30-30 close."

They all laughed except Dotty, whose face broadcast her sympathy for the rat.

"What? You think I should have kept him for a pet? Not me, I'm from the inner city. I know rats, and I don't share my space with them. Not willingly, anyway.

"Actually, I think I'm safer out here than any of you living in the city. People are pretty cautious about approaching a house at the end of a country lane. Too many of the residents keep dogs and rifles handy."

"Well, what about poachers looking for a place to squat?" Scot asked.

"Yeah, I heard that was a real problem down in the hills outside of Santa Cruz, where there are a lot of summer cabins. Homeless people or druggies just move right in. There was an article in the paper a while back about it," Dotty offered.

"And the homeless are getting to be a real problem around here," Janice contributed. "We're seeing more and more of them hanging around. Just last week there were several congregated around the door at the supermarket, approaching customers as they went in and out." She shuddered. "I just see them as potential patients in the ER. They lead such a dangerous life. And Belle Vista doesn't really have any programs to help them."

"Actually, the church Scott and I go to has been talking about that. They're thinking of opening a soup kitchen and shelter. It's a hot topic, because some of the members of the congregation claim it will attract more homeless to the area, while the other half argue it will just keep the ones already here alive during these cold winter nights." He shrugged. "We'll see what they decide to do.

"Well somebody should do something. I don't like it when they approach me. They make me feel creepy, even though I know that some of them get sucked into that kind of life by a series of tragic events and only need a helping hand to get them out of it," was Dotty's response.

"Yeah, and some of them just like the life," Norm said. Then changing the subject, "Doug, I bet you get a lot of deer up here. Do you hunt?"

"Yes, I have lots of deer. But, I don't hunt them and I don't let anyone else hunt them on my property. It's posted. Now pigs are another thing. Anybody who'd like to hunt pig is welcome as long as they cart the carcasses away. There is a pack of wild pigs that come through here, especially when the apples are ripe. They're a bloody nuisance, and they tear up the ground in the orchard something fierce." He looked at Norm. "If you and your buddies are interested in pigs, let me know."

"Pigs? That sounds interesting. I'll talk to the guys. That could be fun."

"I don't know, Norm. Wild pigs are dangerous, aren't they?" Dotty asked with a frown.

"Yeah, but they really taste good," Norm said, smiling at the thought of the meat. "And that little grocery store down at the crossroads could make us some great sausage from wild pig. Yum, I'm going to talk to the guys, maybe we could make a weekend of it."

"And I'd love to get rid of them." Doug couldn't help promoting the idea.

"Speaking of getting rid of someone, I have to go or I'll be late for work." Rich stood up. "Sorry I won't be able to help with the dishes, people." His grin showed absolutely no remorse. "Thanks for the great meal, Doug. It was a nice evening."

Rich headed out while the rest of them started cleaning up. As soon as the kitchen looked reasonable, Karo took her leave.

"Great pie, Karo."

"It was fun meeting you."

"I hope we'll see you again."

Doug walked her and the dogs out to her car and watched as she carefully hooked the dogs to the seatbelts.

"Thanks for coming. You added a lot to the day, in addition to the pie, I mean," he said, leaning down and gently kissing her cheek.

She jerked with surprise, then recovered. "I loved it. It was fun seeing your place and meeting your friends. You throw a pretty good party, mister." And she headed down the little lane, carefully driving over the bridge to head for home, all the while smiling to herself. It had been a fun day.

* * *

Betty opened the door and immediately bent down to pat Captain and Rudy. "How are you guys? Come in, come in."

Then she remembered Karo still standing on the porch. "You too, Karo. I put the kettle on. I thought you might like some tea. Do you have time?"

Karo nodded, "Sure," and followed her into the kitchen.

Betty poured the boiling water into one of her lovely teapots and then went to the sink and filled two bowls of tap water for the dogs. "I bought some doggie treats. Can they have one?" she asked Karo and seeing her nod she gave each of the dogs a green bone to gnaw.

She brought the tea to the table and sat down. "Have a cookie; I know they're not as good as the ones you served Christmas Eve, but I think that little bakery near the supermarket does a pretty good job."

Karo took a bite of one and nodded her agreement. "They are good, thank you." Then with a little scolding tone in her voice she reminded Betty, "I thought you were going to go over to the animal shelter and get yourself a dog. You should really do that."

Betty looked sad and said, "I would, I should, but I just haven't gotten myself to do it. I guess the responsibility scares me. I feel I just can't handle any more responsibility right now what with my husband and all..."

"Oh, of course." Karo was instantly sorry she had brought the subject up. "Dogs do take a lot of care. They're kind of like having a child, one who never grows up. Well, when you're ready for one there will be lots there to chose from." She changed the subject again. "I wanted to drop off this sea glass I've collected." She reached into her pocket and pulled out a packet wrapped in paper toweling.

Betty watched as Karo carefully unwrapped the towel to reveal the glass she brought. "Oh, they are nice. Did you find them recently?"

"Well, the red one I found yesterday, but the others I found around the end of the year. Remember we had a couple big storms then. That yellow one is my favorite. What do you think it was?"

Betty picked it up and examined it closely. "I don't know, but it is beautiful, isn't it. It will sell immediately." She looked up at Karo. "Are you sure I can't give you something for these, Karo? I'd be happy to."

"No, don't be silly. It's been fun looking for it in the sand. I didn't even know about sea glass until you told me. I'm happy to contribute to your supply and if you make money off of it, that's great."

Betty smiled, gathered up the pieces and carefully stowed them in a drawer in her kitchen.

They chatted a while about the neighborhood and then the studio.

"Betty, I know Joy is your friend, but she is very strange. I just don't understand her." Karo thought a lot about Joy, she was such an enigma. She just didn't know what to make of her, and it still bothered her that she discovered Joy owned multiple accounts with various people at the bank, although she knew she could never say anything about that. But it occurred to her that Betty knew Joy rather well and maybe she could shed some light on the mystery of Joy's personality. So she leaned forward and said earnestly, "Connie, from Sandi's class, came in on that Friday workshop you missed. She only wanted to finish glazing a casserole so it could get in the weekly firing. Anyway, Joy made a big thing out of it. She was so rude to Connie, it was embarrassing. And you know Connie, she's such a shy, sweet person, she almost burst out in tears.

"It was too much! I just couldn't help but intervene. I managed to calm Joy down and I convinced her to let Connie stay just this once, but really it was so unnecessary. And Joy was just being mean. Doesn't she realize how nasty she can get? Doesn't she care?"

Betty just shook her head, a concerned expression on her face. "Joy's had some real sadness in her life, Karo. I think she tries, but sometimes she just lets her disappointment with life overwhelm her." Betty tried to defend her friend.

"Well, what is really confusing to me about Joy is that only a few weeks before that incident with Connie, I saw an entirely different side of Joy. A side I would have never believed if I hadn't seen it with my own eyes. I was in Redwood City when I saw her. And you won't believe what she was doing?"

Betty just stared at Karo, not venturing a guess.

"She was distributing coffee and sandwiches to the homeless down in that area near the train station where they live. It was one of those cold and blustery days. It's just amazing those people can survive the freezing temperatures overnight. And there was Joy, moving through the area handing out food and hot drinks.

"I couldn't believe my eyes at first, but I saw clearly it was her." Karo shook her head. "I just don't understand the woman." At the strange noise she heard she stopped talking, noticing the peculiar look on Betty's face.

"Betty, Betty, are you all right?" She was alarmed, wondering if the older woman was having a seizure or something.

Betty shook her head, waved her hand saying, "I'm okay, just swallowed wrong. Give me a minute." She gasped and wheezed, coughed a few times and then seemed to recover, leaning forward with an earnest expression on her face. "Sorry dear, that's so annoying. Now tell me again about seeing Joy. She was in Redwood City passing out food and drink to the homeless?"

Karo nodded. "I saw her there."

Betty shook her head angrily now. "Well I can't believe it, and after she promised."

"She promised? She promised what? Surely her act of charity should be admired..."

Betty's face was now flushed deep red. "No! You don't understand. Joy is not acting out of charity."

Betty closed her eyes tight and sat silently thinking. After a moment she muttered, "She promised she was through with all of that."

She opened her eyes, but didn't seem to be seeing Karo. "I'll have to do something. It has to stop. It has to stop right now!"

She stood up abruptly. "I'm sorry to hurry you, Karo, but I have something I have to do right away. Come again, another time, won't you?" And she escorted the confused Karo, the dogs trailing her, to the door before she had even finished her tea.

CHAPTER 10

"Joy, someone saw you giving out coffee recently. You promised! And now you're doing it again? After you promised me you stopped."

Joy held the receiver away from her ear; the voice was so shrill it hurt. Betty's voice was so loud it hurt her ear. Joy carefully modulated her own voice to a soft, calm tone hoping it would pacify Betty. "Betty, what on earth are you talking about? Why are you so upset?"

"Someone saw you! They saw you giving out hot coffee and sandwiches to the homeless down by the railroad station in Redwood City. And that can only mean one thing to me. You're doing it again after you promised me you were done with all that." The accusation came shrilly through the receiver.

"Calm down. Who? Who saw me?"

"It doesn't matter who saw you. What does matter is whether or not you were there."

"Well, actually I was. It was right after that cold snap and I was worried about some of the guys I've come to know. I just took some stuff down there to make their day a little more bearable." She delivered this assurance in a sincere tone, hoping she sounded convincing. "That's all. I promised you I'd stop and I keep my promises."

"Well you'd better, because I'm warning you, I can't live with the knowledge of what you're doing. If you don't stop, I'll be forced to take some action to stop you, no matter what consequences that would have for both of us. Do you understand me?"

"Oh, relax. There's no need to be so dramatic." She was suddenly tired of this charade. She didn't like having to explain herself to anyone. "I understand. I understood you perfectly when we talked about it. I agreed to stop, didn't I? And I have. You're just acting like some paranoid old biddy." She laughed a bit to take some of the sting out of the words that slipped out of her mouth. "Loosen up, Betty. I admit that I was down there looking for two guys in particular. They were ones I had originally targeted for my program, but after I agreed to abandon my plan, I decided that I would still help them."

"What do you mean?"

"Well, there's no reason I couldn't do what I promised them, help them get their finances straightened out, rent them a place and let them manage their own life, off the streets." Her voice sounded sanctimonious.

"What?" was more a screech than a word. "No way I'm believing you're acting from altruistic motives."

"It's the truth. I found the guy they call Charger and he was desperate to get off the streets. That last cold spell was finally too much for him. I couldn't just leave him there. I've been talking to him for over a year. He needs help and I know how to provide it. He's eligible for a pension in addition to Social Security. In fact, we've already submitted the paperwork for him.

We're just waiting for the funds to begin arriving. Meanwhile we're looking for cheap housing for him in case you know of any."

"Look, I'm not that gullible. You may have convinced this guy, Charger, of your good intentions, but I know you, Joy. I know you don't have any real feelings for these people, so I don't believe you're going to suddenly start to do good works for them.

"I'm going to watch you closely. Starting this week I'm going to be right there helping you load the kilns. Do you hear me? Plan on me being with you each week when you close the doors and turn them on. And I'll help unload when they're finished, too. You're not going to be able to sneak around me, trust me on this!" Betty emphasized this statement by slamming down the receiver.

Joy set her phone receiver down gently, thinking hard about how to get around this nasty turn of events.

She should have never let Mary Louise convince her to help Betty. She had learned long ago that you couldn't rely on the gratefulness of those you helped. Eventually, those people who initially couldn't do enough to show their appreciation became inured to their gratitude, and then they started resenting you for making them feel indebted. She should have remembered this. If she had, Betty would probably be living out on the streets herself, too busy trying to survive to worry about the morality of Joy's activities.

Well, Betty had offered the solution herself. If Betty couldn't live with what Joy was doing, then Joy would have to see that she didn't have to.

Then, deciding she would solve this problem later, she threw a sweater over her shoulders and went up to the apartment over the garage. She knocked on the door, calling out, "Charger, are you up, it's me."

The door opened and the man called Charger stood in the doorway. He looked very different from the man she had brought home only two weeks ago. While he hadn't yet shaved this morning, you could see he had shaved not long ago. He was wearing clean jeans and a sweat shirt. The clothes, while worn and a little shabby, were still clean and in one piece. She had bought his new wardrobe at the Salvation Army store, and he was very pleased with it.

"Good morning. I just wanted to remind you that today we're going into town to open a bank account, so your checks can be deposited directly to your checking account. That way you don't have to worry about someone stealing them from your mailbox."

He nodded, though she thought she saw a gleam of suspicion in his eyes.

"Remember, we talked about this," she reminded him patiently, accustomed to the ways of these men who had lived so long in the wilds of the streets. "We'll open a joint account. That way the bank can use my credit to establish the account and they won't put you through all kinds of grief about not having a recent account anywhere. But, it's important that you look respectable. We're going to say you're my brother, who just moved to this area. So make sure you shave and wear clean clothes. We're going to leave here in about an hour. Afterwards we'll stop at the store and get you a bottle to celebrate. That's how it works, remember, you reward yourself every time you take a step toward establishing your new life."

Charger's eye lit up at the thought of having a bottle later today. Any suspicions he had were quickly forgotten. "I'll be ready."

She smiled to herself as she went back down the stairs. It was really very easy to manipulate these guys. How could Betty possibly be naïve enough to think she would stop before she met her goal?

Maybe Betty was getting senile as well as feeling overwhelmed by guilt.

After Charger she only needed two more candidates to reach her goal. And then she would be happy to stop. Because then she would be ready to initiate the rest of her plan to sell out and move, ready at last to live the kind of life she had always dreamed about. The kind of life she deserved. It was all she could do to suppress her chuckle of delight. She was proud of herself and what she had accomplished. She could have lived her whole life reeling from the nasty surprises life dished out to her, one after the other, but no, after she found herself in that unbearable situation with Hiram, when she found herself cornered, she did what any cornered animal would do. She fought back. And when she found out it could all be so easy, she made her plan. And now, finally, she was close to completing it. And Betty's misgivings were not going to keep her from her just reward.

* * *

Karo had just finished loading her groceries into the back of her SUV when she noticed him standing there. Her heart gave a crazy lurch before she recognized him and relaxed. "Lieutenant Myers, you startled me."

He nodded. "I was afraid of that. That's why I stood back until you noticed me. I didn't want you thinking you were going to get mugged in the Safeway parking lot."

She smiled. "How have you been? Have you solved the mystery of the woman on the beach?"

"No, I'm sorry, I haven't. But don't worry, I will. Sometimes it takes a little more time than I expect, but I'll eventually get the answer. Belle Vista doesn't have very many unsolved murders and I don't intend the number to grow on my watch."

"So what can I do for you?"

"I saw you in the market and wondered if you'd like to have a Coke or a cup of coffee with me?"

"Is this official police business?" she asked, uncertain about the invitation.

He smiled. He looked almost handsome and certainly a lot more humane. "No, it isn't. I was doing my shopping too, and I thought I'd like to hear what you've been up to lately. So...?"

"So, I'd love a Coke, I'm kind of thirsty and nothing I bought will perish from being left for a few more minutes in the car. Where?"

He nodded his head. "There's a little coffee shop over there that could do." And he fell into step beside her.

After the waitress poured his cup of coffee and brought her Coke, they sat a minute longer as if neither could think of anything to say.

"As I remember it, you had just relocated to Belle Vista a few weeks before we met on the beach. How are you adjusting to living here by the beach?"

She nodded, grateful to have a topic. "Actually, I love it here. As you know, there have been a few problems, but I assume that could happen anywhere." She thought a minute. "Of course, it never happened to me before, but naturally you read about situations like these in the papers all the time. So I don't blame them on Belle Vista. And since the explosion, our neighborhood has been serene. In fact, because of the explosion, the neighbors have all gotten together to start a neighborhood watch program, which has progressed to planning a block party for the Fourth of July."

She changed the subject. "How long have you lived here?"

"About ten years. I moved up from Southern California where I lived a long time." He shrugged, looked uncomfortable and then took a breath and went on. "I lost my wife and one of my sons in an auto accident." He saw the shock on her face and said simply, "A drunk driver on the Santa Monica freeway at the same time my wife was driving my son home from the orthodontist and, suddenly, life as I knew it ended."

They were both silent for a while, then he said softly, "I tried to handle it. I had another son in college, and I tried to be there for him. When he graduated and wanted to make his own way in the world, I said to hell with it. It was time for a change. I moved up here, and I believe I made the right choice. Belle Vista was very happy to get someone with my experience, and I was relieved to find the crime here is nowhere near the level I was used to. I feel almost like a normal person again."

He looked at her. "Why did you move here?"

She shook her head. "Mine is not nearly as tragic a story as yours. Mine is the usual one of mid-life changes, divorce, trying to find myself. My daughter went east to college and when she graduated she decided to stay there. My husband and I split up and there didn't seem to be any compelling reason to stay where I was. The beach seemed to be calling me. And the pottery studio was for sure. I'm a potter, and I wanted to work at the studio attached to the Belle Vista Recreation Department. So here I am."

Lieutenant Myers looked down at the coffee cup gripped in both his hands. "I've thought about calling you, but I didn't know what you would think about that. I'm afraid I haven't had a lot of experience dating. But today when I saw you in the market I suddenly decided to take a chance."

She nodded soberly. "Thank you for doing that. I haven't dated for a very long time either, so if you had put the moves on me, I'm not sure I would have even known what you were doing." She brightened, smiling. "But I was thirsty and an invitation for a Coke was perfect."

He seemed to relax. "Then I'm hoping if I call you sometime and ask you to go to dinner or a movie you might not be offended?"

"I probably won't be offended. You should try it sometime and see." She laughed softly. "Meanwhile, what's happening about the woman on the beach. Now that you've identified her, are you any closer to finding out what happened?"

He shrugged. "Much as I'd like to talk to you about it, I can't discuss an on-going investigation. I hope you understand. But while it isn't solved, I haven't given up. Someday, somewhere, somehow, I'm going to find that little piece that will make sense of the whole thing. When it's solved I'll let you know, okay?"

She nodded; she hadn't really expected him to tell her much. "Okay. Now Lieutenant Myers, I think I'd better get going. Thank you again for the Coke."

"Delvin. The name is Delvin Myers. May I call you Karo?"

She nodded. "Of course. I'll look forward to your call, Delvin." And she walked back to her car feeling a little bounce in her step, thinking there was nothing like a little flirtation to make her feel young and sassy again.

* * *

Rich pounced on her as soon as she came through the door. "Okay, no more stalling. Today's the day we do raku."

Karo's immediate response was, oh no, not today, but then she realized Rich was right. She had been finding one excuse after another to delay this project. And now she had about seven pieces ready, glazed with the special raku glazes and waiting for the right time. She slowly nodded her head, agreeing today was the day.

The first thing Rich had her do was bring all her pieces for the raku kiln out to the covered patio where she set them on a table with his things. Then, they separated them into groups which would fit into a kiln. It turned out that they were going to have to fire each of the two kilns twice to finish all the pieces.

"Well, this is going to take us a while. That's what we get for waiting so long. But the good thing is it will be great for training. I guarantee you'll be an expert at raku when we're done firing today, Karo."

She and Rich carefully placed the pieces they had selected for the first firing on the fire brick at the base of the kiln. Rich then showed her how to operate the pulley system to lower the barrel cover into place. Then, they turned on the gas jet and lit the kiln. Once it was firing to Rich's satisfaction they turned their attention to the second kiln. When it was loaded Karo managed to manipulate the pulleys to lower the barrel hesitantly. With Rich's supervision, she lit the gas jet.

"There, that wasn't so bad, was it?"

She shook her head, not even bothering to tell him how wobbly her knees felt. There was just something about lighting that gas jet that terrified her.

They hovered over the kilns, adjusting the gas higher or lower as appropriate for the correct temperature. Meanwhile they prepared the barrels to receive the hot pieces when it was time to transfer them. Each of the two metal trash barrels were stuffed with sawdust and wadded up newspaper. The lid was propped along side of the barrel to be clamped on top to suppress the flames when the hot pottery ignited the contents of the barrels.

"Get your gloves and tongs, Karo, it's show time," Rich sang out gaily. It was time for the transfer.

Karo took a deep breath to calm herself as Rich fiddled with the pulleys that raised the barrel leaving the base of the kiln and the pottery pieces sitting on the fire brick, glowing orange with heat.

"I'm taking the taller vase near me. You take that little piece nearest you and carefully turn this way to put it in the barrel," Rich said as he reached out with the long tongs and securely grabbed the vase.

Karo didn't have time to watch him as she got her tongs fastened on the piece she had targeted. She gripped the handles tightly and swung the piece carefully through the air to deposit it in the barrel, already flaming from the piece Rich had placed inside. As soon as her tongs came out of the barrel, Rich slapped the lid on to suppress the flames.

"Get that other large piece, Karo." And when Karo swung it toward the barrel Rich quickly removed the lid and then replaced it after she deposited the piece.

"All right, let's get the other pieces." He moved the second barrel into position and they grabbed the last pieces and quickly transferred them. As soon as the lid was slapped on that barrel they put down their tongs and gloves and high-fived each other.

"Good job, Karo. See it wasn't so bad, was it?"

Karo shook her head, but secretly thought that it was going to take a lot more work for her to be comfortable swinging those pieces of hot pottery, glowing orange, through the air like that. It just seemed so dangerous.

"Let's get two more barrels ready. The second kiln is going to be ready to transfer soon."

They worked quickly, ignoring the smoke still leaking out from under the lids in the two barrels containing the cooling pottery from the first kiln.

"Rich, how long do we have to wait until we load the kilns again?"

"Not long, we just need the bricks to cool a bit. Probably when we're finished with this kiln the first one will be cool enough to load again. And after that the fired pottery might be cool enough to wash off so we can see what we have."

After they unloaded the second kiln and had loaded the first one again they emptied the pieces from the first two barrels onto one of the tables in an effort to cool them down faster. They filled the trash barrels once again with newspaper and sawdust and turned their attention to loading the last kiln.

"Whew, this is work." Karo took a breath. "Look, everyone is eating. Did we miss the lunch call?"

"I guess we were too busy. Look, while they're all out on the patio, let's go wash the ash off of these pots and see how they turned out. We can eat later while we're waiting for these kilns to finish."

Karo joined him eagerly at the sinks in the studio. It was amazing to see the colors revealed as the ash was washed off. "Oh, this one is a beauty, Rich. What did you use to glaze it?"

"That's Alligator, nice, uh?"

"And look how nice the blue came out on that one, Karo. I love the contrast with the copper."

They proudly carried them back to the patio area to dry and to be admired by the other potters when they came in after having their lunch.

By then it was time to transfer the pieces in the first kiln again, and they barely had time to wolf down their lunch before the second kiln was ready to be unloaded. It wasn't until almost closing time when they had finished cleaning out the barrels, and had swept away the mess on the patio near the kilns that Karo noticed Betty hadn't been in all day. It was too late to ask Joy where she was, so she thought she'd check on her the next day. She worried a little about Betty's absence because she seemed so alone in the world. If something happened to her she wondered how anyone would know she needed help.

The next day when Betty still didn't show up for class, Sandi asked Karo if she would help her by working with the beginning students. It wasn't what Karo had planned for the day, but she was willing to help Sandi out. But now she was really worried about Betty, especially as Sandi told her she hadn't talked to her. She had just gotten a message from the front desk of the Recreation Center saying Betty called in earlier saying she couldn't come today. She might be sick, or worse, her husband might have taken a turn for the worse. Karo knew from her conversations with Betty that even though her husband was unresponsive now, Betty still took comfort in knowing he was alive and she could visit him.

When Betty didn't show up at the studio on Friday, Karo became alarmed and questioned Joy. "Joy, have you heard from Betty? Is everything okay with her? Do you know where she is?"

Joy nodded, a sad expression on her face. "Yes, she called to tell me her husband died. She's very sad about it. They were very close you know."

"Oh no, poor Betty! I guess I'll go by tonight and see if I can do anything for her."

"That's very considerate of you, Karo, but she's not there. Her niece came out from Iowa to help her and Betty decided to go home with her for a little while." Joy uncharacteristically reached out and patted Karo's shoulder. "I think she needed the support of family, Karo. This is a staggering blow to her. She lived so long devoting all her energies toward her husband. It's like leaning against a wall to hold it erect and suddenly it's gone and now you find it was what was holding you up."

Karo nodded, understanding what Joy was telling her. She thought a minute and asked, "Aren't they having a funeral?"

"No service, no notice in the papers. Betty says he's been as good as gone for a few years now, so they decided to just quietly cremate him and move on. It's very sad. Why don't you send her a note. She said she was going to have her mail forwarded. I'm sure she'd appreciate hearing from you."

Karo nodded. "I'll do that, Joy. And please let me know as soon as you hear when she plans to return." She turned away, feeling sad for Betty. She would send a note and a condolence card, but somehow felt she should do something more for her, something that would be more comforting.

CHAPTER 11

"Joy, what's going on? I heard what you just told Karo, but I know better. Where is Betty really?" Mary Louise hissed at Joy in the corner of the studio.

"Not now! Not here!" Joy whispered back, and then seeing by the look in Mary Louise's eyes that she was on the verge of panic, she relented and said, "We'll go out for a walk. We can talk then. Let me finish this up and when you see me go out, you follow after a few minutes. Okay?"

Mary Louise nodded and drifted back to the table where she had her tools spread out. She sat down to finish the lidded casserole in front of her, but surreptitiously watched Joy. After Joy left the studio, Mary Louise casually got up grabbed her sweater and went out the door, as if she was just going to the restroom.

Mary Louise slipped out of the exit door leading to the parking lot and looked around. She didn't see Joy so she walked around the side of the building and caught sight of Joy disappearing into the eucalyptus trees. She hurried after her, struggling into her sweater as she went. She found Joy sitting at a picnic bench a little ways off the path to the beach.

Mary Louise sat down, immediately asking, "So why did you say Betty's husband died? Where is Betty?" She sat shivering and anxious, her eyes glued to Joy's face.

"Betty's gone."

"What?" Mary Louise's voice went up several octaves. "What do you mean by gone? How can she be gone?"

Joy put out her hand, taking hold of Mary Louise's arm, shaking it a bit. "Calm down and I'll tell you everything." She held on tightly until Mary Louise stopped trembling. Then Joy said in a low voice, "Apparently Betty has been haunted by what she did. What we did. She's talked to me about it a couple times, but I thought she just needed to be reassured. The last time we spoke I thought she was okay after we talked, so I didn't even think to tell you about it. You know we don't talk about any of that." She watched Mary Louise's face closely and seemed to relax at her apparent acceptance of this story.

"But I guess she has just been getting more upset. Part of it I blame on her new friendship with Karo. She's been telling Karo all about Ralph and how wonderful he was, how he built her studio for her. Apparently the more wonderful she portrayed him, the more guilt she felt about what she did." Joy shook her head, not understanding Betty's guilt at all.

"Anyway, last Saturday she showed up when I was loading the kiln, acting very weird. She was agitated and nervous. She said she couldn't sleep and she hadn't been eating. I could see she was in bad shape, her hands were shaking and she couldn't seem to be still a minute. I tried to calm her down, but she only got worse. She said she had made up her mind she was going to call the police and turn herself in. Well, you know how that would affect all of us. Naturally, I tried to reason with her, but instead she became more insistent that she was going to do it. She said she was going over to the office to call immediately. Of course I became very alarmed, because she would ruin everything. We all would pay to appease her conscience. I tried to stop her. I still thought I could talk her out of it.

"I grabbed her to keep her from leaving. She's very strong, you know. She always looked a little frail, but she was strong, and she was very determined. We struggled. I suddenly realized I might not be able to stop her." Joy paused, staring away from Mary Louise now; she blinked rapidly and swallowed once.

"I truly don't know how it happened. We were on the covered patio, she was struggling to get free and I was holding her back with all my strength. When I realized she might get away from me I got desperate. I pulled at her with all my might and the next thing I knew, I was falling backwards. I sat down with a thump that drove the breath right out of me and while I was sitting there gasping, I watched her stumble back and fall over that stack of fire brick near the small kiln. She crashed, head first, into the corner of the kiln.

"I couldn't move for a bit, and she didn't move at all. When I finally got to my feet, and was able to check on her, it was too late. She was dead."

She looked at Mary Louise, wide-eyed, and then gave a very convincing sob. "Just like that! She was gone."

They both sat there a moment in shocked silence.

"It was an accident, Mary Louise! And I didn't know what to do. I thought about calling you, because I knew you would come help me immediately, but I didn't want to get you involved if it wasn't necessary. I realized with Betty dead, even though it was an accident, there would be all kinds of questions and a thorough investigation. Most likely it would even involve the police.

"And it wouldn't be long before someone discovered her husband wasn't around anymore and then they would discover his pension benefits were still being paid to him as if he were. I knew that would generate even more questions. More question than we dared have circulating.

"It seemed the best thing would be if Betty just went away for a little while and hopefully that would give us enough time to cover our tracks."

She waited quietly while Mary Louise absorbed all she had told her.

Mary Louise, normally a stalwart, unemotional woman, wiped at the tears leaking out of her eyes with the sleeve of her sweater. "Oh, poor Betty. I didn't realize she would feel so guilty about taking that money. After all, it should have been hers. If her stupid, inconsiderate husband had half an ounce of brains he would have seen to it that she would be protected if he died first." She stared off into the trees. "What is the matter with people? And she thought he was so wonderful because he built her that studio, but he left her with no means of support when he died."

She took a big gulp of air. "Well, you should have told me, Joy. I would have talked to her. It might have made a difference."

Joy nodded, and said in a contrite tone, "You're right, Mary Louise. I should have talked to you about it early on. If I had, if I had thought..., well, maybe we could have prevented this whole awful tragedy."

After a few moments of silence Mary Louise asked almost timidly, "So what did you do with Betty?"

"The usual. I mean we were right there so I fired up the second kiln and then cleaned up the studio. It was a bit of a problem as I had to take her car back and park it in her garage, but I managed. And I had the rest of the weekend to work out the details of the story."

Mary Louise looked at Joy expectantly.

"Well, unfortunately, while Betty is visiting her niece she's going to have a major stroke. Betty won't be coming back, Mary Louise. Eventually the niece will contact me and ask me to clear out Betty's place and then every once in while I'll hear from the niece that Betty is still in a coma. Eventually people will stop asking, they will not want to hear the sad answers to their questions. Betty will only be a memory when she eventually passes on." Joy nodded with satisfaction. She was certain it would work. People weren't usually suspicious of people they knew and interacted with. And while everyone would initially grieve over Betty's tragedy, they would soon get involved in more immediate issues.

Meanwhile, this unexpected incident with Betty had demonstrated clearly to Joy how naïve she was being with her own plan to live happily ever after. She now realized how easily something could happen to upset her carefully laid plans. She had already begun taking the appropriate steps to insure nothing happened to expose her scheme and lead the authorities to her in her posh new life. She had already opened an account in a bank on one of the offshore islands which were known for not asking questions of their depositors and who did not allow agencies to trace the funds deposited in their bank. She had even begun transferring her accumulated savings to the new account. In the coming weeks she was going to set up more automatic transfers to move future funds as they were deposited to the various other accounts she controlled.

"I can't believe Betty's gone." Mary Louise's ragged voice was full of grief as she interrupted Joy's review of her defensive actions.

Joy answered in a harsh voice, "Believe it, and you'd better believe it is lucky for us she is. You know, Mary Louise, this is all your fault. You were the one who insisted we do something for her and now look what's happened. You should have just let it alone. She would have found some other way to eek out a living. It didn't have to be us who saved her, did it?"

Mary Louise had a stricken look. "I only meant to help. Joy, you know I only wanted to help her. It seemed such a rotten situation and one she didn't deserve." She seemed to be fighting against tears again. "I'm sorry, Joy. You're right, I probably shouldn't have interfered."

"Well, no sense crying over spilt milk now, uh?" Joy said gruffly. "I'm going back in. Are you going to be okay? Can you pull this off?"

Mary Louise nodded. "I'll be back in a few minutes. Don't worry about me. I'll be as surprised and upset as anyone when you tell us about Betty's stroke, but I can handle it. I've had to handle more than this in my life." She nodded firmly as Joy headed back to the studio.

* * *

"Hey there, friend." Doug's voice on the phone conveyed clearly that he wanted something.

Karo smiled. "Okay, what do you want?"

"What makes you think I was going to ask for something? Can't a friend just call to say hi?"

"Sure they can, but when I hear that tone in your voice, I know it involves a request for a favor."

Doug laughed. "Well, you're right. I need a big favor from you. Do you know the Friends of Carruthers are having their big fund raising dinner and dance next week?"

"Well actually, I do know that. I've seen some of the articles in the paper. Sounds like a big deal for the members of Belle Vista society."

"Apparently it is. Well, I was just told that as one of the physicians on staff I am expected to be there, in tuxedo, with a date. That was a shocker. I tried to get out of it, as it's not really my kind of thing. But it seems they like to have a doctor sitting at each table to schmooze with the patrons. So every doctor not on duty is required to attend. And it's just my luck that I'm not on duty that night." He paused dramatically. "So I'm looking for a friend to be my date."

"Me?"

"Would you? I'd really appreciate it. It would really be a friendly thing to do."

"Well, I don't know..."

"Please, Karo. It could be fun. Well heck, I cannot tell a lie, it probably won't be fun. But they'll feed us, and I understand the band is one of the best in the area, so if you like to dance that would be a plus."

The silence was making him nervous. "Please, you would really help make it bearable for me."

"Well, sure, I think I still have a formal gown or two. I guess I can act like part of society for a few hours."

He laughed with relief. "I can't tell you how I appreciate it. I'll pick you up Friday at seven, okay?"

Karo hung up the phone and immediately headed for the closet in the guest room where she had hung all the gowns she decided to keep when she cleaned out her closets before moving. There had been no reason to keep them, but some were barely worn, and she couldn't force herself to get rid of them. Now as she skimmed through the rack of hangers each holding a plastic wrapped gown she paused at one. This is the one she had bought on sale in anticipation of wearing it later in the year to an annual fete she and Greg always attended. But she had never worn it, as by the time the occasion had rolled around, she and Greg had already decided to separate and neither was interested in making the effort of going out together.

The dress was a deep blue, not quite navy, maybe midnight blue was a better description. It was a sheer silk, dotted with sparkles, over a simple slip. The material reminded her of a night sky with a handful of stars thrown randomly across it. The neckline was scooped deeply, but not shockingly, and it had little cap sleeves to hold it on her shoulders. It had fit beautifully and was quite flattering. It would be perfect for this occasion.

She smiled to herself, remembering she had some big rhinestone and faux sapphire earrings which would be perfect with it. Yes, she was sure she could put herself together to make Doug proud.

And when Doug came to pick her up he was shocked into a moment of immobility when he saw her. He finally managed to drawl, "Karo, you're looking good."

She realized that except for the Christmas party, he had never seen her dressed in anything other than her jeans and sweaters. He probably hadn't suspected she could look like one of the beautiful people.

"Well, you look pretty good yourself. You might want to consider wearing that tux more often. In fact, you might want to make it your uniform. You actually look yummy." She laughed at his look. "Come on, let's get this show on the road, in case the fairy godmother changes her mind and turns us back into what we normally look like."

They left the house in a happy mood, waving good-by to the dogs. They were going to make the best of this command performance.

The affair was held at the big resort hotel and spa at the south end of town. The food was much better than average, the band was special, delivering very danceable 60's and 70's tunes, which people couldn't seem to resist, and for sure, Karo couldn't. She danced several times with Doug and then with some of the other men who were seated at their table. They had been assigned to a table of ten. The other eight people included a big donor to the hospital, an interior decorator, Cynthia Meredith, and her date, a prominent member of the city council and her husband, and the owner of a big car dealership and his wife, who was a member of the committee which organized the event. Everyone was interesting and cordial and seemed intrigued with Doug's life in the ER.

Karo and Cynthia recognized immediately that they were kindred spirits, as sometimes happens when you meet a stranger. Cynthia was younger than Karo, probably closer to Doug's age, and had her own interior design business. She was currently involved in decorating a show house in Atherton for the Atherton Women's Auxiliary. It was a very prestigious annual event and it made a lot of money for the charities the Auxiliary supported. Karo remembered it well from prior years and had even attended a few in the past. She had been very impressed when she heard Cynthia was decorating the dining room, as she knew it was a much sought-after plum among the local designers.

Cynthia, on the other hand, seemed fascinated to find that Karo was a potter. They talked throughout the night finding numerous subjects of common interest. When the party finally wound down, Karo and Cynthia promised to call each other and do lunch soon.

When Doug delivered Karo to her house they were both still vibrating with energy despite the late hour. "Do you want to come in? I can make some coffee, or open some wine?" she offered, not really wanting the fun to end.

He shook his head. "No, I'd better go home. Norm and a couple of his buddies are showing up early to look for pigs. You remember meeting Norm, don't you, from that dinner at my place?"

Karo nodded. "So you suckered him into getting rid of your pigs?"

"I'm hoping. Anyway, I want to be half awake to make sure they don't hunt for anything else while they're there.

"But, thanks to you I had a great time tonight, and I was truly dreading it." He smiled, pleased with the evening.

"I think you did great on your own. You sure impressed that couple, who were the big donors. Obviously the hospital knows what it is doing when they insist a doctor be at each table. And I had a wonderful time. I forgot how much fun it is to dance to that great music. And Doug, you're a good dancer too. Yep, I've got a closet full of gowns so any time you need me, I'm available."

They both laughed, and he bent down and kissed her gently on the lips. "Thanks, Karo, it was great. You are a good friend." And he left her standing in the doorway, feeling like a young girl again.

* * *

Karo hadn't been surprised to get a phone call from Cynthia a few days later asking if she could see some of Karo's pottery. Karo had immediately invited her to come to lunch.

When the doorbell rang the dogs ran pell-mell for the door, barking and jumping, and generally being dogs. "Captain, Rudy, sit!" Karo said sternly and then to make sure they understood, she held up her forefinger and said, "Stay!" and turned to open the door for her new friend.

When Cynthia came through the door she couldn't help but notice the dogs sitting there. Captain was squirming, trying to stay as ordered, but dying to run to Cynthia. Rudy gazed at her with such soulful eyes Karo almost felt guilty for being so stern with him.

"Oh, what darling dogs." Cynthia bent to offer her hand to Captain's nose and Karo gave up, giving them the sign they could move, and move they did. Captain immediately lay down to expose his stomach for a belly rub and Rudy somehow managed to get his head positioned right under Cynthia's other hand, in case she might want to fondle his long droopy ears.

"Oh Karo, you didn't tell me about your family." Cynthia laughed with delight.

"Aren't they the pair? Okay guys, enough now. Let Cynthia come in." Karo took her coat and hung it on the coat rack in the hall before leading her into the living room. "Welcome to my humble home. Although I can't claim to be a decorator, I do love it."

"Oh what a wonderful Craftman style house you have. You must have done a lot of work to restore it. It looks just like it should have looked when it was built." She stood in the room and turned around slowly looking at everything.

"Actually, I did very little. The house was lived in for much of its life by a couple, who only recently moved to a senior living complex at the other end of town. I had to paint it, have the floors refinished and have some yard clean-up, but mostly it's just as I found it."

"You're so lucky. These houses were built when they knew how to build a good, solid house, but so many have been bastardized over the years so they've lost their good bones. But look at the big, clean lines of the rooms. And are these pocket doors still here?" She pulled on one of the latches. "Yes, and they're original too. What a find, Karo." She walked around looking at the hall and the dining room. "Oh, is this some of your pottery?" She found the display that Karo had put on the dining room table. "Oh my God, this is amazing. I thought you said you were a beginner. These are not beginner pieces. How long have you been doing pottery?"

"Well, about five years now. But truthfully, I feel during the past few months, working at the Belle Vista studio, I have just blossomed. It's like all I learned in the past has suddenly exploded and I've become a potter."

Cynthia was holding the modified vase Karo had only recently fired in the raku kiln. "This is amazing. I love the colors. And the shape is very unique. Do you have more like this?"

"No, that's one of a kind. It's a raku pot. It is for decorative use only because it's not fired at as high a temperature as the other pieces are. Sometimes when a piece is ready for firing it just calls out for raku, so I set it aside to fire later. Here's another piece I did in that same firing." She pointed to a medium size bowl with a white glaze. It had delicate black lines crackling through it making an interesting pattern.

Cynthia had to look at each piece carefully, picking up most of them to turn them over in her hands to look at every surface. Finally she finished looking at all the pottery and Karo led her into the kitchen.

"I hope you don't mind eating in the kitchen."

"Not at all and what is that heavenly smell?"

"We're having quiche and salad. Is that all right with you?"

"Sounds wonderful." She sat down at the table and eyed the plates. "Did you make these?"

"Yes, that's the trouble with potters, they try everything and eventually everything in their houses has come from their kilns."

"Well, that doesn't appear to be a problem to me. These are very nice."

Then after the first few bites of lunch had appeased their appetites, Cynthia said, "You know, Karo, one of the most important parts of decorating is the little accent pieces we put in the rooms. They focus attention and can make or break the most careful design plan. I personally use a lot of pottery for accent pieces and I'm always looking for unique sources. That was why I was so excited to find you were a potter. I somehow think that if you like the person, you'll like their work. So there you were, someone I found I liked immediately and it turned out you were a potter."

Karo nodded, feeling a similar certainty that she would like the rooms Cynthia designed.

"Anyway, I really do like your work just as I expected I would. And I wonder if you would consider entering into an arrangement where you will supply me with pieces."

Karo looked up startled. "Supply you with pieces...?"

"Yes, sell me pieces of your pottery. I will use them in my decorating and sell them to my customers, for more than I paid you for them, of course." She smiled when she said this. "You won't believe what customers using a decorator are willing to pay for these things. And well they should because the decorator has to search for just the right pieces."

"But, but I'm not very good..." she started to say.

Cynthia held up her hand. "Stop right there. You are very good. And you are unique. That's what my clients want. Something different, something you can't find in the big stores. They will pay for that kind of item, and frankly, I'm always searching for a source. So if you're interested, we can have a little business arrangement that will be beneficial for both of us. And I suspect we already know we're going to end up good friends."

Karo nodded, thinking this seemed too easy. "Of course I'm interested in selling you whatever you want. That is my dream, to make some money at potting so I don't have to support myself writing procedural manuals."

"Good, after lunch I'll go back over your pottery and make you an offer on the pieces I want. Okay?"

Karo nodded, curls of excitement starting to bunch up in her stomach. Suddenly she felt like she couldn't eat another bite, but she restrained herself until Cynthia was finished. Then she did the dishes so Cynthia could prowl around the dining room undisturbed with a pad and pencil. When she finished in the kitchen and joined Cynthia, she found she had separated the pottery and assembled almost two-thirds of her pieces at one side of the table. And she had taken the three tall candlesticks holding three inch pillar candles Karo had sitting on the hearth and included them with the pieces she had selected.

"I hope you don't mind. It was obvious you made them and I love them. My clients will be ecstatic about them. In fact, I will buy as many of these as you care to make."

When Karo examined the list handed her, she felt the blood drain from her head. She almost staggered from shock when she saw the total.

"You're kidding?"

"No, I'm not, and remember I'm probably going to charge twice that amount. My clients won't consider it, if it's not priced right. They are paying for 'art', and they won't value it if the price they pay doesn't reflect the value."

Karo shook her head, dumbfounded. "Of course you can have the candlesticks, take anything you want. I just never imagined I could sell my pieces at these prices."

"Well, how much time does it take you to make a piece?"

"It depends on how complicated the piece is. For one of those pillar candlesticks, it probably took me about ten hours over several days. And then I lost three in the process of making six."

Cynthia nodded. "So you have to factor in for the ones lost, and then there is the artistic factor, that's worth money. And when you add that all together the prices I listed seem more reasonable, don't they?"

Karo nodded. "It's just no one sells their pieces for these prices. We all want to, we really think they're worth it, we just don't find a market to support those prices."

"Well now you've found your market. And by the way, do you ever produce big pieces." She held her arms out to indicate size. "I'd love to have a source for some really nice big pieces."

Karo shook her head. "They're so difficult to work with. The clay weighs so much, you see. You have to have long arms and be very strong to make large pieces successfully. And then there is the whole problem of kiln space to fire them. But a friend of mine likes to make big pieces and they're beautiful. Perhaps you'd like to talk to him?"

"I would. Now Karo, you see which of the pieces you've done I really like. There is nothing wrong with these other pieces, but they're just not special enough for the accent pieces that I need. Keep these in mind as you're working. Whenever something comes out of the kiln that is similar to these, set it aside so I can have first dibs, okay?"

Karo nodded.

"I know we'll stay in touch, lunch and things, but I'll want to review your work every few months to select new pieces if that's all right with you?"

"Fine, that would be fine. Do you want to take these with you today?" At Cythnia's nod she went to the mud room to get some of the newspapers she stacked for use in the studio.

Then, while Karo was wrapping and taping the pottery, Cynthia asked if she could look around her house.

She returned full of enthusiasm. "You know, Karo, you've managed to achieve that special feeling in these rooms I try to provide in the rooms I decorate for my clients. It's a good thing more people can't seem to strike that balance between comfort and beauty or I'd be out of a job. And the thing I like is how you've kept it simple yet the house still seems to reflect your personality."

"That's very nice to hear. But I'm afraid I didn't really think about decorating when I did it. I just was trying to furnish it so I'd be comfortable living here."

"Well, whatever the reason, it works. It's warm, comfortable and beautiful. Of course these rooms lend themselves to that feeling. No, I don't think I would change a thing." She paused and then said, "Well, maybe I'd put a grouping of handmade ceramic pedestal candlesticks on the hearth. Yes, that would probably be the perfect final touch."

Karo laughed.

CHAPTER 12

"Where's Doug? I thought you said you were going to ask him to come?" Rich asked when he opened the car door.

"I did ask him, but he said this wasn't really his kind of thing. He's doing something with those boy scouts he had out to pick apples last fall. They were going to track pigs or some other manly sport."

"Well, I hope they don't find them. I've heard feral pigs are dangerous."

"I don't know about that, but I think the fun is in tracking them, you know? Besides, I think Norm and his buddies got most of them already. I understand there are only a few left."

Rich smiled, settling in and buckling his seat belt. "Well, I'm kind of excited. Cynthia said she used that giant round vase I made. You know the one with the tiny little spout? I can't wait to see what it looks like in her fancy dining room."

"Wow, that is exciting. I don't know if she used any of my pieces or not. Frankly, I'm just so excited about selling them to her, I don't care what she does

184 • MUD TO ASHES

with them. Well, I guess that's not exactly true. I'd really be pleased to see them displayed in one of the rooms for everyone to see."

"I know exactly how you feel, and I really appreciate you referring her to me. I had just reached that point of desperation, wondering how I could possibly fit one more of those big pieces in my small condo. I was actually thinking about renting one of those storage units. I mean, I tell myself to make things smaller and then I'd at least have a chance to sell them in our sale, but I just keep going bigger and bigger. It's almost an obsession. Now she's made it possible for me to go as big as I want. All I have to do is convince Joy to give me the kiln space."

"Yeah, how do you do that? She can be so disagreeable, you never know how she'll react, especially if she doesn't want to do something."

"I charm her, of course. Well, last time we used the soda fire kiln. She only fires that when she has a load for it or in this case it was easier for her to use it than to fire the other kiln an extra time. But some of my really big pieces just won't fit into the high fire kiln with everyone else's pieces. So when I cajole Joy into agreeing to use the soda kiln for my pieces, I bring a buddy in and we load the kilns for her. That way she doesn't really have any reason to refuse me." He grinned, remembering the last time they fired a load. "She grumbles and grouches, but I just jolly her along. Eventually she does what I want."

"Well, you're the only one who seems to get his way. Wait, that's not fair. I really can't complain about her treatment of me as she seems to cut me some slack, maybe because I've spoken up a few times so she knows she can't bully me. You know like so many people who bully others, she's very sensitive when people confront her. But I've heard her be so mean to some of the potters it makes me cringe. I mean, what is her problem? It's not natural for someone to be so nasty. She acts like that studio is there for her express use and the rest of us are her minions, only there to take care of the chores she assigns us."

Rich raised his eyebrows. "I'm guessing she must have done something recently to get you riled up. Fess up, what happened?"

Karo had to laugh. "I guess you're right. She and Mary Louise ganged up on me the other day about the condition of the studio after the Wednesday class. They seem to think since I'm helping Sandi while Betty's gone it's now my responsibility to make sure the studio is spick and span before I leave. Mary Louise said the newspapers were in a mess and some of the lids on the glaze buckets were mixed up. I mean, come on, I don't run around the studio and check everything. And it probably wasn't even the Wednesday class that did it. It could have been the night class on Thursday or even from the Tuesday workshop, which is Joy's responsibility.

"The newspapers weren't stacked up evenly? Give me a break." She looked at Rich indignantly, then catching his eye she started to laugh. "I guess I'm starting to sound just like them, aren't I?"

"Well, I wasn't going to mention it, but it did occur to me."

"Careful or you'll find yourself walking home," Karo said, glowering at him. But she couldn't maintain it, laughing again. "Okay enough about Joy.

"What I'm really upset about is the situation with Betty. Joy said when she last spoke to Betty's niece, she was optimistic about her recovery. Poor Betty, I guess the shock of losing her husband after so many years was just too much for her."

"Unfortunately, that happens a lot with couples who have been together for a long time. One dies and the other, who may not even be sick, suddenly goes into a decline and dies right after." Rich shook his head. "We see it a lot. I think it's what people call a broken heart. There is no other explanation."

They were both quiet for a while. The image of Betty in a coma was very sad. She had seemed so capable, so energetic, it was hard to think that she would most likely never recover.

"Some people do come out of it, don't they?"

Rich was slow to answer. "It doesn't sound like there is much hope of that, Karo. Sorry."

They were both silent until they turned onto the exit from the freeway. Rich spoke somberly, "You know, Karo, we should keep quiet about selling our pieces to Cynthia. If the word gets around the studio there's liable to be trouble."

"Trouble? What do you mean?"

"I mean that there will be some noses out of joint, questions about whether or not professional potters can use studio facilities, and lots of petty jealousies flaring up. While initially people might be happy to hear we found a market, before long they will be wondering why us? Why not them? And then they'll start thinking we're getting preferential treatment at the studio."

Karo thought about it a minute and then nodded. "I guess you're right. Would they make us leave the studio? Is it against the rules to work there if we're selling our work?"

"Well, they may not come right out and say it, but the studio isn't really meant for professional potters' use, you know?"

She nodded. "Well, I always intended to set up my own studio. I guess I'd better start thinking seriously about doing that. It's just that I don't feel I'm ready to work on my own. I'm still learning so much from working at the Rec Center."

"I know what you mean. There is a creativity that seems to be in the air." Rich thought for a minute. "Maybe if you had a studio at home, then it would seem reasonable to also work at the Rec Center studio. Betty did that. She made and sold her pottery at the flea market and she still worked at the studio."

"Yes, she told me she took the pieces she wanted fired in the reduction kiln to the studio to fire. And some of the pieces she made at the studio she might bisque or fire it at home in her electric high fire kiln. Everyone seemed to think that was all right."

"Well, for now we should just keep our mouths shut and think about alternative plans. One thing to think about would be to set up a co-op studio somewhere. I bet some of the other potters in the area might be interested in joining. We could lease a big industrial building and build our own kilns and then work out a system for sharing the work. After all, we all do the work at this studio, except the firing of the big kilns." He thought a minute and then continued with enthusiasm, "Everyone could have their own space and wheel, and we could share the glazes, the firings and those kinds of things."

"Wow, that sounds like a lot of expense and a lot of work."

"Yeah, but it's not as much work as doing everything yourself in your own studio. Then you have to mix every glaze and pay for all the chemicals. You have to load and unload every kiln. That is a lot of work."

They were distracted from finishing this conversation when Rich pointed. "There, see."

Karo rolled to a stop. She showed their tickets to the man at the gate and he directed them up the long sloping drive to the lot near the house.

"Wow, this is some place."

The drive took them through the curve of the undulating yellow hills, spotted liberally with the dark green of bunched up oaks and then into a pasture that was being used temporarily as a parking lot. They left the car and headed on foot towards the big Italian Villa type house nestled in the vee where three hills seemed to converge.

Cynthia had given both Karo and Rich tickets for the event, insisting they needed to see how she was using the ceramic pieces they made. "It will help you understand what I need," she said. "And besides I have to buy some of these tickets or they'll never use me again."

So Karo and Rich accepted happily. They could immediately see the event was very well organized, probably due to the years of practice by the Women's Auxiliary. Visitors were free to wander from room to room as they wished. The members of the Auxiliary acted as docents, policing each room open for viewing. In every room docents were stationed to answer questions and hand out flyers listing the source of the furnishings and art, the decorators and any sponsors of the room. It was amazing what had been done in each room to make the decorator's vision come to life. The house was big and old, probably built in the nineteen-twenties when money was plentiful. They wandered through the library, the living room and the entrance hall with eyes wide and mouths open.

"Come on, Rich, the dining room is this way," Karo hissed impatiently.

They walked through the double pocket doors and paused as the drama of the room opened up to them. In front of them a long, dark table with chairs dominated the room, back lit by a bowed wall of French doors looking out on a flagstone terrace surrounded by oaks. The room itself was painted a strong burnt orange. The cream colored ceiling was a series of recessed sections which glowed from invisible lights tucked into the folds, effectively lighting the room without any lights actually to be seen. On one side of the room a long credenza matching the table in the center stood against the wall. Over the credenza hung an enormous painting in vivid colors and sitting on the end closest to the French doors was Rich's large vase. The Shino glaze of reddish brown and orange to gold looked perfect, as if it had been made expressly for that spot.

"Ooh," escaped from Rich. He couldn't conceal his pleasure at seeing how beautiful his piece looked.

On the opposite wall was a large, tall, obviously old, Chinese cabinet flanked by two standing black and brass candelabras, each holding more than a dozen altar candles. The floor was gleaming dark hardwood in a herringbone pattern covered by a large, fine Persian carpet pleasingly worn, glowing in a pattern of burnt orange, gold, beige, dark blue and brown. The room was warm and inviting and Karo loved it. She didn't even notice until her second look around the room that the middle of the table held her own three ceramic pillar candlesticks with dark brown three inch wide candles in them. They were so much a part of the room, she had actually not recognized they were hers the first time she saw them.

They lingered a long time. They didn't want to leave. But finally they noticed the docents were looking at them warily, so they reluctantly moved on. They toured the bedrooms where they admired the master bath. They examined every detail in the remodeled gourmet kitchen, which contained all the latest fads, the granite counters, the dishwasher drawers, the Wolf Range, the Sub-zero side by side freezer and refrigerator, the separate ice maker, the wine cooler and even the warming drawers. Finally, they escaped to the covered lanai where the Auxiliary women were selling tea, soft drinks and sandwiches to squeeze every possible dime out of their captive audience. Rich claimed a table three women vacated and they both collapsed, waiting for refreshments.

"Your vase is perfect there and look, here you are on the list of artists. Aren't you thrilled?"

Rich nodded. "It's hard to believe I didn't have that exact room in mind when I made that vase. Maybe Cynthia decorated the room around the vase?"

Karo nodded. "I didn't know she was going to use my candlesticks. I didn't even have them out to sell, you know. Cynthia took them off the hearth and added them to the pieces she wanted. Look, here I am on the list, too." She smiled, still thinking how right they looked on that table, in that room, with all those other beautiful things. "I'm going to ask Cynthia for a picture of them, in case I ever forget." She paused while the lady delivered their soft drinks and sandwiches.

"I'll never forget," Rich said simply. "I've never come to one of these before, have you?"

Karo nodded. "I've been a couple times to this one and I went to one in Hillsborough and one in San Francisco once."

"I loved that kitchen. Wouldn't you love to cook in that, Karo?"

She shook her head. "Not really. Been there, done that and I wasn't really happy, you know, Rich."

He looked surprised. "You had a kitchen like that?"

"Well not exactly like that but almost, the Sub-zero, the Wolf range, the warming drawers. My house in San Mateo had a great kitchen and we entertained a lot. But you know what? I enjoy cooking up a pot of soup in my old outdated kitchen now and I'm much happier than I've been for a long, long time. Somehow, all those trappings that everyone thinks they need don't necessarily add anything to the happiness quotient of life."

After they finished their sandwiches and drinks they agreed they needed to take one last look at the dining room before leaving. This time there were different docents on duty, so they didn't have to try to ignore the suspicious glances while they closely examined every detail again.

"It's simple, clean, but bold and beautiful," Karo whispered to Rich.

"Yeah, and where did they get that wonderful pottery?" Rich winked.

They were on their way home when Rich casually mentioned he had been dating someone new. In fact he was so casual about it Karo immediately knew this was important to him.

"Oh Rich, how wonderful."

"And I want you to meet her."

Her? Karo glanced over at him with real surprise. Recovering she said enthusiastically, "Well why not bring her over some night? Saturday night? I could invite a few people and we could play games. I know you have to go to work later but what do you think?"

"Sounds good."

"Come about seven. I'll serve dessert and we can talk and play Charades. Or if you think Charades demands too much activity, we could play Mexican Train Dominoes." She nodded, already thinking about who else she should invite.

* * *

"Hi Mom, how are you?"

"Hi sweetie, I'm fine. How was your week?"

"Good. You're a little late calling today. Did you have a big night last night?"

Although Karo knew Lisa was being facetious she admitted, "As a matter of fact, I did. I had a few people over to play Charades. It was a lot of fun and I'm afraid I waited until this morning to clean up. So I was a little behind my normal schedule today."

"So... who came? Rich? Doug?"

"Yes, and Rich's girlfriend."

"Girlfriend? I thought you said he was gay."

"Well, I think maybe I was wrong about that, especially after seeing him around Anna." She felt a little defensive. She had been surprised at how smitten

Rich obviously was and how solicitous he was of Anna, as if she was the most precious thing in the world.

"Anna? Tell me about her."

"She's very nice, and smart. She's a lawyer with a prestigious firm here in town. They met in the emergency room when she brought a friend in who had been hurt. Judging by how they are now, I imagine sparks flew. Anyway, they've been dating a couple of months. But it was only last week that Rich told me about her, so obviously he's now at the point he wants everyone to know. I wouldn't be surprised if there was a major announcement from them before the year's end."

"Wow, it sounds like one of those romantic movies starring Meg Ryan." Then her voice became kind of wistful. "I guess there is still hope for any of us."

"Of course there is. You're still very young Lisa. You don't want to find your true love so early. Enjoy your life for a while. Trust me on this, experience will only help you make a better choice."

"Sure, like you and Dad?"

"That was kind of low."

Now Lisa's voice was full of contrition. "Oh, Mom, I'm sorry. That was mean of me. But really, you were in your late twenties when you got married and it didn't make the marriage last."

"Sometimes those things happen. I don't think people fully mature until they are in their thirties, so many times when you marry young you're still growing. You and your partner may grow in a way that just enhances your relationship, but sometimes you change and go in opposite directions. That's what happened to your dad and me. We found we no longer shared the same goals, the same interests, except of course, those of raising you. So one day we woke up and found we didn't really want to be married to each other. It just happened."

There was a momentary pause on the line. Then Lisa spoke, obviously trying to steer the conversation in another direction. "So if Rich isn't gay, does that mean that Doug isn't gay either?"

Karo had to laugh. "I just don't know, but it really doesn't matter to me, Lisa. I told you we're just friends. I'm not romantically interested in him."

"Oh, Mom." Now she sounded just like the teenager she was not so long ago.

"Don't 'Oh, Mom,' me. I'm happy, I'm busy and I don't need to complicate my life with romance."

"Oh, Mom, now you sound like an old lady saying that. How can you not want romance? Everyone does."

"Because, Lisa, as you grow older you realize that romance is sometimes fleeting, and sometimes it brings more pain than joy. Right now I'm enjoying my life and I'm not looking for anything romantic or sexual. Maybe later, just not now!" She was firm about it, refusing to feel guilty about not mentioning she had gone out with Lieutenant Delvin Myers last week and had enjoyed herself immensely. She firmly pushed the memories of their "date" out of her mind. She didn't want to tell Lisa, or anyone, about him. She admitted she was foolishly superstitious and didn't want to risk blowing the relationship by talking about it before they even had a chance to see how it would work.

So she asked Lisa about work, knowing it would distract her from any further thoughts of a love life for her mother and sat back to listen to the newest chapter of adventures and irritations that made up her daughter's life.

CHAPTER 13

The banging on the door wouldn't stop. Finally, Joy couldn't ignore it any longer. She checked to see where Charger was and then went to the door.

"Who's there?" she called out angrily.

"Hey Joy, it's me, Rich."

She unlocked the door and opened it just a few inches. Just enough for her to scowl through the crack. "Go away Rich, I'm right in the middle of loading and I don't want any interruptions."

"I just thought you might like some help loading. And maybe I could help you fit in a couple of those big pieces I have waiting. I know they're too heavy for you to handle alone."

"For God's sake, Rich, no! I told you I'd fire them when I had room. There is not enough room today. Anyway, I told you I'd let you know ahead of time so you could load them. I don't need your help today, thank you very much. Just leave me alone to do my thing, can't you?"

Rich shrugged. "I guess I was just anxious. You're sure?"

"Go away!" She closed the door and twisted the lock and then stood quietly waiting to hear his footsteps as he walked away.

Of all the luck, she thought with disgust. Now she wouldn't dare finish what she had planned for the morning. She shuddered. What if she had already started it and he came by and interrupted? It made her knees weak just thinking about how that scenario would play out. She was starting to feel she was losing control at the studio. A while ago Karo had barged in on a Monday, asking to save a piece she had forgotten to wrap up. Now she realized she had foolishly allowed her to come in and do that. Now here was Rich! His visit could have been disastrous if he came in at the wrong time. And she couldn't forget about Betty.

Betty's unwelcome intrusion had been very upsetting requiring immediate action and then a continuous chain of lies to cover up the results. She shook her head wearily, wondering who would make the next attempt to breach her rules. She decided then and there she would have to renew her efforts to enforce them. No more acting like the *nice guy*. She was not going to allow any more exceptions to the rules. It was just too dangerous. She walked back into the covered patio and forced herself to calmly look at the pottery pieces Charger had loaded in the kiln for her. She adjusted two of the pieces and then nodded at him to continue. He was doing a pretty good job. She had been bringing him with her for the past few weeks, thinking she may as well get some work out of him while they were waiting for the paperwork on his pension to be approved. That little task had taken much longer than she expected, and during that waiting time she had to deal with Betty. But today was the day she had finally planned to finish with Charger.

It had been a simple plan. Bringing him to the studio under his own power and even having him load the reduction kiln for her was smart. How typical, she thought. You're just getting really good at something at about the time you quit doing it.

But now Rich's interruption had spooked her. Today wasn't going to be an auspicious day. No, it was not going to happen today. After they finished here, she would buy Charger the bottle she promised in return for his help and wait for next week. But it had to be soon. She was going crazy being around him. He had no manners, he asked too many questions and he made messes for her to clean up. And she was afraid people were beginning to notice him. They had already run into Karo at a bank in San Mateo when they were opening the account which would receive his pension funds. Joy felt she had no choice. She had introduced Charger as her brother, and while Karo hadn't said anything, she saw the surprise on her face. Karo was going to remember Joy's brother. Joy hadn't realized that Karo worked at that bank and she didn't like knowing that Karo might have access to information about her accounts. She knew she was going to be very careful not to give Karo any reason to ask questions about her brother later.

* * *

When Karo arrived at Betty's house there were already several of the pottery people there. This was a work party, organized by Joy, to help pack up Betty's personal effects to ship to her in Iowa, and prepare the rest for an estate sale to be held the following weekend.

The shock Karo felt when she first learned Betty wouldn't be coming home soon, probably never, was receding. Joy reported Betty's niece said it would be a blessing if her friends could turn Betty's furnishings into cash to help cover the cost of the special care she needed. So Joy had gotten them organized. This weekend was the prep work. Next weekend they would hold the sale.

"Look at all the bisque ware sitting here. I think we should glaze it. The finished pieces will be much easier to sell," Evy said to Karo and Rich. They had been assigned to clean out the studio.

"Great idea. Does anyone know how to work this kiln?" Rich said looking at the big oval kiln.

"I bet Joy or Mary Louise will. It looks like the same brand we have at the studio. We just need to know what temperature to fire it to."

Rich nodded. "Okay, I'll go talk to them, and you and Karo can start glazing those pots. Do a good job. You know how precise Betty was. She wouldn't be happy if we messed up her pots."

Karo and Evy got busy preparing the pots for glazing. It was fun working in Betty's studio, selecting which of her glazes would look best on which pieces. It took them most of the day, but finally, the pots were glazed and waiting to be loaded in the kiln. Rich had left a while ago, reminding them he had been working while they had been sleeping the night before. But Marge had come to help and had started pricing some of the finished pottery sitting on shelves in the studio. Mary Louise had promised to come and turn on the kiln once they had it loaded. Meanwhile, they were gathering up and sorting out Betty's tools.

"I feel so bad about helping to dismantle this studio. She was so proud of it," Karo said with regret.

"I know, but remember she won't be using it again and she needs the money so we're doing what we can to help her. Joy is going to put an ad on the board at the Clay Shop for the equipment. She thinks it will go fast listed there. If I didn't already have everything I need at home I'd be first in line to buy it," Evy said, and then, looking at Karo, she suggested, "Why don't you buy it? Couldn't you use some equipment at home? It's a really good deal, much better than buying it new."

Karo nodded. "I know it is. And I do plan to set up a studio some day, but I'm just not sure I'm ready yet."

"Well, you don't often come face to face with a deal like this will be. You could just store it until you're ready to set up. This will cost a fraction of what it would cost new, and Betty has all the best brands. You know she took good care of it. If you want it, Karo, you should talk to Joy about it before she posts the notice, because then it will be gone in a flash. Trust me on that."

Karo nodded, thinking. She did want to set up her own studio space, but she was reluctant to take Betty's. Somehow she felt as if she would be gaining by her friend's tragedy.

She knew that was a silly sentiment. They were going to sell everything except Betty's papers and photographs. Her niece didn't want any of her things, and Betty could no longer use them. Karo shuddered. It was awful. Thank God, she had Lisa, who she hoped would at least look through all the things precious to her mother.

She looked around the studio, assessing how much of it she would want. The kiln, the wheel, the shelves, even the stools would be useful. Then she looked closer, taking out a pencil, she started making notes on a sheet of paper. After she finished in the studio and Mary Louise had the kiln firing, Karo searched for Joy. She found her directing Hal and Liv, who were sealing the boxes of personal effects that would be loaded on Joy's truck so she could ship them.

"Joy? Evy says you're planning on posting the pottery equipment for sale at the Clay Shop."

Joy nodded, still watching the loading carefully.

"I'd be interested in buying quite a bit of it, if we can work out a price I can afford." Karo handed Joy the piece of paper she had noted her choices on. Joy looked at it and nodded.

"When could you pick it up?"

"Probably some time this next week, whenever it would be convenient," she said, hoping Doug and Rich would be available to help.

"Okay, selling to you would save me a lot of trouble. If you buy it all, I'll include the clay, the chemicals and glazes she has already mixed up. What do you think?"

"Well, it sounds like a great deal, but it really depends on the price. I have to be careful about what I spend."

Joy nodded. "Wait a minute, I have the prices I worked out inside." She soon returned with a paper listing the prices.

Karo swallowed hard at the total, but still, she realized it was a great deal. "Are you sure about this? I don't want to take unfair advantage of Betty in any way."

"Well, I'd like to get more for her, but I came up with those prices from comparable items on Craig's List. So I think they're fair. If you agree, we're done."

Karo nodded.

"Okay, just let me know when you can pick it all up and bring your check."

Later, walking the beach with the boys, Karo was torn between excitement and concern over her impulse purchase. It was true it was a great deal. It was also true she intended to buy her own equipment someday, but the thing that was bothering her was the "someday." Still, she reminded herself, she had the money from Cynthia and a promise of more sales to come, so she should regard this solely as a business proposition. She had an opportunity, so she took advantage of it. Then she started thinking how to make room in the apartment behind the garage by stacking all the stuff she had stored there in the tiny bedroom. That would give her enough space in the living room to set up space for her wheel and the shelves. And in a few months she could have the apartment wired for the kiln. That led to speculation on the cost of removing the little kitchen unit and replacing it with a utility sink and counter which would be much more useful in a studio. Soon she was smiling, forgetting her second thoughts about the money she spent. It wasn't that she didn't have it; it was more that she was trying to conserve what she had and be practical. But the truth of it was, she was excited by the thought of having her own studio in her house.

* * *

"Petrale sole for you, madam?"

At her nod the waiter placed the plate in front of her, putting the other plate piled high with fish and chips in front of Delvin. It all looked wonderful and she was hungry. After a few bites she was able to slow down and enjoy the delicate fish, sautéed in an egg wash and served with a butter sauce and capers.

"So did you get it all done? Are you ready for the sale next week?"

She nodded. "It was amazing how fast it went with everybody working. Joy was in charge. Joy is the manager of the workshop and studio at the Rec Center and usually she irritates me a lot with her brusqueness and her rude orders, but I have to admit she's efficient. She had us all organized and she was everywhere making sure it was done just as she wanted. And everything did get done. She's put a sale ad in the paper, posted it on Craig's List and had the potters plaster the town with notices on store bulletin boards. Next week we're having the preview sale on Friday night and then everything will hopefully be sold on Saturday and Sunday. Anything left will be sent to the Goodwill for their resale shop."

"Your friend Betty is lucky to have a group of friends willing to step in to take care of this for her. I'm afraid if something happened to me, everything would just sit there until it turned to dust."

"Wouldn't your son step in?" she asked, wondering what kind of relationship he had with his only remaining child.

"Maybe, but he's so wrapped up in his career right now, I'm not even sure he'd notice I was gone until several months had passed." He grinned. "That's why I'm going down to visit him soon. I need to make sure we stay connected."

"That's a scary thought. I'm sure you're just kidding about your son, but can you imagine how tragic it would be to lead a life so isolated no one would even notice when you're gone." She paused, a bite of potatoes halfway to her mouth. "That's one of the reasons I've been so haunted by the woman on the beach. I mean, why wasn't she reported missing for such a long time?"

"Well, actually she was. It was just that they reported her missing in San Francisco and somehow it wasn't connected to the Jane Doe we found down here. But there are people like you described out there. Some go missing every day. Homeless people, recluses, people who don't keep connected with other people. Sometimes one of them just seems to fall off the edge of the earth and no one notices."

Karo stared at him, clearly upset at the situation he described.

Delvin changed the subject. "How's your fish?" At her nod he continued, "I've heard about this place for a while and I've been meaning to try it. I appreciate your willingness to take a chance with an untried restaurant."

"It's kind of fun, don't you think? You never know what will happen. And if it was someplace you recommended and I didn't like it, then it would be your fault. This way we're both taking a chance." She smiled. "This is a great dish, done just right. How are your fish and chips? Or can you tell after sousing it in all that vinegar?"

He laughed. "I do like the vinegar, but don't worry I can tell they did a great job. Want a bite?"

"No, it would spoil the taste of this, but it looks good and they certainly gave you a generous helping." She looked around her and noticed the dining room was full. It was a popular spot. The restaurant was rather funky looking, weather-beaten as you would expect sitting so close to the ocean, and somehow comforting. The food listed on the menu was mostly fish, cooked in traditional styles, but that seemed to go with the feel of the place.

"I like this place. I'm sure I'll be back."

He nodded. "Yes, I like it too." His face changed and he grabbed his side, retrieving his phone from where it was attached to his belt. With an apologetic smile he put it to his ear and said, "Myers." He nodded several times, his face changing to a frown. When he finished the conversation and folded his phone back up, he said, "Karo, I'm very sorry, but I have to go. Can you get a cab?"

She nodded, somewhat taken aback at the interruption.

"I'm really sorry, part of the problem of socializing with a policeman, you know?" He stood up and hurried out, leaving her to finish her meal by herself.

She passed on dessert and asked for the check.

"No check, madam, the gentleman paid before leaving. He said you would want a taxi? Should I call one now?" The waiter was very kind as he picked up the plates.

So Karo arrived home much earlier than she expected, to be happily greeted by Captain and Rudy. She laughed out loud when she realized her whole long conversation with her friend, Eileen, was for naught. She had called Eileen after she accepted this date with Delvin. She knew she was being silly, but she hadn't dated for years and she knew the dating scene had changed a lot since her last date. She realized she had no idea what was expected of her or how she should respond if Delvin wanted to become intimate. She and Eileen had giggled like school girls as they discussed every possible scenario, but now, she realized she had just postponed that whole issue until the next time she dated Delvin, provided, of course, he called her for another date.

She smiled again. He'd call. She knew he was interested. She could feel it bubbling not far below the surface. And, she admitted, she found him attractive, too.

* * *

Joy reviewed the balance sheet on her computer with pleasure. Now that Charger had been settled she found it much easier to be optimistic. But, she reminded herself, March was almost over and signs of spring were already appearing. It was always harder to convince the homeless to accept her offer to escape the streets in the milder months of the year. That seemed to be the time when they enjoyed the freedom of the street life.

She clicked on the file she kept with profiles she made up for potential targets. Since it had taken her so long to resolve Charger's issues she was now off

206 • MUD TO ASHES

schedule. She realized she would only have time for one more before the warm weather was on them, and that was when she planned to wrap things up and move on. She reviewed the profiles she had, pausing to consider a woman on her list.

She had never tried it with a woman, but she didn't know why it wouldn't work. And the advantage of using a woman would be most likely her size would be more manageable. That had been a problem with Charger. He was too big. She didn't know what she was thinking when she selected him. Then in a moment of honesty she admitted she hadn't really been thinking clearly. She had been so surprised at his sudden willingness to go with her, she just fell all over herself to get him. Well, she thought, he did have that nice pension due him from the union. And while it had been a real challenge to get it started, the amount was well worth the effort. And, she had cleverly worked around his size. He was amenable to anything that would earn him a bottle and when she realized how to manage him, she was able to get a lot of work out of him while he was with her. But it still didn't make up for the inconvenience of his too long presence in her life.

She nodded with satisfaction. Yes, after all the worry and the problems, Charger worked out very well for her. And just thinking about it, she realized she wasn't going to take a woman. She didn't know if it would work as well with a woman and this close to the end, she didn't want any surprises. No, she was going for one more target and she was going to select the best of the ones she had profiled. The one she was thinking about used to hang around the freeway ramp in San Francisco. She hadn't taken anyone from San

Francisco since Gus. When that woman had shown up looking for Gus it had spooked her enough to stay clear of San Francisco for a while. But that had been months ago and if her target was still there he might be interested in her offer after so many months of hard life on the cold streets. And he was the right size, a small wiry man, who had turned sixty-five last year. He was eligible for Social Security and he told her when he retired he would get a pension from the state. He was typical of the people she helped. He should have retired and applied for his pension as soon as he was eligible. But no, he planned to retire later. And she would make sure this was as late as it would get for him.

Then just before she closed the file she saw the last entry, Billy Harder. She paused looking at his profile. Did she dare?

Billy Harder was a fixture in town. He hung around Belle Vista panhandling, until he was shooed away by the shop owners, then he would only move to another location. He was the right size. He was the right age. She knew he was receiving some retirement benefits already because she had seen him at the main post office where he collected his checks. But, she remembered he told her he hadn't applied for Social Security benefits, and she was sure he would now be eligible for them.

Billy Harder had been around so long no one really noticed him anymore. It would certainly be no loss to the community if he just disappeared one day. In fact, it was bound to happen as he wasn't getting any younger. And he was close, so it would be very handy for her.

She glanced at the calendar, noting that this weekend was the second in the month. The Flea Market would be open at the Fairgrounds and Billy always showed up to panhandle the customers there. She would be there too, she decided. Let's see if she could pull this off. It would be quite a coup for the last one. She nodded, pleased. She was thinking about what it would take to convince Billy to accept her help. She was confident she could do it. She would do it!

CHAPTER 14

Scott was down on his knees looking under the sink. Doug and Rich were standing to the side waiting for his opinion.

"What do you think, Scott?" Karo asked anxiously.

"Well, it's certainly doable. I'll shut off the water and disconnect the pipes and unplug the stove unit. Then the guys can get in here with their crowbars and remove this unit. Meanwhile, I'll see what it's going to take to install that piece you bought." He gestured to the big industrial stainless steel, double sink unit Karo had purchased at a store which carried fixtures from dismantled restaurants.

"Well, okay then, let's do it." Doug was holding his crowbar at readiness.

Scott waited, looking at Karo. "It's really not a big project, you know. We can probably have it all done in a few hours. The biggest problem will be getting the kitchen unit out the door and on Doug's truck."

Karo still hesitated, remembering the few hours Doug and Rich spent cutting down her tree. It had turned out to be a much bigger project than they expected it to be. She didn't want this to take their whole day.

"Karo, let's do it. You have us here, willing workers, take advantage of it. I have a date later." Rich was impatient, too.

"Okay, let's do it. I really appreciate this, guys. I hope nothing goes wrong."

"Forget it, what could go wrong? And if it does we have Scott here to fix it. He's a whiz at plumbing, aren't you Scott?" Doug grinned.

Scott nodded, soberly. "Actually, I am. If I had stuck with it instead of getting my accounting degree, I'd probably be ready to retire by now." But then he was on his knees again, his upper torso hidden inside the cupboard below the sink.

Karo looked around the living room of the apartment built behind the garage. They had already moved all the boxes and furniture she was storing into the tiny bedroom. The floor was stripped of the faded, worn shag carpeting so now there was only the concrete showing. Once the all-in-one kitchen unit had been removed and the new sink unit installed, Doug and Rich were going to help her move the pottery equipment sitting in the garage into the new studio. Of course it wouldn't be complete until she had the electrician in to install the ceiling lights and wire the room so the kiln could be plugged in, but she wasn't planning to do that right away. Meanwhile, having the studio available would mean she could work on her pottery whenever she had some free time, instead of waiting for workshop days.

Since Betty had been gone she had been assisting Sandi on class days and her own production was suffering. But Sandi needed help and no one else in class seemed to be interested in taking on that responsibility. So Karo felt she would be leaving Sandi in a lurch if she didn't help. And she appreciated the free workshops she got in exchange for her help. She found explaining the procedures and techniques to the new students was actually helping her, as it made her analyze every little thing she did which seemed to improve her own techniques. But still, it was cutting into the time she had to experiment. Having her own working studio was going to solve that dilemma. She just had to be very careful she didn't allow it to tempt her to neglect her writing. She couldn't afford to jeopardize her bread and butter work.

Cynthia had been excited to hear Karo had decided to set up her own studio and insisted she look at the space in order to offer advice. She had immediately noticed the concrete floor under the ugly carpeting and urged Karo to just pull up the carpeting and throw it away. She pointed out that a cement floor was perfect in a studio where clay, water and glazes were likely to end up on the floor.

And when Karo mentioned installing an industrial sink to replace the little kitchen unit, Cynthia knew just the place to get a used one. They had gone there immediately and Karo not only found a sink, but two stainless steel tables at just the right height to use while standing up. And they were very reasonably priced.

When she asked Doug for his help and truck to transport the pieces she bought, he asked her who was doing the plumbing.

"I don't know. I guess I'll just call someone in the Yellow Pages unless you know someone."

"I do and you do, too. Remember Scott from the dinner out at my house?" Seeing her nod, he continued, "He's a plumber. Well at least he was, while he was putting himself through college. His uncle owns a plumbing business and he worked for him until he got his degree. He still does a few jobs for friends. I think he would be happy to help you out and it wouldn't cost much. He doesn't charge the going rate. In fact, I'll bet you could barter some of your pottery and perhaps a pie or some cookies for an afternoon's work." He grinned, pleased to be able to help. "Shall I ask him?"

Karo couldn't believe her luck. "Please, but I have to pay him something, as well as bake him something. If he will do it, find out what he likes to eat."

So her studio was quickly becoming a reality and she could hardly wait.

* * *

"So, let's see this new studio you have."

Karo beamed with pride. "Really, you'd like to see it?"

"Hell, yes. You've been talking about it for weeks now. I'd like to see what all the fuss is about."

"Come on then." Karo led Delvin out the door of the mud room and across the backyard to the path alongside the garage. She pushed open the door with a flourish, flipped on the light switch and stood aside for him to enter.

She followed him inside and stood looking. It impressed her, but then she knew how it had looked before and she knew what each piece of equipment was used for. She wondered what Delvin would think of it.

He stood quietly, looking around with that careful way he had, as if he was examining a crime scene. He nodded. "It looks very professional, but I have no idea if it is or not. Tell me what you use all this for. I can see those pots sitting there. Are they done?"

So she went piece by piece, place by place and explained the whole process of making pottery.

He seemed impressed and interested. "Wow, this is much more complicated than I imagined. Just mixing the glazes sounds a lot like chemistry and firing the kiln is almost rocket science, isn't it?"

She laughed. "I'll tell you next month when I do my first kiln load. The electrician will be here in two weeks and then I'll fire these pieces I have setting here. The first firing is a bisque firing. That's to remove the moisture so they don't explode when they're fired at a high temperature. The bisque makes all the pieces dry and brittle so they can take a wet glaze. Then I will fire them in the same kiln, but to a much higher temperature. The high fire takes them up to about 2200°F where the glazes will mature and set. Then when they're cool, they're done."

"And all these pieces are things you've made here?"

She nodded. "I could take them to the studio to bisque them, but they're very fragile at this stage. Rather than risk breakage in transport I'll wait and fire them when I test out the kiln."

He looked at the buckets of glaze and the samples attached to the bucket handles. "Is this what the glazes look like when they're fired?"

"I wish. No, if you use the same clay body and fire to the same temperature they will look very much like that. But I use about four different kinds of clay and each of them will take each glaze differently. You have to learn what glazes look like on each clay body or you will get some nasty surprises when you open the kiln."

"So if it doesn't turn out the way you want? What then?"

She laughed. "Well you shrug and hope someone else will like it and buy it. Or you can fire it again; sometimes that works. Or you can add a different glaze and refire it. Or the final solution is to use that." She pointed at the heavy mallet lying on the table.

"Karo, I'm impressed. You've done a lot of work on this place and I didn't even help. Why didn't you ask me? I would have been happy to roll up my sleeves and help, if only to paint the walls."

"Well, in fact we didn't need to paint the walls, because I had the whole place painted before I moved in. And I did have a couple of work parties, but that was when you went down south to visit your son, so I knew you weren't available."

She pointed. "There was a kitchen unit in here I had to remove and a friend installed the sink unit for me. Then it was just a matter of bringing in the pieces, setting up the shelves and arranging things. But I appreciate your offer, late though it may be."

"Busted." He grinned. "But seriously, it looks great. Someday I'd like to come watch you when you're working out here."

"Maybe. I don't know how it would work with someone watching, you know?"

She turned out the lights behind them and led the way to the house.

"I noticed you locked it up. Do you have it alarmed?"

She shook her head.

"Well, okay, that will be my contribution. I'll bring some stuff over and do it for you. May as well protect your investment, huh?"

They hurried through the cold rain which had started while they were in the studio. The kitchen smelled good. The pork tenderloin and vegetables roasting in the oven announced it was almost dinnertime.

Karo poured them each a glass of wine, and Delvin sat at the table telling her about his visit with his son while she made a salad.

"So you had a good visit."

"Yes, I was a little nervous about it, but as it turned out we had a lot of time to talk and we did. He really shared his thoughts with me and I appreciated it. I guess after the accident both of us were trying to make the best of it for each other, but that meant we were hiding our true feelings. Somehow we just closed ourselves off to each other. I feel like we've really turned that around. He promised he would come up here for Christmas this year and maybe we'll even get to do some deep sea fishing."

Karo smiled at him. "That would be really good. How's his job going?"

"He says great, and you should see how his eyes light up while he's talking about it, so I guess he means it. I really don't understand what he does, it's all so technical. I don't know where he gets it from. I can barely use the computer to get my e-mails and file my reports at work. And I know Jill, my wife, used it, but she really wasn't big on computers either. However, Jason's been into computers since he was a kid. When he was in junior high school he built one for a science project." He shook his head in wonderment. "It's just amazing."

Karo took the roast out of the oven to rest a moment while she dressed the salad and sliced the bread. She dished up the tiny new potatoes, the red, orange and yellow bell peppers, the sliced Portabella mushrooms and the quartered onions layered in the bottom of the roasting pan. She sliced the pork tenderloin and laid the pieces on top of the vegetables and put the platter on the table.

"Here you go, simple but hearty. I hope you're hungry."

"Well, if I wasn't, I would be after sitting here smelling this."

Neither spoke as they ate, and Karo watched Delvin to make sure he was enjoying the meal. They had only met once since that aborted dinner, when they met at a local bookstore for a signing by one of Karo's favorite mystery writers. Afterwards they had coffee and talked for a while. The weekend following that date, Karo had helped with the sale at Betty's and the week after that Delvin left for his trip to Southern California. Of course, they had several conversations over the phone during that time which helped Karo calm her nervousness about venturing into the romance arena at what she felt was a ridiculous age.

It turned out Delvin was as anxious as she was about the whole prospect and they laughed together about their dilemma. When he called a couple of days ago to see if she wanted to try dinner with him one more time, she countered with an offer to cook for him.

"You're afraid of getting left in the lurch again, huh?"

"Of course not, I told you I understood. You can't control when crime happens and someone has to take charge. It's just that it's been a very busy week and the weather has been nasty. I thought a cozy dinner in and maybe an old movie might be nice. What do you think?"

"Well, the price is certainly right. I just feel I should shower you with lavish dinners and dancing and such."

"Sounds good to me, but another time?"

It didn't take much to convince him. He showed up this evening with flowers and a bottle of wine. As soon as he set them down in the kitchen, he wrapped his arms around her and gave her a kiss that curled her toes.

"There, now we don't have to wait all evening to wonder if a kiss will make the bells ring." He looked at her closely. "Or didn't they ring for you?"

She was speechless, but nodded, staring at him with wonderment in her eyes. He kissed her once more, this time gently, but just as thoroughly.

"Very nice, don't you think?"

Delvin interrupted her reminiscing when he noticed her staring at him across the table. "What's wrong? Do I have lettuce in my teeth?"

She shook her head. "No, I'm just enjoying you enjoying my cooking. I like to cook and I love it when someone appreciates it."

He grinned. "So how's your day job coming along?"

"Oh, pretty well, I think. I've finished the manual for the bank and it's been distributed. I think they're using it; at least that's what they tell me. And already I have a list of updates to do for it. That's good because if they let it get outdated, it will be useless. And I'm not ready to come to the end of the paying job.

"I've started the product manual for their marketing department. That's a real project. You should see all the brochures and bulletins I have to plough through to find all the features of each of their products. It's amazing to me that the staff knows enough to select the right product for each situation. But to tell the truth, I have to be very disciplined to sit in my office and force myself to write when I really want to be out in my new studio working with the clay."

Delvin laughed. "You've set yourself up, haven't you?" Then a shadow passed over his face. "Karo, do you remember our discussion a while back about people just going missing?"

She nodded.

"Well, the strangest thing happened. This old, homeless guy who has been hanging around town for years has disappeared. I think it happened while I was gone. At least I haven't seen him since before I left."

"Who is it? Would I know him?"

"Probably, but you might not know him by name. His name is Billy, Billy Harder. I suppose I wouldn't have even noticed he was gone, except I usually see him a couple times a week near the place where I stop to get coffee in the mornings. If he's there, I buy him a coffee. But he hasn't been there for a while. I asked around about him, but no one knows what happened to him."

"That's terrible. Do you know where he lives?"

He shook his head. "People like him move around a lot. Sometimes he sleeps under the overpass from the ocean highway where it connects to the road to the peninsula. For a while he was camping out behind the fairgrounds. Sometimes they've rousted him and others out of the campgrounds at the beach. I've looked in all those places and no one seems to know anything."

She shook her head, appalled. "How do people get to that point? Wandering from place to place with nowhere to be safe?" She wondered out loud, "Isn't there anything we can do for them?"

He shrugged. "I don't know. I tried to help Billy at one time. He had helped me out with a case, so I thought maybe I could help him out in return." He looked at Karo's face. "I found out Billy was once a prominent surgeon in Dallas. His drinking got out of control until one day he made a terrible error in the operating room. I guess it was very ugly, and it was plastered all over the media with newspaper and TV coverage. There was a very public trial, and of course his license to practice was revoked. But apparently none of that was as bad as Billy's own self-loathing. When he emerged from jail he apparently hit the bottle and the roads trying to escape his demons. Until he reached the edge of the earth as he knew it, here in Belle Vista. For some reason he stopped running here. As near as I can tell, he's been here around five years or so. No one remembers exactly when they first noticed him. But now he's gone."

"Do you think he started running again? Or did he get hurt and crawl off to die somewhere?" Karo asked with concern.

"Or someone killed him and dumped his body. I just don't know. I hope he's okay. I know we have lots of whackos around here, and I know we have our share of crime, but I'd like to believe the citizens of Belle Vista are too kind to hurt the old man."

Karo nodded her agreement. It seemed so sad.

"Coffee and dessert now? Or later?"

Delvin groaned. "Don't tell me what it is. I just don't have room. Later is better." He got up to help with the dishes and when they were finished they moved into the living room.

Karo loaded the DVD with the movie they had agreed on earlier, while Delvin pet the dogs. Then they all settled down to watch. Delvin sat on the couch with his arm around Karo, the dogs curled up near their feet. The fireplace crackled from the two logs Karo had added and the movie started.

* * *

"What are you doing?"

"Nothing much. I'm going to take the dogs to the beach and then clean the house a bit. What are you doing?"

"It's such a beautiful day I thought I'd go fishing. I wondered if you'd like to join me. You could bring the dogs if you want."

"Now?"

"Hell, yes. The sun is shining, the sap's running, as they say. I feel like I need to get out. Of course, if you want to join me I'll wait until you get here."

"Well, it will take me about a half hour to get there. What do I need to bring? Lunch?"

"No, just bring yourself, and the boys. I've got plenty of fishing gear and we'll either have fish for lunch or we can scrounge for something in my kitchen. Are you coming?"

"We're on our way." Karo hung up smiling to herself. It wasn't what she had planned to do with her Sunday, but it sounded like fun. And Doug was right, the day was too beautiful to stay indoors.

It was actually only twenty-five minutes until she carefully crossed the little bridge and took the winding road up to Doug's house. As soon as her car rolled to a stop near the corral, Doug appeared with a backpack on his shoulders, holding a tackle box and some fishing poles. The dogs were excited. As soon as they were free of the restraints in the car they were running here and there to smell everything.

"Well, you made good time."

"Listen when someone suggests something fun, I'm ready." Karo grabbed the small pack she brought and slipped it on her back. She looked around at the trees, noting the buds on the apple trees straining to burst, the grass green from all the rain now reaching toward the warmth of the sun. "Doug, it looks and smells heavenly. No wonder you love living out here."

Doug nodded. "This is the best time, these days early in spring, when the sun starts warming us up." He took a deep breath. "I feel a little like those buds on the apple trees, ready to burst out of my skin." He led the way through the orchard and then followed a faint path into the forest behind.

They didn't talk, they both enjoyed the quiet. The dogs stayed with them, sticking close lest they be left behind. When they came to the stream it was flowing fast as a result of all the rains they had recently. The place they sat when Doug had first shown Karo the stream was now too close to the water for comfort. He selected a different spot where a series of rocks included a big flat one on top. He tested it for stability and then nodded, laying out the poles and shrugging off his pack.

"I think this will do. We're close enough to cast our lines in the pool and we don't have to worry about the water lapping at our toes."

Karo settled herself and peered into the water. "Do you think there are many fish in here?" she asked doubtfully.

"Don't worry, there are plenty. Whether or not they'll take our bait is an entirely different question."

Karo looked over at the little containers Doug took out of his tackle box, pushing Captain back and grabbing Rudy's collar. "No, no you guys, that's not for you." She fished around in her pack and found a couple of doggie treats and tossed them on the ground behind the rocks they were sitting on. "You go eat these and leave us alone, we're fishing," she told Captain and Rudy with mock sternness.

She watched Doug bait the hooks on two poles with wiggling worms, and then he handed one to her. "Do you know what to do with it?"

She laughed. "Well, I've never actually been fishing before so I'll watch and do what you do."

He casually flipped his rod a couple of times and then sent the line zinging out over the water to drop in a dark pool in the shelter of the far bank. It looked easy.

"Okay, I guess I need a lesson," she admitted after the third attempt, her line now caught in some bushes behind them.

She waited holding Doug's rod as he untangled her line, put another worm on the hook to replace the one she lost and reeled in the line for another cast. He showed her how to release the reel when she gave the last flip of the rod so the line could sail out over the water. She tried to follow his instructions exactly, and this time she was successful although she didn't get her line to reach the deep pool on the other side. They settled down, mesmerized by the current, content to hold their poles while the lines danced in the water.

While they sat in dappled shade, the sun shone directly on the water and the rocks below them reflecting the heat pleasantly. The birds were singing and the squirrels scolding, while butterflies and bees flitted around. The dogs were even content to sit in the shade behind them, stirring only occasionally when something intrigued them.

Karo had no idea how long it was before the pole almost fell from her hands. She grabbed it before it went into the water and felt something pulling the line from the other end.

It was exciting. She had a bite. She followed Doug's instructions, pulling on the pole and reeling in the line, bit by bit. She could see the fish now.

"Oh, look, it's really big."

And then the line snapped and she was left with disappointment.

Doug handed her his pole while he added another hook and bait to hers. And then they had a flurry of activity, catching three fish in a rather short time. Doug had strung the fish on a line and dropped them in the stream to keep them cool while they hoped for more.

Now they talked intermittently while they fished, catching up on the news of their friends.

"I guess Rich's relationship with Anna is getting serious."

Doug raised his eyebrows. "You think?"

"Well, it sure sounds like Rich is serious, so I hope she feels the same way."

Doug nodded. "She seems nice."

They were quiet for a while, then Karo said, "Did I tell you that someone is building on the vacant lot at the end of the block?"

"No. That didn't take long, did it?"

"I guess after it was cleared it looked appealing. One of the neighbors told me it was sold a while ago. When I went down to the beach on Monday, they were starting to put in the markers for the foundation. The whole neighborhood is waiting anxiously to find out who is moving in. We're hoping for a nice normal family."

"Well, for sure, no one will be getting away with putting another Meth house on your block, will they?"

She shook her head. "No we've been there, done that. Now we're keeping our eyes open. But it's nice to know the neighborhood is attractive enough to attract a builder. As a homeowner, that's always a concern."

"Yeah, I suppose it is." Then changing the subject, Doug asked, "What about the woman you found on the beach? Did you hear if they ever solved that?"

Karo shook her head. "Delvin says he's still working on it."

Doug looked at her surprised. "Delvin? Who is Delvin?"

Karo actually blushed, and because that embarrassed her, she felt her face get even redder. "Delvin Myers is the police lieutenant handling that case. You met him, didn't you? He was the one who came by to question us all after the Meth house burned down."

Doug shook his head. "Didn't question me, don't know him." But his eyes were questioning Karo.

"Well, I met him that day on the beach and he's questioned me a few times about it. You know, when they identified her, and after the fire, that kind of thing." She thought a minute and then decided she'd better be up front about this. "Actually, I've gone out with him a few times. We kind of hit it off, you know?"

Doug nodded, looking at her intently. "Sometimes that happens. Is it serious?"

"I don't know. We like each other, but I'm not really interested in a serious relationship. I'm still trying to sort myself out after the last one."

Doug nodded again. "Look Karo, I can see you're uncomfortable about telling me this, but you shouldn't be. We're friends, remember?"

She nodded, smiling. "Yes, that's how I feel, but...well, I don't know. It seemed a little awkward."

He reached over and patted her on the shoulder. "Well, don't worry about it. If you like him, I'm sure I will. And probably Rich will and your other friends will, too. You should invite him when we have a get-together, and we can all check him out for you."

She laughed. "I don't know about that. It seems a little dangerous to me. I think I'll wait and see how much I like him first."

She checked the sky for the sun's position. "Hey, I'm getting a little hungry. Isn't this enough fish for lunch?"

Doug nodded. "Sure, let's go. I think you're due for the second part of your fishing lesson, learning how to clean the fish."

CHAPTER 15

It was late when the phone shattered the peaceful silence. Karo glanced at the clock wondering who would be calling at nine-thirty on a Sunday night.

"Hey Karo, this is Sandi. I'm not calling too late, am I?"

"Sandi, no, I'm still up. What can I do for you?"

"Look Karo, I'm sorry to bother you, but I need a favor."

"Sure, what can I help you with?"

"I have a large blue celadon bowl in the kiln I made for a friend who is moving to the East Coast. I just found out her goodbye party is tomorrow at lunch and not Wednesday as I thought. I'm stuck in a meeting tomorrow at the University and I can't get out of it, but I really want her to have the bowl. I hoped you could stop by the studio in the morning and take it out of the kiln and then drop it off at the office at Belle Vista Middle School. My friends there will see it gets to her." She paused to draw a breath, adding anxiously, "Is that too much of an imposition?"

Karo thought through her plans for the morning. "Well, I have time to do that, but you know Joy doesn't like anyone messing with the kiln before she looks at everything," she broached tentatively.

"Oh, that woman! Well, she'll just have to deal with it. Everyone goes out of their way to accommodate her little peculiarities, but I can tell you I'm getting fed up with her rules." Sandi's voice was full of indignation. "You have a key, just go in and open the kiln and take it out. If she says anything, just tell her I sent you."

Karo nodded, realizing that little riff between Sandi and Joy still hadn't been mended. If anything, it sounded as if it had only gotten worse. "Well, yes I can do that if you want me to." She still wasn't enthusiastic about it. After all she was the one who would have to deal with Joy on one of her tears and she knew how unpleasant that could be.

"Would you, Karo? I'm afraid I really messed this up. I thought the luncheon was going to be Wednesday when I'm working in Belle Vista, so I could just dash over at lunch time. Now I find out she's leaving Wednesday, so of course, they can't have the party then. I must have just mixed up the dates in my head."

Then she said as a final thought, "You could go anytime in the morning; it doesn't matter when. Do you know where Belle Vista Middle School is?"

"Yes, I know. Sandi, is there only one of your pieces in the kiln?" She didn't want to take the wrong piece.

"Yes, I don't fire much there as Joy's rules are just too annoying for me. I do most of my firing in the kiln at the University. But this is a piece I made when I was demonstrating for the class, and so I thought I may as well just glaze it and fire it there. You can't miss it. You recognize my work, don't you?"

Karo hung up the phone feeling slightly apprehensive about her agreement to do this favor. Sure it was easy for Sandi to say just tell Joy she sent her, but she was the one who would have to face Joy's wrath. Then she shrugged, she was making too big a thing out of this. After all, Sandi was right, Joy made too many rules. And she did have the key assigned to her, so she could open the studio on Wednesday mornings for the class and for when she stayed to lock up at night.

She thought she would go in early Monday and maybe Joy wouldn't even know she had been there. No, she realized, Joy would see the empty place in the kiln. She would know someone had removed a piece without her seeing it.

She remembered Joy had been okay that one time she had stopped by unexpectedly, but Rich had told her he had stopped by one morning recently to see if he could help her load his pieces in the kiln and she wouldn't even let him in. Karo laughed grimly to herself, thinking that working with Joy was always a challenge.

The next morning she left after breakfast to take care of the favor for Sandi before attending to the errands she needed to run. When she drove into the Recreation Center she decided to park in front and pay for some clay at the front desk instead of going around to the side parking lot where the door nearest the studio was. She paid her money and tucked the receipt for the clay in her wallet to exchange for a bag of clay on Tuesday, and then walked down the long hall to the studio. The door was locked as she expected. She didn't bother knocking, just used her key to let herself in and proceeded to the covered patio. The lights were on and both the high fire and the soda fire kilns had their doors open. The noise was horrific. She realized Joy was running the Ball Mill again. But she didn't see Joy.

She assumed she was taking some of her pieces out to her truck or perhaps she was in the restroom. She took advantage of being alone to head right for the high fire kiln. With the door open and the shelves exposed, it was easy to locate Sandi's bowl in the center of the second shelf. Great, she was going to have to unload several pieces to get to it. She set her purse down and carefully unloaded the pieces between her and Sandi's bowl. Finally she was able to reach the piece she wanted. She carefully slid it off the shelf and transferred it to the table, looking it over carefully before setting it down. It was a beautiful piece. Not only was the shape lovely but the blue celadon glowed with almost an iridescent look. She had to credit Joy for that. She had placed it in just the perfect place in the kiln. She was already thinking how she could use the celadon on some of her pieces.

She wondered briefly if she should put the other pieces back in the kiln, but then decided that it was too much trouble, and anyway, Joy was bound to notice the empty space.

Joy still hadn't returned. But she did see that there was a stack of shelves and pillars by the open soda fire kiln, so she realized someone had removed them to make space in the kiln for big pieces. She walked over to see if some of Rich's pieces had been fired.

The shelves on both outer sides of the kiln were in place and had a few pieces sitting on them. The space in the middle was where the shelves had been removed leaving a large empty area, but there were no pieces sitting there. She noticed something on the shelf and moved closer. She walked around the door to see better and saw what appeared to be a pile of ashes and some pieces of white porous material that looked suspiciously like bones.

Of course, she remembered, Joy sometimes used beef bones to get a flash of color on unglazed high fired pieces. And the Ball Mill was going so that must be what she was seeing. But these didn't look like beef bones. In fact, she thought one fragment looked very much like...

She caught the movement out of the corner of her eye and instinctively jumped back as the heavy mallet skimmed past where her head had just been to crash viciously into the shelves still stacked in position on the side of the kiln.

For a brief moment time seemed frozen.

Joy must have felt numbness all the way up her arm from the force of the mallet meeting the shelf, which had split the heavy shelf in two.

Karo didn't quite get what had just happened, what she had just seen. But she had processed enough of it to be already moving before Joy recovered enough to lift the mallet to swing again.

She didn't try to reason with Joy. She could see by the murderous expression on Joy's face, she best get out of her reach quickly. They circled the large table in the middle of the covered patio where Karo had placed the pieces she had removed from the kiln earlier. She managed to keep the table between them, and herself out of reach of Joy's swinging mallet.

The adrenaline was rushing through her veins, but her mind was quickly sorting through her options to escape

The gate to the patio was still locked.

She assumed Joy had locked the door leading to the corridor when she came in, so she knew she had to have enough time to turn the lock and open the door before the mallet could hit her. With a sinking feeling she realized she would have to somehow immobilize Joy in order to gain enough time to escape, because she could see that Joy didn't intend to let her out alive.

Her hand reached out and grabbed a small heavy bowl she had taken out of the kiln. It was about the size of a soft ball, but it weighed a lot, so it was probably one of the beginning students' work. She heaved it at Joy as hard as she could and then while Joy was dodging it, she picked up two more and threw them with all her might. One shattered against the kiln while the other scored a hit directly on Joy's shoulder. Karo raced toward the door leading into the studio, dodging behind one of the rolling racks which now held only a couple pieces waiting to be fired.

When the mallet hit the rolling cart, Karo shoved the cart at Joy and charged through the door into the studio. She paused on the other side of the wedging table to see which way Joy would choose to chase her. Here the noise from the Ball Mill wasn't so loud, and so she tried to reason with Joy.

"Joy, what are you doing? Are you crazy?"

Joy's face, already red and contorted, turned almost purple. Karo realized crazy was a poor choice of a word to use.

"Joy, put down the mallet and let's talk about this. What's wrong with you?" she said with authority, trying to keep her voice calm which was very hard since she was panting. She ran toward the other end of the tables they used for hand building, looking frantically for something to use to protect herself.

Joy was right behind her, swinging the mallet dangerously close. She grabbed another of the rolling carts, this one loaded with works-in-process, and shoved it with all her might right into Joy.

Joy's angry roar was either because the heavy cart hurt her, or it was a shout of rage because Karo had risked damaging so much work. But now there was nowhere for Karo to go, there was nothing to use to save herself. Karo wondered if she could leap out of the reach of the mallet one more time and somehow overwhelm Joy as heroine's did all the time in the movies.

Joy pushed the cart to the side and advanced slowly, deliberately, and with deadly determination. She raised the mallet, ready to smash Karo's skull, a cold smile of satisfaction on her lips.

Karo grabbed one of the chairs, holding it as lion tamers did, hoping somehow to deflect the blow she knew would be coming. Joy paused, her face twisted into a hideous grimace, and then she dropped the mallet as she sank to a heap on the floor.

Karo couldn't believe it. She watched to see if it was a trick. Joy didn't stir so she carefully stepped around her and then raced for the door. Her hand was shaking so much she had trouble turning the knob to unlock it, but finally she was successful and she sprinted down the hall to the reception desk in the lobby.

"Help! Call the police. An ambulance. Help! Get help."

The woman could see how distraught Karo was and didn't spend any time asking questions. She just picked up the phone and punched in nine-one-one before handing the receiver to Karo.

Karo suspected she wasn't coherent, but the operator seemed to understand it was an emergency. The lady behind the desk moved to run to the studio to see if she could help, but Karo grabbed her arm and held it firmly, shaking her head. What if Joy was on her feet again? Who knew what she would do? She wasn't rational. She could be deadly.

And with the phone receiver still to her ear, her knees gave out and her hold on the receptionist's arm couldn't save her as she sat on the floor in a heap, unable to suppress her sobs.

Karo really didn't know who arrived first, the police or the ambulance. And she didn't realize she was bleeding until they were bent over her with their equipment.

"No, no. It's not me." She tried to push them away. "It's Joy. In the studio! She collapsed. Maybe it was a heart attack, or maybe a stroke. I don't know." She tried to control her shaking hand as she pointed toward the studio down the hall.

When the medics saw she only had some superficial cuts, probably the result of some pottery shards, they both sprinted for the studio, the police officers right behind them. That's when Karo remembered the importance of the kiln.

"Officer, officer wait!" she called to the retreating backs. "I think there has been a murder." She struggled to her feet and lurched after them. "Call Lieutenant Myers. Tell him there has been a murder. He'll know what to do." She insisted and when they got to the studio she didn't even glance at where the emergency team was crouched over the prone figure that was Joy, but went directly to the covered patio and switched off the Ball Mill.

In the sudden silence she said softly to one of the policemen behind her, "I found bones in the kiln, they may be human remains." She pointed to the soda fire kiln and than sank down on a convenient stool while they checked it out.

She sat there quietly. The ambulance crew was busy with Joy. She saw the police officers look warily into the kiln and then radio for help. She wondered anxiously if she was wrong. Maybe the bones in the kiln were not human. Was there some reasonable explanation and she had just jumped to the wrong conclusion?

She felt the tickle of fear in her gut as she wondered if she was making some big thing out of some silly misunderstanding. But then, she reasoned, what would be the reason for Joy's murderous attack with the mallet? She shuddered remembering how close the heavy mallet had whizzed past her head when she jerked back at the kiln. If Joy hadn't been swinging it so hard that she couldn't stop, Karo's own head would be shattered instead of the kiln shelf. Now she was shivering in earnest, whether from nerves or the coolness of the patio she didn't know. She hunched in on herself, trying to keep warm while she waited.

"Karo, are you hurt?" Delvin bent over her, concern in his voice as his eyes checked her out.

When she shook her head, he turned and told one of the officers to get her a blanket. He waited with her until the officer returned and then he patted her and said, "I'll be right back to talk to you. Will you be okay?"

She nodded, very grateful for the warmth spreading through her from the blanket she now clutched around her shoulders. She watched Delvin talk to the ambulance attendants, nodding at them. They then rolled the stretcher toward the door to the hall, followed closely by a police officer.

Delvin went over to the kiln to talk with the officers, who had first responded to the call. They leaned in and peered closely at the bone fragments in the kiln, not touching anything. Soon several more people arrived, and Delvin came back and sat on the table facing Karo.

"Karo, you do lead an exciting life, don't you?" His slight smile let her know he sympathized with her. "Are you ready to tell me what happened here?"

She nodded and he helped her to her feet and led her back into the studio and sat her down at one of the tables. Another man joined them and took out a pad and pen, preparing to take notes. Delvin signaled a third officer, "See if you can find some hot coffee and put cream and sugar in it, will you?" While it sounded like a request, they all knew it was an order.

"Now Karo, before we get started, tell us who the lady was who was just wheeled out of here."

"That's Joy Ledbetter. She's in charge of the studio. She manages the kiln and the workshops and assigns all the studio tasks to the potters who work here. She's been here since they built this studio."

Delvin nodded. "Okay, now tell us what happened here."

Karo tried very hard to tell everything in order and not go off on tangents. She stopped only long enough to take a big drink of hot coffee when the policeman returned with it.

"And that's when I told them to call you. Oh, and I came in and turned off the Ball Mill." She could see the question on Delvin's face. "The Ball Mill is a very noisy machine that grinds hard material into powder. It was running this morning when I came in, so I assumed Joy was grinding up what was left of some beef bones she had fired in the kiln..." She looked up, distress painted on her face. "But I was wrong. It probably wasn't beef bones."

"Do you have any idea whose bones were in the kiln?" Delvin asked.

Karo's eyes widened with horror. Until Delvin asked that question she had never even thought it could be someone she knew. She shook her head. "As far as I know everyone in the class is still around, the only person missing is Betty..." She shuddered, praying it wasn't Betty.

"After Betty's husband died, she went to Iowa to visit her niece. She had a massive stroke while she was there and is still in a coma. Remember? I told you about us cleaning out her house and having a sale to raise the funds to help with the hospital bills. Joy took care of all the financial part of it. Joy was in contact with Betty and later with her niece." She stared at Delvin. "Joy is the only link we have with Betty. You don't think that could be...? No, it couldn't be...?"

"Calm down, Karo. Hopefully it isn't your friend, Betty. But for sure it is someone. We have a lot of information to gather and process here. Something very nasty is going on, and we're going to find the answers."

Delvin then led her back through her story asking specific questions, going over several aspects thoroughly before finally relaxing. "Okay. I think that's all for now. I have to caution you not to talk to anyone about this. You don't want to interfere with our investigation by alerting people to what's happened before we interview them. We will be talking to everyone who works at the studio and everyone connected to Betty and Joy.

"Can you do that? Keep mum about it?" He looked at her intently and she nodded. She didn't want to talk about it to anyone; she didn't even want to think about it.

"I imagine the media will be arriving soon, and I know it will be hard to ignore them. If anyone causes a problem just let us know."

She nodded, shrugging off the blanket. She stood up, now anxious to go home.

"And Karo, you did good, you know? Speaking as a policeman, I appreciate your quick thinking. Speaking as your friend, I'm very grateful you escaped with only a few superficial cuts." He gently squeezed her shoulder and then turned back to join the people working in the covered patio area.

She turned to go, but paused. "Uh, Delvin?" He didn't hear her so she called louder, "Delvin?"

When he turned back to her she said, "Did they say how Joy was? What was wrong with her?"

"They think it might be a stroke. They said she was in a coma. Don't worry, Karo, we'll be keeping a guard with her."

* * *

When Karo got home she noticed how much of the day had passed. It was somehow already early afternoon. Before she did anything she sat on the floor to hug Captain and Rudy. She buried her face in Rudy's neck while she held the squirming Captain close. "You guys almost lost your momma today," she said, shuddering at the memory. She cried while they licked her, trying their best to comfort her. Finally, she got to her feet and let them out in the backyard while she assembled some crackers, cheese and a pear for lunch. When she finished she sat down with the phone to call Eileen. Delvin told her not to talk about it, but she reasoned he didn't mean she couldn't have the support of her family and friends. And she really needed to talk to someone who cared that she survived this morning.

It was while she was explaining the whole situation to Eileen that she remembered that conversation she had with Betty just before Betty disappeared. She realized she needed to tell Delvin. It might be significant information.

"Eileen, I just remembered something. I have to hang up now and call the police to tell them."

"Okay, you do that, and I'll call the airlines and get tickets. I'm coming out."

"Eileen, you don't have to..."

"Karo, I'm coming. Expect me sometime tonight. I'll just rent a car at the airport. That's what friends are for, to be there when you have troubles."

Karo hung up, feeling slightly guilty for pulling her friend from her life, but feeling better just knowing she was on her way.

She vacillated a bit about calling Delvin, then realized he would have to decide if her information was important or not. She punched in the number for his cell phone.

"Myers," was his abrupt greeting.

"Delvin, I was talking to my friend Eileen and I suddenly remembered something that might be important."

"I thought you agreed you wouldn't discuss this?"

"Eileen is my best friend and she lives in St. Louis. I hardly think talking to her will interfere with your investigation in any way. Do you?"

"Well, I guess not. So, what did you remember?"

Delvin's manner was rather short, definitely not the caring interested beau she had been getting used to having around. "Well, it was a discussion I had with Betty the last time I was at her house. I was telling her about seeing Joy down near the railroad station in Redwood City, you know, where the homeless people hang out? Anyway, I saw Joy dispensing coffee and food. I was amazed to see Joy there, because she doesn't seem to be the charitable type. In fact, she's been very vocal with her negative opinions of anyone using public assistance.

"Betty became very upset when she heard Joy was there. I can't really remember what she said but something about promises and she would put an end to it. She just hustled me and the dogs out of her house before I had even finished my tea. I had forgotten all about this conversation, but now I'm wondering what she knew about Joy that upset her so. Do you think it has something to do with all this?"

"Don't know yet, but that's good information. We haven't found out anything about your friend Betty. So far no one knows her niece or even that she had a niece. We will be searching Joy's house and Betty's too.

"Is that it?" He sounded a little friendlier now. "How are you doing, Karo? Will you be okay?"

"I'm fine. No, of course I'm not fine, but my friend, Eileen, is on her way. She'll be a comfort. And Delvin, you have to let me know what's going on if you don't want me to talk to any of the other people from the studio. I have to know what you find."

"Don't worry. I'm sure you'll hear all about it. The newspapers have shown up. It's only a matter of time before the TV remote vans arrive. But I will try to keep in touch. Take care, and call me if you remember anything else."

CHAPTER 16

"I'm so sorry, Karo. I had no idea." Sandi stood on the porch, pale and shaken.

"Come in, Sandi." Karo reached out and took her arm pulling her in the house just as she saw the news van with a satellite dish on top pull up to the curb.

"Of course you didn't have any idea. None of us did, did we?" She looked at her closer. "Are you all right, Sandi?"

"Yes, no, I don't know. I just spent about five hours at the Rec Center with the Director and the police. It was grueling, to say the least. I'm just so upset about placing you in danger, and," she suddenly hugged Karo tightly, "Karo, I can't tell you how thankful I am you weren't hurt."

Sandi stood and looked Karo over carefully. "I had to come and see for myself. I had to know you were really okay."

Then as if she were waking from a long sleep, she looked around her and, seeing the prancing dogs, she absently bent down to pet each of them. "I have to go. My family is frantic with worry, but I told them I had to come by here first."

"Are you sure you don't want something to drink, a Coke, coffee?" Then when she saw the shake of Sandi's head, "Of course you must go. Thank you for stopping by. I don't blame you, Sandi. How could you have known? None of us suspected anything." She stood at the door and watched Sandi run for her car, refusing to even look at the camera sitting on one of the men's shoulders while another held a microphone out, hoping for a comment. Karo shut the door firmly when the camera swiveled hopefully in her direction and went back into the kitchen.

"Well, the TV vans have arrived. One is in front and another was just pulling up. The next time the doorbell rings I'd appreciate it if you would answer it for me, Rich."

Rich nodded. "Be happy to, and we can answer the phone if you want us to."

Doug, who had arrived shortly after the first radio report hit the airwaves, was busy at the stove. He nodded his agreement.

"No, right now it's easy to just hang up if it's someone I don't want to talk to." And the phone rang yet again. Karo made a face but picked it up.

"Karo, are you all right?" It was Greg and he sounded worried.

"I'm fine, Greg. How did you know I was having problems?"

"How did I know? Karo, you're on every news channel. How could I not notice? Do you need help? A lawyer? Do you want me to come down to stay with you?"

"Greg, that's very thoughtful. No, I don't need a lawyer. I didn't do anything wrong and the police don't consider me involved. I have some friends here with me and they're helping me hold off the media hounds. Eileen is on her way and she'll lend moral support. It was a really a scary situation, but now it's over, thank God."

"Karo, have you talked to Lisa? I'd hate for her to hear about this on the evening news."

"Oh, my God, that would be terrible. I haven't called her, but I will as soon as I hang up. You're right, thank you, Greg. And thanks for calling." She pushed the button down to disconnect and immediately punched in Lisa's cell phone number.

"Lisa, how are you dear? I'm sorry to disturb you, but something's come up and I wanted to tell you before you saw the news."

She managed to give her a brief update of the events of the morning, assure her that she was perfectly safe, and that she didn't need her to rush home.

"Eileen is on her way here and should be arriving in an hour or two. I'll call you tomorrow and give you an update. Frankly everything is very chaotic right now and no one really knows what was going on. Doug and Rich are here. Doug is making a big pot of his special stew, so the house smells heavenly. They are giving me moral support and fending off the paparazzi for me. Yes, yes I'll tell them. Take care, dear. I love you."

Karo hung up the phone and went to the kitchen table and sat down heavily. "I need something stronger than a Coke, Rich. I need some wine. I think I need lots of it."

When Rich put the glass in her hand she drank about half, held it out for a refill and then heaved a big sigh. "Thanks both of you. I really appreciate you coming over."

She had been surprised and relieved when she answered the door earlier and found Doug standing on the porch with plastic bags filled with groceries hanging from his hands. He had immediately headed for the kitchen, unloaded the groceries, stopping only long enough to pet the dogs and give Karo a comforting hug, before he started making a stew.

Rich had arrived a short time later, coming directly from his interview with the police. He said he couldn't discuss the case, but he could hang out and help protect Karo from the nuisance of the press until it was time for him to go to work.

"But frankly, Karo, I'm a bit shook up myself. I don't know if I'm here to give comfort or to be comforted." He shook his head perplexed. "Life is sometimes full of nasty surprises, isn't it?" He patted her on the shoulder. "Anna will be over as soon as she gets off work. That's all right with you, isn't it?"

Karo nodded. "Of course she's welcome. I'm sure Doug's got enough stew there for a dozen people." Then she remembered her conversation with Greg. "Rich, Greg said it was on all the TV news channels. Should we turn on the TV?"

Rich reached it first and turned to the CNN news channel. The report was scary. They all looked at each other with horror.

"It looks even worse on TV, doesn't it?"

Karo nodded. "It kind of makes it seem real, you know? Like those horrible stories that happen to someone else."

Rich changed the channel to NBC, and after that he caught the last part of ABC.

The phone rang again.

"Karo, are you all right? What's going on over there? I could hardly get into my driveway."

"I'm fine Diane. I guess you haven't been listening to the news."

"No, I don't like Tiffany to hear all that stuff. Why, what's happened?"

"Diane, it's too long and complicated to tell you over the phone. Why don't you come over and have some stew with us. Doug is cooking."

"Are you sure?"

"Sure, come through the back and spare yourself the need to fight through that crowd on the sidewalk." She hung up announcing, "Diane and Tiffany are coming over. Rich can you entertain Tiffany while I explain what's happened to Diane. There is no reason that child needs to hear any of it, and that way you won't hear my version either." They both remembered their instructions. Karo added, "Don't worry, I'll only tell her what is on the TV and radio. That should satisfy Lieutenant Myers. Diane can read the details in the paper tomorrow if she wants to."

The dogs ran joyfully barking to the back door. It was strange how their barks sounded different almost as if they recognized Tiffany.

Rich took Tiffany and the dogs into the living room, where he could monitor the front door. Karo poured Diane a glass of wine and briefly explained what had happened this morning. The phone rang four times, but three times it was newspaper reporters, so Karo just hung up. The fourth was the neighbor down the block asking if she was all right.

When Doug finally decided the stew was ready, Karo went out to get Rich and Tiffany and found Anna there playing a game with them.

"Hi Anna, thanks for coming over. You must have been one of the door bell rings."

Anna gave her a warm hug. "How are you doing, Karo? This is a nasty business and I'm sorry you're involved."

They all trooped into the kitchen and crowded around the little table to eat the hearty, fragrant stew.

Diane and Tiffany left by the back door a while after dinner, because it was almost Tiffany's bedtime. Rich and Anna left about ten, because Rich had to be at work by eleven. Karo and Doug settled on the couch with an old movie on TV when the doorbell rang yet again.

Karo bounced off the sofa thinking Eileen had arrived, but when she looked through the little peek-hole in the door she saw it was Delvin. He looked tired and worn, every month of his fifty some years seemed etched on his face. She noticed when she opened the door that the reporters kept their distance from him even though they watched with interest.

"Come in, Delvin."

She turned around after closing the door and found him and Doug eyeing each other warily. She introduced them and then offered, "Delvin, are you hungry? Thirsty? We have some leftover stew I can warm up."

"That sounds great. I'm sorry to come so late, but I had a few more questions. I hoped you hadn't gone to bed yet."

Karo led the two men to the kitchen. "No, somehow I'm not expecting to get much sleep tonight.

Anyway, my friend Eileen is on her way here and when she gets here, which should be any time now, I'm sure we'll be up late talking."

Doug took the dish of leftover stew from the refrigerator, waving Karo to the chairs at the table. "I'll do that, you talk to Lieutenant Myers."

So Karo sat and looked expectantly at Delvin.

"Karo, remember you said you told Betty about seeing Joy ministering to the homeless? And you said she got upset and muttered about promises and she'd take care of it? Can you remember precisely when that was? What actual date it was? And is that the last time you actually saw or spoke to Betty?"

Karo looked at him thinking, and then she went over to the counter where she kept a calendar near the base of the remote phone. She brought the calendar over to the table and looked at the previous months. Finally, she pointed to a Thursday. "That's it. I remember because the following Tuesday she didn't come to class. I helped Sandi the first time on the following Wednesday." She looked at Delvin, surprise on her face. "I never connected the two. Are you thinking...? I mean, do you think...? It couldn't have been Betty in the kiln?" She couldn't stop the shudder that rippled through her.

"No, I'm sure it wasn't Betty, Karo. But according to all the information we've collected, the last time anyone saw Betty was that Friday. And no one had heard of Betty's niece before Joy talked about her. So far we've not been able to find any trace of either Betty or the niece."

Doug brought a bowl of steaming stew to the table and sat it in front of Delvin. He then brought a hunk of sourdough bread, butter and a cup of coffee. Delvin turned his attention to the food while Karo sat thinking about Betty. Remembering how sad she had been to hear Betty's husband had passed away. She had been even more distressed to learn about Betty's stroke which incapacitated her. But it was just too horrible to think that Betty might have been a victim of a vicious attack by Joy.

"What about Betty's husband? Did you locate the care facility that took care of him?"

Delvin, his mouth full, shook his head.

"Well, surely you located the funeral home that handled his body? That couldn't have been too hard."

Delvin looked at her and soberly shook his head.

Karo was stunned, speechless. She sat fingering the glass of wine Doug had retrieved from the living room while Delvin finished his stew. Doug came and sat down at the table with them.

"Do you want more?" Doug asked, and when Delvin shook his head, offered, "More coffee?"

Delvin nodded holding out his cup. "That was a great stew, Karo. I was starved."

"Doug made it. He's been here all afternoon, cooking and answering the door and just being with me."

Delvin nodded, looking at Doug. "Nice of you. People who survive trauma such as Karo experienced need someone to lean on. But, I guess you know that being in ER and all."

Doug nodded.

Delvin faced Karo again. "I'm sorry to tell you, Karo, this situation is going to get worse. This is not for general knowledge, but we have reason to believe that there have been multiple victims. We have found records on Joy's computer to lead us to believe she has been using the studio's kiln for her nefarious purposes for quite a while. How she has gotten away with it is incredible." He paused a moment letting that information seep into Karo's brain. "We think Joy has befriended homeless men, set up automatic payments of their retirement benefits to be credited to a bank account in their joint names and then disposed of them.

Karo looked up her eyes wide with shock as she suddenly remembered the two accounts she had seen at the local bank. Each of them was with Joy and a different man. She shuddered, remembering running into Joy at the bank one day with a man she introduced as her brother.

"Are you sure? I mean couldn't these people be related to her somehow? I met a man with her once, she said he was her brother." Karo didn't want to believe Delvin. It was just too terrible.

Delvin shook his head. "And we found a connection between Joy and Alison Burkhouse, the woman you found on the beach," he reported gravely.

Karo's mouth fell open.

Delvin nodded. "Augustus Aurelieus is currently a co-owner of a bank account with Joyce Ledbetter. His Social Security payments are being deposited automatically to that account. Subsequently these monies are transferred to another account in the Bahamas. What is very interesting is that prior to the check being credited to the joint account with Joy it had previously been sent directly to the mission in San Francisco where Alison Burkhouse worked. And the people at the mission found a box of items Alison was holding marked with his name.

Karo and Doug just stared.

"We think this Augustus Aurelius was one of Joy's victims and that Alison Burkhouse may have come looking for him, so Joy killed her to protect her scheme.

"But that made us wonder why Alison was found on the beach? If Joy had murdered her, why wouldn't she have used the kiln to dispose of the body as we suspect she did so many times?" Delvin paused, letting the question hang in the air, and then shook his head an expression of disgust on his face.

"Well, in talking to the people at the Recreation Center we find that during the time, when the forensics people think Alison was killed, the entire Rec Center was closed for some maintenance work. There was a period of about three weeks when the kilns couldn't be fired, when the studio was closed." He looked at them and shrugged. "So maybe she had to use the ocean?"

"But why? Do you have any idea why she was doing this?" Doug asked, keeping his voice steady.

"Greed is my guess. Some people will go to any length to get money. We found several accounts with her name and another person which have automatic deposits coming in from various sources. We found financial records on her computer showing a sizable fortune deposited offshore. We're trying to track all that now. But, I'm guessing we're talking about a couple of dozen people here who may have been victims."

"I need more wine," Karo whispered.

Doug got up immediately to fill her glass. He offered some to Delvin.

"Thanks, but no. I've still got a few hours more to my day." He pushed his chair back from the table. "I've got to get going. The FBI has been called in and they're now in charge. This case is way too big for us to handle alone. Belle Vista just doesn't have the skills or the resources to handle a case as big as this one. The FBI has already started digging and we think we're just seeing the tip of the iceberg. The media folks are going to have a circus with this and I believe they already know it. Every hotel room in town is taken; each of them wants to be the one to get the juiciest tidbits. You can expect to be hounded for a while. You'll be called down for more interviews with the FBI, and the reporters will be dogging you wherever you go.

"You're a key player in this, Karo, through no fault of your own. So it's good you have friends to support you." He nodded at Doug. "Thanks for the food, and the information. I'll try to check in with you from time to time, but call me if you need me. Or if you remember something that might be pertinent."

"I'll walk you out," Karo said, standing.

The men shook hands solemnly. "Keep an eye on her, Doug. She needs friends now," Delvin said gravely. Then with a nod he turned toward the front door.

At the front door he put his arms around Karo for a hug and kissed her chastely on the cheek. "Take care, Karo. Someday this will be over and hopefully we can try dinner again."

Karo noticed when he left the TV vans followed him leaving her street empty for the first time since early evening.

* * *

The incessant ringing of the phone finally dragged Karo out of a deep restless sleep. Eileen had arrived late and Doug had left them to their talk. It had been the wee hours of the morning before she finally slept. Now she tried to ignore the phone, but it just wouldn't stop. She staggered out of her room to find Eileen had gotten it.

"It was your friend, Doug. He's on his way over with all the newspapers and plenty of donuts. He just wanted to warn us to watch for him and let him in so he doesn't get trapped by the paparazzi on the sidewalk."

"Okay, but I have to go brush my teeth and wash my face; will you keep watch until I get back."

"Go! Hurry up. He said he'd be here in ten minutes." Eileen made shooing motions then wrapped her robe around her and headed for the kitchen. "I hope I can remember how to work this hi-tech coffee machine you have," she muttered as she went.

Karo quickly dressed, did her ablutions and headed for the coffee machine when the pounding on the front door caused her to detour.

Doug was loaded with papers and holding a bakery box when she let him in, ignoring the pleas of the crowd on the sidewalk. The TV remote vans were back in force, their numbers were augmented by several other cars and SUV's parked up and down the block. Karo only opened the door wide enough for Doug to slip in, and then she said firmly to the three men crowding behind him on the porch, "You're on private property. If you don't leave I will call the police immediately." Then she closed the door, leaving them trying to peer through the windows. The dogs were barking and growling and lunging at the door and windows; they didn't like the intrusion.

Karo called the police station and begged them to send someone out to manage the crowd. She was embarrassed to be such a nuisance to her neighbors.

She then joined Eileen and Doug in the kitchen where they turned on the television in time to watch the stiff cold FBI spokesperson's report, while they read the papers and washed too many donuts down with their coffee.

"Ugh, take those donuts away or I'm going to be sick. I just can't seem to stop eating them." Eileen did look a little green, but it might have been lack of sleep on top of the distressing reports in the papers they were reading.

MURDEROUS MONSTER IN BELLE VISTA
COFFEE LADY SERIAL KILLER LOOSE IN BELLE VISTA
POTTERY STUDIO REVEALS GRUESOME REMAINS
ANGEL OF DEATH STALKS AMONG THE HOMELESS

The headlines were just a sample of the salacious stories to come.

"It says they found traces of human bones in some of the clay stored on Joy's shelves at the studio, but they can't identify DNA from the bones after they've been fired at that high a temperature."

Karo nodded. "I saw the beef bones she fired in the kiln. They were only fragments, porous, leached white and very brittle. They were very easily turned to dust in the Ball Mill." She had a sudden thought and her face went chalk white. "I hope they were beef bones. You don't suppose she would be bold enough to have been processing human remains and tell me they were beef bones, do you?"

Doug said calmly, "I think you would have seen the difference. Beef bones would have been three or four times larger than human bones. After all, you realized the bones you saw in the kiln weren't beef bones immediately, didn't you?" At her nod, he continued, "So I'm sure the bones she showed you were beef bones just as she claimed."

The phone rang and Doug picked it up. After a few words he went to the front door, returning with Rich.

"Your request has been honored, Karo. There are two police officers in front keeping people off your property. Luckily Rich had his cell phone with him or he'd still be trying to convince them it was okay to let him in."

"I just heard on the car radio that Joy died. She never regained consciousness," Rich reported.

Doug turned on the TV again to get the update. They had turned it off when they realized that it was the same information being repeated over and over again.

"Now they'll never get all the answers, will they?" Karo shook her head sorrowfully.

"Maybe not, but don't worry. I bet the FBI already has a bunch. And from the looks of these articles, the media is finding a lot of answers already." Doug pointed at the papers strewn over the top of the table.

"Or they made up the answers," Eileen added cynically. "I mean listen to this one:

> *Joy Ledbetter, known amongst the homeless as the coffee lady, dispensed more than hot coffee and sandwiches to the area's indigents. Known as an Angel*

of Hope she frequently assisted willing recipients of her largess to get their life back on track. However, none of the takers of her help has ever been seen again.

Rumors have been spreading rapidly through this segment of the community as they are now even more suspicious of attempts to help them. They say authorities don't count them as part of the community, and therefore, no one notices when they disappear. Yet apparently Joy Ledbetter took notice of them, and in particular, the large number who were eligible for Social Security and other retirement benefits.

Authorities are trying to piece together the pattern of her system of befriending homeless men, helping them claim their benefits, having their retirement funds credited to an account which bore her name jointly with each of them, and then conveniently causing the homeless men to disappear. Speculation is she has killed as many as three dozen people."

"Oh, my gosh, I don't want to hear any more about it. Enough, already!" Karo got up and headed into the living room. Standing in front of the window where she could dimly see the crowd outside through the sheer curtains, she wrapped her arms around herself and rocked to and fro.

"So girlfriend, what do you want to do?" Eileen asked.

"I think going to the beach will be a little difficult right now." She nodded towards the crowded sidewalk.

"How about we play a game?" Rich had joined them.

"Okay, I vote for a little poker. That should keep your mind focused, if you let it wander, it will cost you bucks." Doug had followed Rich.

And so they cleared the kitchen table of newspapers and started a game of poker. When the FBI came they found them still at it.

"We'd like to take you downtown for an interview, Ms. Meisner." They were very polite, but they scared Karo to death.

"Is she being arrested?" Eileen demanded. When the agents shook their heads, she announced, "If she goes, I go too."

Karo was very relieved when they agreed that Eileen could accompany her. They followed the agents outside to the dark four-door sedan, the policemen and the FBI protecting them from the media, who were clamoring for answers to their shouted questions. Karo knew she should be grateful for the protection, but somehow she felt as if she was a prisoner being taken off to jail. She ducked her head in an attempt to avoid the flashes of the cameras, envisioning the headlines under her picture in the next edition of the papers.

CHAPTER 17

Eileen went home. There was a limit to how long she could abandon her family in order to support her friend. The satellite vans and the crowds of reporters had dwindled until now Karo was now only bothered occasionally by the most persistent. She had been questioned by the FBI two more times, but they made it clear that she was not suspect of anything, merely a good source of information to help them tie up loose ends.

The Director of the Recreation Center had a meeting to discuss the future of the studio. The room was packed with opinionated people. Some thought it should be closed and dismantled, but many who found working with clay had become an integral part of their lives suggested alternatives. The final plan adopted would have Sandi continue teaching classes and acting as the expert for studio. The man who taught the evening class would also continue, and in addition, he would offer a much requested class for children on Saturdays. The workshops would continue, styled on a co-op system. All firings would require two people to participate, assigned on a rotating basis. The

Recreation Center would assign a witness to oversee the closing of the kiln and the initiation of the firing. This would ensure that no potter could misuse the kiln again. In addition, they would hire a person who would act as Workshop Coordinator. Interested and qualified people were encouraged to apply. It would be a paying position, although with a modest salary, and the incumbent would need organizational, management and people skills in addition to being a skilled potter.

At any rate the studio wouldn't open again for a few weeks. When the police finally released it, the potters and the maintenance staff at the Rec Center would have to spend some time and effort putting it back together again. It was going to be a big job.

Meanwhile, Karo was thankful she had set up her own studio. She had offered to share it with Rich, so they worked out a schedule they both felt would work. Karo's kiln had been plugged in and she and Rich had already fired two bisque loads. They were planning to do their first high fire load soon.

While life hadn't returned to normal, at least Karo was sleeping, only haunted by nightmares occasionally. She didn't see much of Delvin these days, but she understood why. Besides him being so busy, she knew it was awkward for him to be involved with a key witness in the big, messy case he was involved with.

She was content to wait. She didn't even want to get involved in a relationship at this point in her life, so it was easy to be patient and just see how their relationship developed, if it even developed.

* * *

Karo wasn't surprised to see the latest article in the paper, just by what one of the local reporters wrote.

LOCAL MAN LAST VICTIM OF MURDEROUS MAVEN

Billy Harder, the homeless man known to many Belle Vista residents, disappeared suddenly several weeks ago. Billy a common sight on Main Street where he frequently panhandled for spare change had another life. He was a benefactor to the children at the local orphanage. Sister Mary Katherine of the Little Sisters of the Poor notified police this week that Billy Harder was missing. She reported Billy Harder appeared at the door of the orphanage each month with his pension check. He would endorse the check over to the orphanage, and Sister would give him fifty dollars in cash for pocket money. The rest of the $3,600 check was used by Sister Mary Katherine to cover expenses for the children.

"He was a generous man," reported Sister Mary Katherine. "I often told him he didn't have to give us so much of his income. I told him the Lord and the children would understand if he used that money to rent a room, or bought clothes and food. But he said he didn't need it. He felt the children could make better use of the money than he could. And he was right; sometimes that money was all that kept us going.

"But he didn't come last month. And he hasn't arrived this month. I contacted the police department because I am concerned

about what has happened to him. They say no one has seen him for weeks. They thought he had just started wandering again; but I think something has happened to him. He was devoted to the children. I know he wouldn't have left without saying good-by. He knew how important his contribution was to the children. He wouldn't have just stopped giving his money to us. I know that."

This reporter learned that Billy Harder's check was issued from funds he set aside in retirement accounts when he was a well known surgeon. Later his life was destroyed by his addiction to alcohol. After a botched operation he lost his license to practice and spent four years in prison. On his release from prison he spent years wandering before finally settling in Belle Vista about five years ago. He applied for his retirement benefits shortly after he first arrived in town and received a check each month delivered to the Main Street Post Office. He had been contributing the majority of those funds to the orphanage run by the Little Sisters of the Poor since he started receiving them. This reporter learned that the checks stopped coming to the Post Office last month when the bank dispensing his retirement funds received instructions to credit the amount automatically to a checking account. The checking account was owned jointly by Billy Harder and Joy Ledbetter. The FBI reports there is some question as to whether or not those instructions were signed by Billy or were forged by Joy Ledbetter. They do admit that Billy Harder was present at the bank office in San Mateo when the account was opened for him and Joy Ledbetter.

As readers will no doubt remember, Joy Ledbetter suffered a stroke while attempting to bludgeon Karo Meisner and subsequently died without gaining consciousness. Karo Meisner found bones in the pottery kiln at the Belle Vista Recreation Center Studio which the authorities confirmed were human remains. That was the start of an investigation which has subsequently identified seventeen victims of Ms. Ledbetter's scheme. The fact that Billy Harder has so recently been identified as another victim only demonstrates that this nightmare is not over. How many more victims...

Karo laid the paper down without bothering to read further as she could see the rest would only be repeated from prior stories. Her hand was shaking slightly when she punched in Delvin's cell phone number.

"Myers, here."

"Delvin, I just read the paper. I'm so sorry about your friend, Billy Harder. I know it must be hard for you."

His voice changed from the abrupt tone he used to answer the phone to one softer. "Thanks Karo, I appreciate it. It was a nasty surprise. And I wondered why it never occurred to me before. I guess because she mostly selected her victims from the streets of San Francisco and Redwood City. And perhaps it was because I really wanted him to be okay, you know."

"Yes, it's like me with Betty. Somehow I can deal with nameless, faceless homeless people being victims, but the thought of Betty being one of them is almost more than I can stand."

"Yes. And can you believe Billy was giving all his money to the orphans. Here he was living off of what he could scrounge when he really had enough money to live on. And Joy tried to take it all. But Billy was smart as well as kind, no matter that he never rid himself of his dependency on the bottle. He had named the orphanage as the beneficiary of his retirement account. He will be declared dead as one of the Joy's victims and the kids are going to get the rest of his money. I understand there is a substantial amount left, as he had only been drawing on it for a few years."

They were both silent a moment, thinking about Billy.

"How are you doing, Karo?" Delvin said softly. "Are you picking up the pieces of your life?"

"I'm doing okay. I try to keep to a schedule which keeps me busy and limits my time for remembering. I'm taking the boys to the beach in the mornings these days. After that I work in my office on my writing or in the studio on my pottery. My friend, Rich, is also using my studio. We take turns. But soon the Rec Center studio will be open again. Many of the potters won't be coming back. They just can't deal with what happened there. Several of them feel some guilt, because it never occurred to them to challenge Joy. One told me they all shared the guilt of those poor homeless people because if they hadn't let her have her way, she wouldn't have been able to continue her scheme. And there is some truth in that. She had us all trained.

"So the studio is going to be very different, but I think that's going to be good. Maybe we'll attract new students. Some of the potters had become too demanding and opinionated over the years. With them gone, we'll have a more pleasant environment to work in. For sure we won't have to work around all Joy's rules and restrictions."

"I'm glad it's working out. I had heard they were thinking of closing it down and I thought that would be a shame, say nothing about the waste of all those resources."

Continuing, he said, "I've missed you, Karo. Things are slowing down a bit here. Maybe one day next week we could have dinner together? Is that possible?"

"I'd like that, Delvin. Call me."

She smiled as she tucked the phone in the leather pouch she wore on her belt. Since that incident with Joy she kept her phone handy at all times. It gave her a feeling of safety.

She noticed the dogs watching her carefully; they knew it was time for a visit to the beach. When she got up from the kitchen table they were already prancing around, eager to start. She snapped on their leashes and while they raced to the front door to wait for her she gathered up the plastic bag she always took in case she needed to clean up after them and a handful of doggie treats. She had been working on their training and they were minding very well, but treats for a bribe or a reward were always handy.

Finally, she was ready, and she shrugged into her jacket, picked up the leashes and opened the front door.

They were happy to be out. They loved their outing to the beach and truthfully Karo did too. She had a hard time remembering how it had been when she didn't live next to the ocean. They passed the house being built at the end of the block. Most of the work seemed to be going on inside, so it was harder to see what progress was being made. But, there were a lot of trucks parked around it and workers going in and out so she assumed the new neighbors would be moving in soon. She climbed over the dune separating the houses from the beach and was in a different world. Here was the vast empty stretch of sand and the endless ocean. The sky was gray with fog, but it was high, overcast, not down-on-the-ground fog. She unsnapped the leashes and followed the dogs down the beach. When it was time to go home she headed back for the path over the dune, Captain running around her, Rudy trailing behind as he nosed every item of interest on the way.

She didn't see her until she got right to the dune then she stopped abruptly, surprised by the woman in front of her.

"Mary Louise? What a surprise. I didn't know you live around here."

"I don't. I came down to see you."

"Oh, well come on to the house. We can have tea. How did you know I was at the beach?"

But Mary Louise didn't move from where she stood blocking the path. "No, I wanted to talk to you here. It's more private. I saw you come down here so I just waited for you."

Captain approached her, growling low as he tried to sniff her ankles. Mary Louise kicked out viciously, catching Captain in the nose. He yelped and backed away, then started barking.

"Mary Louise, that was mean of you. He wouldn't have hurt you."

"I don't like strange dogs threatening me."

"I don't know what your problem is, but don't be kicking my dog." She was mad. When she saw Captain didn't seem to be seriously hurt she gave him the hand signal to sit. "Stay, Captain.

"Now, Mary Louise, what do you want to talk to me about that is so private you want to talk on the beach?"

"I wanted to talk about Joy." Her face changed and her voice became softer. "You know, Karo, this whole thing has been blown way out of proportion? The papers, the police, you, have made Joy out to be some kind of a monster. In fact the paper this morning called her a Murderous Maven. That's so unfair.

"Joy wasn't like that. She was a caring, thoughtful person. She was a wonderful friend. Actually she was an angel, not an Angel of Death as they said."

"Mary Louise, get real. The woman tried to kill me. She was not an angel." Karo was indignant.

"See? That's the problem. You go around saying these things that aren't true. You make her sound like some mad demented person. And you caused this problem, Karo. You did!

"You have poked your nose in everything since you came to the studio. You were always asking questions and wanting to do things different than we did them. You're the one who got Joy so upset it triggered her stroke. Then you've fed these rumors. The television and newspapers have been going crazy with stories about her. They make you out to be the heroine, and no one looks at all the good Joy did.

"I mean, so a few homeless people have disappeared? So what? Who really cares? How does that really hurt society?

"I'll tell you. It doesn't! Those people were a nuisance, vermin. They were a blight on society. Good riddance, I say! And probably a lot of other people would agree with me if they dared."

Karo stood there, her mouth opened in shock as she listened to Mary Louise rant.

She shook her head. "Mary Louise, what are you saying? Are you listening to yourself defend what Joy did? Can you honestly think it was alright for her to just select people, steal their money and then kill them? Are you..."

She stopped mid-sentence realizing in time it wouldn't be wise to call Mary Louise nuts, or even crazy because now that she was looking at her, she was beginning to see that was the problem.

She took a deep breath and said in a calm tone, "Look Mary Louise, I didn't call Joy any names. The reporters and television didn't get any of that information from me. What I did was run for my life when Joy tried to brain me with that mallet. I would guess you would have done the same thing if you were in my place. It's too bad Betty wasn't able to save herself." She watched Mary Louise's face darken and decided to change tactics.

"If you think Joy is being given unfair press coverage why don't you talk to the reporters or the police about it? I'm sure they would be interested in what you have to say."

Mary Louise sneered, "Sure, you must think I'm very stupid. No Karo, I'm not going to tell anyone but you. I blame you. You've been disruptive since you arrived. Poking your nose in where it's not wanted, asking questions, offering to help, even befriending Betty. It was you, you know. You caused Betty's death."

She paused watching for Karo's reaction. Apparently satisfied by the shock she saw on Karo's face, she nodded smugly. "Yes, you told Betty you saw Joy giving out coffee to the homeless, so Betty assumed Joy was recruiting a new guest. Joy had promised Betty she was finished with that whole process, that she wouldn't do it anymore. I know Joy meant to keep that promise when Betty insisted, but as she told me, she then realized what a waste it would be. There were so many of them out there and who cared about them? Joy was getting close to retiring to Florida and she felt a few more targets would add a layer of financial protection for her. And she deserved to build up a retirement fund for her old age.

"But after you told Betty about seeing Joy, apparently Betty went over to the studio to confront Joy. Betty was very agitated and Joy tried to calm her down, to reason with her. During their struggle Betty fell back against the kiln, hitting her head.

"Joy told me all about it. Betty was our friend. Joy would have never intentionally hurt her. But after Betty died, Joy had to do something about her body. There would be too many questions asked otherwise.

"Betty was another person who Joy had saved. You just didn't know Joy or how generous she could be. When Betty's husband passed away leaving Betty totally unprotected financially, it was Joy who solved the problem for Betty. We told everyone he was in a full care facility and we destroyed the body. No one questioned Betty. Why would they? Everyone knew how Betty had been struggling to take care of him. He needed to be in a full care facility. Everyone just accepted that she had finally made the difficult decision to place him in one and they were supportive of her decision."

Karo shook her head. "Stop, I don't want to hear this, Mary Louise! I don't need to know any of this. Tell the police. Tell your priest. Now, move aside and let me pass, I've had enough."

"No you haven't." Mary Louise stood her ground, but somehow she was now holding a revolver in her hand. It had a rather nasty look to it, black, squatty and deadly looking.

"I've been thinking about this. Planning what I would say to you. No one but me is left who knows what happened. I'm the only one around to make you accountable for what you did. Because of your interference, Betty is dead. And now Joy is dead, again, thanks to you. The studio will never be the same. The potters there will never produce the same quality of work we were able to achieve. But you won't know because you won't be there."

She nodded her head, her eyes gleamed with malice. Karo realized with dread that Mary Louise was completely mad. She was every bit as crazy as Joy had been.

"Mary Louise, think a minute. You don't want to use that gun. You don't want to spend the last years of your life in jail. Someone will hear the shot. There are workers just over the dune who will hear it and come running. There is no way you can get away with shooting me.

"And for what? What did I do? I didn't kill Joy. I didn't do anything but try to save my life."

"Shut up, Karo. No one will hear the shot. The wind, the surf and the dune will block the sound. See, we can't hear their hammers, they won't hear my shots." She gave a short bark of a laugh. "I'll just stroll down the beach a ways and take the path back to where I parked my car. No one will ever connect me to this shooting on the beach, or to the tragic death of yet another potter. I'm just an old lady, one of the ones who unwittingly worked at the studio. No one will ever think to suspect me of being involved with this shooting."

Karo realized, with a sinking feeling, what Mary Louise was saying was true.

"But before I kill you I want to tell you what kind of friend Joy was. I want you to understand what kind of person you destroyed.

"I lived with my stinking, drunken, abusive husband for thirty-one years before I finally had enough. My kids were long gone and I didn't blame them. We had no more friends. Who wanted to be our friend? Everyday it was only a matter of getting through it alive. Sometimes I almost didn't make it. I had to make up stories about accidents and clumsiness to explain my injuries. And he just lolled around and demanded I wait on him. One night after he beat me almost senseless and then passed out in his chair, I pulled myself up off the floor, dragged myself to the kitchen and got my cast iron skillet and whacked him on the head until it was only a pulpy mess. And then I passed out. In the morning I woke up to what I had done.

"Oh, I wasn't sorry. Not in the least. It fact I wondered why I hadn't done it long before, but I was worried about what to do about it. What to do with him."

She glared at Karo. "So I called my only friend in the world. I called Joy Ledbetter."

She took her free hand and wiped at her eyes. "She didn't ask me any questions over the phone. She just arrived at the door. She helped me roll him up in the shower curtain. We scrubbed down the living room. She loaded the blood soaked carpeting and the chair he was sitting in into her truck bed. She helped me go through the house and clear out all his things and we loaded those in the truck, too. Then we left the body and drove to the dump to empty the truck. That night we went to the studio with the body and we loaded the kiln for a special firing." She waved her empty hand dismissively. "End of problem. No one doubted that my husband deserted me. My husband hardly worked those last years, so I didn't even feel a financial burden with him gone. In fact, the proceeds I received from my grandfather's estate suddenly seemed like plenty when my husband wasn't there to spend most of it on booze. My life improved immediately, and I owed it all to Joy."

Captain, perhaps sensing Mary Louise's threat, started growling again.

"Now my only friend is dead. And I hold you responsible, Karo. I owe it to Joy to make sure you pay." Her tone was sharp and angry.

It was too much for Captain. He leaped for her ankle, and her vicious kick to his ribs sent him flying with a shriek of pain. That was too much for Karo who lunged at Mary Louise, but the gun had already swung around towards her. Mary Louise squeezed the trigger just as Rudy leaped, grabbing her gun hand in his fangs. The impact of his body knocked her to the side, and then she was on the ground screaming, struggling, flailing at Rudy, as she tried to dislodge his jaws clamped painfully on her wrist.

Karo felt the burning and then the cold in her thigh, but she didn't fall. She pried the gun from Mary Louise's hand before she could squeeze the trigger again. Then she hobbled to Captain lying so still on the sand a few feet away. That's when the pain hit her and she sat hard on the ground. She heard Mary Louise screaming hysterically, but didn't waste any time worrying about her. Blackness was creeping over her and she knew she had to get help fast. She fumbled for the phone in the little leather case attached to her belt and managed to poke in nine-one-one. "Help, I need help. On the beach, I'm on the beach near Sunset Lane." The blackness was spreading, she tried once more desperately. "Shooting..., need help...."

CHAPTER 18

"Can you hear me?" The face loomed very close.

Karo felt as if she was coming up from the bottom of a swimming pool. She nodded, and tried to say she was okay.

"Can you call your dog? He won't let go of the woman's arm. Call him off, will you?"

Karo tried to call him, but even she could tell the words were garbled and indistinct. She tried again. "Rudy, come." Still not loud enough, she took a deep breath and shouted, "Rudy, come!" And in a moment she felt Rudy push his nose into her face, licking her cheek.

"Captain? Where's Captain?"

"The little dog?" The man asked as he was doing something with her thigh.

"Yes, she kicked him. She hurt him." The horror of seeing his still body on the sand came back in a rush. "Is he okay?"

"He's hurt, but not too badly, perhaps only bruised ribs or maybe a crack. He probably had the air kicked out of him, and now he's trying to get his breath back. I think he'll be okay."

Things were happening around her, but it all seemed a long distance away. She remembered. "My dogs, someone has to take care of the dogs..."

Then as they were moving her on a gurney she said, "Wait! I don't want to ride with Mary Louise. Don't put me in the ambulance with her. She tried to kill me."

She was strapped down and someone was sitting next to her. She could hear the siren, but it was muted. She knew they were taking her to the hospital and she tried to remember what she wanted to tell them.

* * *

"Karo? Karo can you hear me."

Karo felt a sense of well-being. Doug was there. He would take care of her. She would be all right.

Later someone asked if she was in pain. She said no, but suddenly the pain hit her with an intensity that took her voice away. "Yes, pain..." she managed to croak and blessedly it went away. She was wrapped mummy-like in warm blankets and she felt safe, warm, good.

When she woke up, Greg was sitting by her bed holding her hand, the one not connected to the tubes. She lay there for a moment wondering if it was all a crazy, scary dream, about living at the beach, about the divorce, about Mary Louise and Joy and Betty.

"You're awake. Good. Lisa is on her way, Karo. She'll be here soon. Just sleep. The doctors said you'll be fine."

She did sleep. Several times she was awake for a short time. Once Delvin was holding her hand. Once Rich was there. A couple times a nurse was doing something with the tubes attached to her arm.

"Oh, Mom, how are you feeling?"

She tried to say something through the cotton balls her mouth felt it was stuffed with. "Water," she croaked and sucked greedily at the straw Lisa put in her mouth.

"Better?"

She nodded, gripping Lisa's hand tightly.

"How did you get here so soon?" she rasped trying to sort everything out in her mind.

"Well I got in late last night. You've been here since yesterday. They had to operate to repair some muscle damage. And you've lost a lot of blood, too much blood. The paramedics said it was lucky they got to you when they did. Mom, thank God you had your cell phone with you."

"Lisa, where are Captain and Rudy? Is Captain all right?"

"Relax Mom. They're at home. Your friend, Lieutenant Myers, sent them both to the vet. Captain has a nasty bruise and so is not moving like his usual self, but otherwise they're fine. They're both moping a little because you're not there, but I'll watch them. I'm sure they'll perk right up when you're home again."

Karo nodded, feeling better already.

"Mom, Lieutenant Myers and a guy from the FBI are anxious to talk to you. Do you think you're up to it?"

She nodded, closing her eyes while she tried to conjure up the memories.

"That Lieutenant Myers seems to be hanging around a lot. Is there something going on between the two of you?" Lisa watched her mother's face.

"Well, I suppose he's worried because I keep getting into trouble. But really Lisa, it hasn't been my fault. It's truly just a case of being in the wrong place at the wrong time." She reached for the water again and took a long drink. She just couldn't seem to get enough water.

"Lisa, Rudy saved my life, you know? He attacked Mary Louise just when she pulled the trigger so she missed."

Lisa looked at her strangely.

"Okay, maybe she didn't miss, but she didn't kill me. And she meant to."

Lisa nodded. "Right. Oh Mom, you say you love your life here at the beach, but it's been very dangerous. First you found that dead woman, and then the house at the end of the block blew up, then that mad woman tried to bean you with a mallet when you found the bones in the kiln, and now this. Are you sure you won't move back to San Mateo?"

"No, Lisa. No way. This is my home."

There was a rap on the door and Delvin came in and went directly to the bed. He took Karo's hand and gave it a gentle squeeze. "How are you doing, Karo? You gave us a real scare." He watched her face closely as she smiled at him.

"Thanks for taking care of the boys, Delvin. Lisa said you took Captain to the vet."

"I was happy to do it. Karo, do you think you're up to some questions? Riley Hill from the FBI is here and has some questions for you. We're treating this as a part of the Joy Ledbetter case for now."

"I'll do my best, but I sometimes just go to sleep so if that happens, please don't think I'm bored."

Delvin smiled and stepped back to allow a young man in a very business-like dark suit to come closer to the bed.

Agent Hill nodded cordially at Karo and held out his badge for her to examine. He then sat down in the chair Lisa had vacated and took out his tape recorder. "Do you mind if we record this?"

Karo shook her head and waited for the questions. She had some questions of her own she fully intended to get answers to while he questioned her.

Agent Hill went through the usual questions; who she was, what day it was, and where they were doing the interview. Then he asked, "Ms. Meisner, how did you get shot?"

"Mary Louise was waiting on the beach for me. She had a gun. She blamed me for Joy's death and especially for all the bad press about Joy Ledbetter. She said Joy was a saint and I caused her stroke when I upset her the way I did. She said I soiled Joy's memory by starting the brouhaha of press coverage. She said she was the only one left to see I paid for what I had done.

"I thought she was going to kill me, truly. But when Captain went for her ankle and she kicked him so hard he flew through the air, well..., I just lost it. I lunged at her just as she pulled the trigger and at the same time Rudy arrived and jumped on her. I felt the bullet hit me. But it didn't stop me right then. I grabbed the gun from her hand and ran to Captain. That's when I realized I was blacking out and I somehow managed to call nine-one-one and.... Well, you'll have to tell me what happened after that because, frankly, it all got pretty hazy."

Delvin offered up his part of the story. "Luckily when you called in you said it was a shooting so the operator notified me at the same time the call went out to the nearest unit. The police and the ambulance arrived at the same time. They came down the beach from an entrance a couple of blocks from where you were. The officers were pretty puzzled over what they found. You were unconscious, wounded, bleeding profusely and holding the gun and the cell phone. Captain was out. Rudy was sitting on top of Mary Louise with her arm in his mouth and growling ferociously every time anyone came near. And Mary Louise was hysterical, screaming for help, saying that Rudy was vicious and attacked her as she walked by.

"The EMT's were taking care of you, so the officers tried to coax Rudy away from Mary Louise, but he wasn't having any of that. They were discussing whether or not to shoot him when I got there. I parked at the end of your street and came over the sand dune path. That was just about the time one of the EMT's asked you to call your dog. You did and Rudy left Mary Louise."

Delvin shook his head. "That woman is really weird. She whined and moaned and threatened. She said she was walking on the beach when your dog attacked her. She was so busy trying to fight him off she didn't see what happened to you, but she heard a shot. She said she was suing you for your dog's attack." Here he actually chuckled. "Rudy hadn't even broken the skin on her arm, but you should have seen him, he wasn't going to let her move.

"Anyway, you had called in a shooting and somehow we didn't quite believe Mary Louise. It was hard to imagine you could have shot yourself at the angle the bullet went in. I told the officers to bag her hands and your hands and we tested for gun powder residue. That pretty much proved who had fired the gun."

"Where's Mary Louise now?"

"In jail. Her lawyer has been parading a bunch of doctors in and out. She's still insisting she's suing you for what your dog did to her. But she's as loony as a fruitcake. It's hard to believe that she has been able to hide how crazy she is."

"She never was a very nice person, but I think this thing with Joy and Betty sent her over the edge. I mean after listening to her, I couldn't help feeling sorry for her, but frankly, she scared me witless."

"Well, apparently not. I mean, you did attack her." The FBI agent commented sardonically.

"She kicked my dog," Karo said indignantly. "What would you have done?"

He smiled. For once his face had a pleasant expression, not so stern. "I wasn't criticizing you. Actually, I think you did great. Now, I have a few more questions. Do you mind?"

He asked his questions, but Karo was finding it more and more difficult to answer and finally she just faded out all together.

When she woke the next time Rich was with Lisa in her room.

"Oh, so you're awake? How are you feeling?"

"Thirsty. I need some water."

"The little girl next door sent you this, Mom." Lisa handed Karo a card made out of construction paper.

"Isn't that sweet?" Karo smiled, handing it back to Lisa. "Can you put it over there on the ledge with the others so I can see it from here?"

"Oh, these are nice flowers. Who are they from?"

"Your dad sent those. Wasn't that thoughtful of him? I was very surprised when I woke up that first night to find him here."

"Well, you were married for a few years. I'm sure he still cares about you."

"Of course, still it was a surprise."

Changing the subject entirely, "Rich, have they opened the studio yet?"

Rich nodded. "Yesterday. We started the clean up. Evy said some people go to extreme lengths to get out of clean up."

They all laughed.

"Seriously, Karo. People were really upset about Mary Louise. It was like they felt responsible for not noticing she had lost it. She's always so sharp and caustic in her manner, and she isn't really chummy with anyone. So if she had been this way for a while we're not sure we would have noticed."

"I know. When I first started talking to her on the beach I thought she was acting a little odd, but then I noticed how weird her eyes looked. That's when I realized that she was seriously crazy. I started to tell her she was nuts and I caught myself in time, because I knew then she really was." She shivered. "You just never know how close to the edge people around you are, do you?"

"I heard they are going to commit her to a facility for the criminally insane. She won't even stand trial for assaulting you. They don't think they can build a case about her knowledge of what Joy was doing and no one wants to tackle the disappearance of Mary Louise's husband all those years ago. The authorities apparently feel locking her up where she can't harm anyone and where she can have some treatment is the best course of action for her."

"She won't be able to check herself out, will she?" Karo was a little concerned.

"No, it will require a court ruling and they would have to address the assault charges then. So it probably is the best solution for everyone, don't you think?"

Karo nodded. "Well, truthfully, I'm glad I won't have to go to court. I can just imagine what the media would do with that. It would be the whole circus all over again." She paused, thinking. "Actually, I'm surprised I haven't been bothered here by the reporters. I would have thought they'd be all over this."

Rich and Lisa looked at each other. Lisa smiled sheepishly. "The hospital has been very good about protecting you. And there has been a policeman stationed outside your room until yesterday, so no one who wasn't approved could have access to you. And you've been sleeping a lot, Mom, so you haven't been watching the news or reading the papers. This has been a front page story and all the networks have it. I've gotten several calls from the morning programs and when they found out you couldn't talk to them they offered me the opportunity. I just told them, no thanks. Eileen called, she was ready to come back out here, but I assured her you were okay and would call her in a few days. It's all dying down now. And with the decision about Mary Louise today, I expect by the time they release you tomorrow, things will be very quiet when you go home."

284 • MUD TO ASHES

"Oh, I'm going home tomorrow? Thank God. I know I'll heal much faster in my own house, with my dogs, and my friends around me."

They were all quiet for a moment, then Karo asked, "Lisa, how did you get the time off to come home?"

"I'm on emergency family leave. I've got to go back on Monday." She looked at her mother, the distress plain on her face. "But you know, Mom, I've been thinking about it while I've been here. Boston is a very long ways away. This whole episode has shown me it's too far away. I love it there, but I'm thinking how much San Francisco is like Boston. It's about the same size. It has that big city feeling, with a lot going on. And my company has an office in San Francisco. So I called them yesterday."

Karo found herself holding her breath, "And...? What did they say?"

Lisa laughed. "They said they had openings and they'd be happy to consider my transfer request."

"Oh, Lisa, that would be so great! I mean I know you want to live your own life, but I keep thinking about what's going to happen when you fall in love and want to get married. And then the kids will start coming and you'll all be across the country from me. I was thinking I might have to move east when that happens." Karo had tears in her eyes. This was the best news Lisa could have given her.

"Mom, give me a few years before you burden me with a passel of kids." But then a shadow passed over her eyes. "But seriously, I realize I can live my own life here, just a few miles from you and Dad.

"And you're right about the getting married and having a family. Two of my friends just got engaged.

One is from Colorado and one is from Arizona. They're going to be starting their own families, miles from where their families live. I don't want that. When I settle down and have kids I want their grandparents to be part of their lives. I want to be near you and Dad."

Lisa couldn't suppress her sob. "It took hours to get here and I was so worried about you, Mom. Dad was here while they operated, but I should have been here, too. I was just too far away."

EPILOGUE

"Merry Christmas, Karo. Merry Christmas, guys." Doug came in the door smiling, loaded down with gaily wrapped packages. He dumped the presents on the coffee table and struggled out of his jacket. "It's cold out, but no rain, thank God. I'm getting a little tired of it already."

"Don't get too comfortable. We've been waiting for you to go to the beach with us, and the boys are ready. Aren't you guys?"

The dogs danced around with excitement as if they understood every word.

"Well okay, I'm up for some fresh air, but wait, let's open these first." Doug fished out two packages and gave one to each dog. They immediately started tearing the paper off.

"Oh, Doug, that was nice of you. They love presents." Each dog soon had clamped in his jaws a rubber ball on a heavy rope, tied with a knot at each end. It was a perfect toy for fetch or tug-of-war.

Karo gathered up the leashes, the doggie treats and the plastic bags, and zipped up her parka, while Doug put his coat back on.

"Did you and Lisa have a nice Christmas morning?"

"Lovely. We slept in and then opened our presents after a leisurely breakfast. She left an hour or so ago to meet her dad for the rest of the day. Then she'll head home. She has to work in the morning. I'm so happy she moved to San Francisco. I love seeing her more frequently and I confess, I don't worry nearly as much."

The day was overcast with a high cloud cover. The wind was sharp and crisp, stinging their cheeks as they headed down Sunset Lane.

"Hey, this house looks almost finished. Have the new owners moved in yet?"

"No, but soon. Clyde said last night that he talked to the new owner a few days ago and they will be here in February. He has two kids, a wife who stays at home, and a dog and cat. So that will be a nice addition to the neighborhood. And I understand the little girl is about the same age as Tiffany, next door, so she's very excited."

Karo fell silent as they climbed over the sand dune to the beach, needing all her breath for the climb straight into the wind. On the other side she unfastened the leashes. She took the toy from Rudy's mouth, held it by the rope and spun it around her head a few times before letting it fly across the sand, Rudy bounding joyfully behind it.

Captain, in the meantime, was growling playfully as he held onto his toy, not about to let Doug get it away from him. With it securely in his mouth, he followed Rudy across the sand, happy to be free to run.

Karo and Doug walked behind the dogs, willingly throwing the toy again each time Rudy returned it. Captain wasn't giving his up. He was content to follow after Rudy, but he wasn't letting go of his treasure yet. After a while, even Rudy was tired of the game, leaving the toy safely in Doug's hand while he nosed around in the driftwood and seaweed littering the beach at the high tide mark.

"How did your party go last night, Karo? I was really sorry to miss it. I remember how much fun we had last year." This year Doug's shift at the hospital ER lasted until Christmas morning so he hadn't been able to attend Karo's second annual Christmas Eve bash.

"It was really nice. Most of the same people were there. Except you, and well, of course, Betty. Rich brought Anna. Diane brought the guy she's been dating. He was very nice. Everyone seemed to like him. And he's very nice to Tiffany as well as Diane. And Delvin came with his son."

Doug's eyebrows shot up. "And how is Delvin? Are you still seeing each other?"

"No, not really. Somehow that whole mess last summer at the pottery studio kind of killed any thought of romance between us. Now we're just friends. His son was up to spend Christmas with him and so they both came. Funny thing, his son and Lisa seemed to really hit it off. I wouldn't be surprised if they didn't get together again.

"The same neighbors were there as last year, and this year I invited my ex with his girlfriend."

Doug's eyebrows waggled again.

"Well, I decided I should be more adult about our relationship. After all we share a child. And truthfully, I really appreciated his support when I was in the hospital. It was nice of him, and it reminded me that we shared too many years together to just throw everything away. I knew Lisa would be happy to have him there, and..." she grinned, "maybe I was just a little curious about this young chick he's seeing."

They both laughed.

"Anyway, it worked out fine. She's nice and they obviously are fond of each other, so it turned out they were a nice addition to the party. I'll probably do it again."

They walked down the beach, skipping out of the way when one of the waves threatened them. "How did it go at the ER? Were you busy? I imagine that's not the best place to be on Christmas Eve."

"No, it's not. But if you have to be there you're really grateful to find it fully staffed. We weren't too busy. The usual kind of cases, plus maybe a few more of the people who suffer depression at this time of the year. I would have rather been at your party, but I was useful in the ER."

They walked a little further and then turned to go back to her house and dinner.

"So are you disappointed that your relationship with Delvin got sidelined?"

Karo thought a minute. "No, I'm really not. I think I'm just not ready for a relationship or a romance. I turned my whole life upside down less than two years ago and I've truly been enjoying finding myself and making a new life. I think I'm just not ready to focus on one person the way you need to do to build a successful relationship. I have my friends, my dogs, my work, my house at the beach and my pottery." She laughed. "Why would I want anything more?"

She noticed Rudy wasn't with them and called back to him, "Rudy, come!"

They walked a little further and still the dog was missing. She stopped and turned around to see Rudy nosing enthusiastically in the rocks.

"Oh no! Not again?" She stared at the dog, willing him to come to her, the feeling of dread spreading over her like an awful pall.

"I'll go check, Karo. Wait here."

Doug easily loped back to the pile of rocks stretching out into the waves and soon was beside Rudy, grabbing his collar. He turned and waved Karo over.

She reluctantly moved forward, gingerly climbed on the rocks and carefully moved over to where Rudy was standing, nose down, barking enthusiastically at the red starfish caught in a pool between the rocks.

Karo looked at Doug and burst out in laughter. "Good dog, Rudy." She patted his back. "You're a good dog. You found a beautiful starfish." She snapped his leash on his collar and this time when they headed back to the path over the dune and dinner, Rudy trotted docilely beside them, while Captain danced around them. Their beach adventure was over for the day.

The End

If you enjoyed this book, or any other book from Koenisha Publications, let us know. Visit our website or drop a line at:

Koenisha Publications
3196 – 53rd Street
Hamilton, MI 49419
Phone or Fax: 269-751-4100
Email: koenisha@macatawa.org
Web site: www.koenisha.com

Koenisha Publications authors are available for speaking engagements and book signings. Send for arrangements and schedule or visit our website.

Purchase additional copies of this book from your local bookstore or visit our web site.

KOENISHA PUBLICATIONS
Founder of the Jacketed SoftCover™
Books You Can Sink Your Mind Into